Hunted

by

Doug Riebock

DORRANCE
PUBLISHING CO
EST. 1920
PITTSBURGH, PENNSYLVANIA 15238

Dorrance Publishing Co
585 Alpha Drive
Pittsburgh, PA 15238
Visit our website at www.dorrancebookstore.com

ISBN: 979-8-88925-401-0
eISBN: 979-8-88925-901-5

Dedication

"To my wife Janet who has supported me through all of this."

He knew from the night before it was going to get warm the next day, a Sunday in late August, and for that reason Virgil had risen at five-thirty this morning to get his planned six-mile run finished. Amongst the many things he had learned from his father, discipline was the most prevalently applied within his middle-aged life. Sometimes, to a fault. He relied on having a plan for his day, week, and month. It was required, he felt, for his business to run smoothly and efficiently. He had just ended a week in which Ditch Repair was quite active in Michigan. Three repairs and some travel time proved profitable but wearing. He had returned home mid-afternoon yesterday, drained of any desire to do anything. He was happy though because it was the one day he and his father, Earl, reserved for college football. They always picked a game either the night before or definitely by eleven the morning of. They had been together for at least part of a game every Saturday for the twenty years since Virgil had started the injection molding machine repair company. When he arrived, Earl was watching the second half of the Illinois versus Northwestern game they had negotiated about the night before on their cell phones. Illinois was the better team this year, but the Wildcats were leading by three. Virgil plopped down on the couch and took a gulp from the bottle of beer Earl had provided.

"Good to have you home, son," Earl said.

Virgil sighed and smiled at his dad, "You know, it really is great to be home."

Now today, like most of his runs, he left the business end of his world behind for a while. This time was his time no matter who he might meet and converse with. His only companion this morning was a working Ipod with a soundtrack containing anything from Andrea Boccelli to ZZ Top. He struggled to find a comfortable pace. In his mind, Virgil replayed the ending of the in-state rivalry game, from yesterday. Due to injuries on both teams, a true freshman made the winning catch in the waning minutes for the Fighting Illini and snatched them the bragging rights for a year. Then, "The Shape I'm In" by The Band came through his ear pieces, helping him find a comfortable rhythm for his distance.

The early humidity, clinging amongst the trees from the previous day, aided in the slowing of that rhythm and the drenching of his shirt. He knew next week was going to be busy as well, so this was an opportunity to get his miles in at the Blackhawk Forest Preserve. After the mile to the preserve, he enjoyed his newfound pace and ran his normal four-mile course by the river, savoring the music, time alone, and outdoors. Now, he was finishing the sixth mile down an empty Raymond Street to John Prine's "Souvenirs" as he safely hugged the curb.

He was two blocks from his childhood home he shared with his father. The house his grandfather, he barely remembered, and relatives helped build. He noticed a big man stumbling down their driveway towards Raymond Street on which he now slowed his pace to a walk. He pulled the earphones out and let them hang over the back of his shoulder. He reached into his pocket and with a push of a button silenced the Ipod. Upon getting closer to the person, he realized it was Tom Kalsow, their neighbor from the other side of the street. He no longer lived there and only visited his mom and dad when he was in the area, though his own home was only twenty minutes away.

"What's going on Tommy?" he asked the bigger but younger man by three years.

Tom mumbled something incoherent then stopped and faced Virgil who grabbed him by the shoulders. He looked Tom up and down for any sign of injury, Virgil asked, "You alright?"

"Yeah, I'm fine," Tom replied, half-smiling and looking him in the eyes. "How are you doing Virgil?"

"You sure you're alright?" Virgil asked again, ignoring Tom's question. He was concerned with the distant and confused look on his former neighbor's face. The glassy-eyed look of Tom's face showed he was anything but fine.

Tom weakly grabbed at Virgil's shoulders, seemingly to steady himself,

"I'll be okay," he said, holding on but swaying slightly side to side, "Just need to get over this bug I've been carrying around lately...and my allergies."

Virgil nodded in agreement, "Okay, just hold on to me. Let me help you over to your mom and dad's house." Then he heard the sound of a vehicle coming from behind him. He eased his grasp on Tom, looking around to see a black Escalade turning from Bent Street two blocks away to the street they stood on. He moved backwards towards his driveway holding Tom by the arm and pulling him with. Tom grasped at Virgil's forearm as they moved.

"I think this is my ride," Tom suddenly said, wresting away from Virgil's grasp and walking towards the oncoming vehicle.

"Where are you going, Tommy?" Virgil asked, reaching out in an effort to pull him back.

"Plan on going fishing," Tom said, not looking back. "You want to go with?" he then asked, stopping, turning, and looking over his shoulder at Virgil, flashing a smile.

"Some other time, Tom," Virgil said, laughing at the situation but still concerned. "You sure you're alright?"

Tom turned, waving the back of his hand at Virgil. The Escalade, lacking any chrome, abruptly stopped just past them in the middle of the street, narrowly missing Tom. The tinted windows prevented Virgil from seeing the driver or anyone else who might be in the vehicle. The passenger's door behind the driver opened. No one showed themselves, only the flash of a hand and a deep voice beckoning Tom to "get in" the large SUV. Virgil started to follow Tom towards the vehicle in an effort to see into it, but Tom swayed in front of him, blocking any clear view of the interior. Tom then climbed in and shut the door. The vehicle slowly headed down Raymond Street then made a left onto Harrison Street. He heard the SUV's engine rpms pick up after it went out of sight.

Virgil stood at the apron of the driveway staring up the street not quite sure what he had just experienced. He looked back where the car had come from, then turned and walked up the driveway. He was tired from the run, but his interest was piqued by what had just happened. He entered the house through the back door from where he had left an hour and a half ago. He climbed the four steps to the kitchen where Earl had been preparing his breakfast before going to church. He was sitting at the table enjoying his efforts.

"If you plan on coming with you better get a move on," Earl said, looking towards Virgil as he entered. "Made some extra eggs and bacon if you're interested."

Virgil laughed, then opened the refrigerator and took the water jug out. He grabbed a glass out of an upper cabinet then filled it with water. "I'm good, Dad, and thanks for the bacon and eggs."

The morning news played on a small flat screen at the end of the counter facing the table Earl now rose from, and where they ate most of their meals together when Virgil wasn't traveling for work. The anchorwoman informed any viewers of a possible new virus slated to hit this coming flu season. The government was working on a vaccine. Beyond that, she possessed or shared little information.

"Have you seen the Kalsows lately?" Virgil asked his dad while grabbing a plate, fork, and paper napkin. He set the plate on the counter.

Earl grabbed the cast iron frying pan and scooped the extra food onto Virgil's plate with the spatula. "They went to Galena this weekend," he said, dropping the pan back on the stove, then returned to the table to finish his meal and orange juice.

"When I got back here, I found Tom walking down our driveway into the street."

"Probably returning a shovel or rake," Earl said, looking up at Virgil and revealing a sly smile.

"Very funny," Virgil said, responding to the inside joke. "He didn't look like he would be able to do any yard work."

"From what Ellen and Gene told me he has had some problems lately," Earl said. "You know, he came out recently."

"What?" Virgil exclaimed, feigning surprise by raising his forearm to his forehead, then dropping his fork on his plate for effect.

"You know, as being gay."

Virgil smiled, picked up his fork and calmly probed his food, "You didn't know that, Dad?"

"How would I know that?" Earl shot back, raising and shaking his fork at his son, appearing upset.

"I suspected it for a long time," Virgil said, returning fire. "Then one night I ran into him at a bar, and he blurted it out. 'I'm gay!' It wasn't at the top of his lungs or anything. He just leaned over and told me. Guess he came to terms with it. You know, Dad, like a hatchet to the face," Virgil said, referring to an episode that helped define his and Earl's lives together.

"Water under the bridge, Virgil."

"I know, Dad," Virgil said, then changed the subject. "You mean Ellen and Gene never said anything to you about Tom's lifestyle?"

"I guess they are old fashioned like me," Earl replied. "You know, there are some things people just don't ask or talk about."

"Dad," Virgil said laughing. "Men have been getting married for years now. I can't believe Gene never tipped you off."

Earl lowered his head and consumed the rest of his breakfast. Ten minutes later he started laughing, "I guess I just never picked up on it when he did. I mean when he called him that."

"Called him what?" Virgil asked, eating his breakfast.

"Cocksucker," Earl nonchalantly said, then tilted his head back, finishing his juice.

"That's not funny, Dad," Virgil said, pounding his fist, fork in hand, on the table, unhappy with his father's comment, but getting the attempt at humor.

Earl slyly smiled while still chuckling under his breath, "Kinda is, now that I know."

"He got picked up in a black Escalade. Said it was his ride," Virgil further explained the meeting in the street and successfully changed the subject.

"I do know he was going on a fishing trip sometime soon," Earl informed his son, trying to help solve the mystery.

"He was in no condition to go fishing either," Virgil said. "He wasn't even dressed for it."

"Maybe they were stopping at his place before they left on the trip," Earl offered.

"Maybe," Virgil said. "Just didn't like what I was smelling out there, Dad."

Earl rinsed his dishes and put them in the dishwasher, then started laughing to himself as he leaned against the counter "Actually, I think it was little cocksucker."

"You better take communion twice today," Virgil said, shaking his head.

"Sure you don't want to come along?" Earl said. "It's been awhile since we've gone together."

"I believe in Him, Dad," Virgil said. "I just can't deal with some of the hypocrites at that church."

"Aren't we all hypocrites in one way or another?"

The comment got Virgil's attention and he set his fork aside for a minute. "I suppose so, Dad, but I try to be a man of my word like you taught me."

"I know you do, we can all do better is all I'm saying," Earl said then shut the backdoor behind him as he walked out.

Virgil Ditch never cared what anyone said about him, or for that matter what anyone thought about him. He knew who he was. A flawed human being like the rest of the people he dealt with on a daily basis. No better, no worse. He was very much like his dad with this outlook on life. He had been influenced by Earl, and embraced it, no matter its limitations or their opposing views about the happenings in their lives. They disagreed at times but always found a compromise they both could live with. All the while, poking fun at each other along the way.

Virgil also knew his limitations. Except for his technical and mechanical skills, and successful repair business, he was not a sought-after prize by any means. He wished he had twenty bucks for every time a woman passed by him at a bar or party to have a conversation with one of his buddies or a random guy standing near him. He was six foot two and a solid two hundred muscular pounds. This from being a two-sport high school athlete, wrestling and baseball. Beyond those days, he had played local baseball and softball to stay in shape. Now, it was three times a week in his basement gym lifting and completing runs which he made time for around his work schedule. He always took a set of dumbbells with him on the road. Depending on where he was at and the time constraints, he was able to lift. Well-traveled in the Great Lakes region and fit he was for sure, but God rested on that early mid-October Sunday Virgil was born, the fifteenth of the month, three-thirty-three in the afternoon on a cool cloudy day.

In the looks department, he had received token attention. His oversized ears made his head appear larger than it actually was. When he became conscious of it, he compensated for it with a collar-length blond-tinged hair style. That revelation helped cover his ears and bolstered his confidence, but offered little help for his equally big nose and crooked lower teeth. Braces were never mentioned by either him or Earl. The deflection of a downward thrust hatchet by his father towards an overhead branch had left an eternal telling mark to his left cheekbone but not his self-awareness. Earl had felt terrible about it but insisted he had asked Virgil to stand back. The intended target had been a dead branch for the kindling of a campfire they were building in the backyard that night. There was to be no fire or sleeping in a tent that evening for either of them. The fifteen stitches equaled the apologies Earl offered his son, until then at age twelve, Virgil cussed in front of him for the first time. "Screw it, Dad. Shit happens." Virgil and Earl then moved on from it.

After The Call

That memory was one reason Earl Ditch was now slowly navigating the property around his son's cabin deep in the northern Wisconsin woods. The other was his love for him and the constant need to look out for his forty-seven year old son. At eighty, though tough and resilient, Earl should not have been looking for him here, or anywhere, but after the phone call this past Wednesday and his amped up concern for Virgil's well-being, he refused to wait for anyone to clear their schedule and tag along. He and Virgil shared two traits, discipline and stubbornness, or as they agreed to call it, perseverance. Like surviving a hatchet to the face.

The rustic but modern three-bedroom log cabin sat forty yards from the Booth Lake wooded shoreline. An upward incline behind it led to Forrest Road at the top. A winding gravel and dirt driveway had brought Earl exactly one hundred yards to the front door of the A-frame cabin. Due to technology, it wasn't remote enough to be without electricity but the nearest town, Lac de Flambeau, was still twenty miles away. Virgil and Earl had always spent Memorial Day weekend plus two days to open the place up for the year and make sure the winter hadn't been too unkind. Two weeks in July were for Virgil and whomever was available to come fishing. Labor Day weekend and a week in mid-October were reserved for some fishing but mostly fall color. Both Earl and Virgil loved fall so they started at the cabin and followed the colorful cascade down to Illinois and the Galena area. The rest of the time Virgil rented it out to fishing and hunting guides and their clients. It was never officially closed until after deer season. This latter arrangement paid for the taxes on the place and any repairs required.

Ten percent of the profits were given to local Native American needs.

Earl was now walking amongst the preview of that fall color, wondering why his son hadn't come home on Friday as promised. "Virgil," he yelled towards the woods four times, changing direction each time. He hoped his aged voice had the volume required to be heard by his son. However, the wind rustling through the maples and aspens was the only response he received each time. He took a much-needed deep breath while trying to remember the details of Virgil's last call. Who had come along with him on this trip he wondered, then realized he had never been told during their last conversation. His level of anxiety increased as did the incline he now climbed back towards the cabin on this cool and cloudy day in the third week of September. His son had always given him names of people he came to the cabin with, surprising him sometimes with the class of people he entertained and hung with. Not this time though, and this fact made Earl's heart race along with his thoughts, neither able to claim a satisfying peace.

He never tried to tell his son how to live his life, yet he felt, as his father, he had a right to at least offer some wisdom or advice. Recently his advice to Virgil had been to steer clear of those two guys. That bearded duo was no good. Get on with your life was his suggestion. He now knew from their last meeting with the men, it was no longer possible.

Virgil's Business

"He doesn't know everything, but he knows where to find the answers," Bryant Industries.

"A man you can count on to get the job done." Helper Plastics.

"Relentless, no quit, until the job is finished." Meeker Container.

These were some of the comments left on Virgil's website from satisfied customers. The few negative comments were twenty years old when his business, Ditch Machine Repair, was first begun. Tired of working for a plastics company that knew his value but failed to compensate him appropriately, Virgil, with his father's backing, started his own business. He covered the northern part of his own state, Illinois, as well as lower Wisconsin, northern part of Indiana, southern Michigan with an occasional venture into Iowa and Missouri when a good business opportunity presented itself. He prospered because of the comments found on his website. But his intelligence and work ethic were the main reasons. His long-time buddy, Mark, once asked why he used the testimony from someone who claimed he didn't know everything. "Because it's true," Virgil had replied, "I have to find answers like everyone else. Nobody knows everything."

"But it sounds a little negative and you might not want that on a business website," Mark followed with an attempt to make his point.

"But what is our slogan?" Virgil asked.

Mark sat quietly then nodded his head, "Ah, I see."

"Say it," Virgil demanded, smiling.

"It's right there on your website," Mark, his friend for thirty-five mostly fun-filled years, said playfully, but not giving an inch.

"Say it, you sonofabitch," Virgil yelled in mock anger and stood over him with fist raised.

"It's lame," Mark countered.

"I'll rip your nipples off and stuff them up your nose," Ditch threatened, laughing.

"Not that again. My other ones just grew back," Mark shot back now stoned faced, "While you're up get me another beer."

"Only if you give me the password which is also my slogan," Virgil said, grabbing Mark's empty Smithwick.

"Ditch Machine Repair, cause we won't." Mark said slowly and sarcastically. "What a classic."

"That's right. And we don't. And I'm sure glad your dumbass accounting mind came up with it. I'll get the beers and you can load the pipe. And if I haven't told ya, thanks for doing my books."

"Hey, every week after the fourth of July we have the best times up here and besides that you have helped me out as well."

"Oh, shut up and fire that thing up," Virgil said, returning with the next round.

That had been the fourth of July earlier this year. Since then Virgil had made his usual rounds throughout his region but with one glitch. In late August he had stopped to help a client in West Allis, Wisconsin, near Milwaukee. The company was Chase Products. The job required two days because of parts availability. On Monday he had taken a defective pump off the machine then relaxed that evening at a local bar, Benny's, which served great burgers, had his beer, and usually good music. It was there he was approached by two tall, bearded men dressed alike in all black clothes. Their hair was also cut the same. Both sides trimmed closely, about an inch over their ears. Above that was an inch tall mohawk greased down from the front to the back of their heads. This was only the third time Virgil had been at

Benny's, yet he was quite sure these guys were not regulars. The sparse crowd that evening made them stick out even more. Each man took a chair on either side of him at the round table Virgil had chosen. It was in the corner, furthest from the bar.

Virgil looked them over, then took and enjoyed another bite out of his burger as they settled into their chairs. He chewed, waiting for them to introduce themselves. They didn't, instead they stared at him until he had finished the bite, all the time looking and nodding at each other. Virgil remained silent, not wanting to give into these guys that were beginning to annoy him. He smiled at them, took a sip of his draft then tried to excuse himself, "I gotta hit the head boys, I'll be right back," he said, moving his chair back.

"Wait one minute," the man to Virgil's left said. "This will only take a moment of your time."

"Relax, we're not here to hurt you," the man to his right added.

"Then you guys can wait five minutes while I relieve myself. Talk amongst yourselves," Virgil said, rising from his chair.

"We'll be right here, friend," the first man said.

"Yeah, we'll be right here, Virgil," the second one said.

Virgil hesitated because they knew his name. That he didn't like, but he maintained a stoic persona. He left his chair with no intention of returning to the half-eaten burger and equally downed bottle. Let them finish it, he thought, throwing two twenties on the bar as he passed. He nodded towards the bartender, "Will that cover me?" Virgil asked.

"Gotcha ya, hoss," the older bartender, Don, who had recognized Virgil from his prior two visits, said, smiling and nodding in return.

Virgil took a left before the main exit double doors. He had to maintain the guise of going to the bathroom. Then of all times Virgil suddenly had the urge to actually go. I can hold it, he thought, maybe piss in the parking lot. The more he thought the worse the urge became. His mind relented to his bladder, and he took the left into the men's bathroom, quickly finding a stall. He unzipped his pants as he locked the door. This had to be quick. The half gallon of water he had consumed that afternoon while removing the pump had started all of this. Once the seal on his bladder had been broken, whatever he consumed the rest of the day flowed through him without hesitation at times. The beer he had recently consumed now pressed his bladder and necessitated the act again. In his fumbling state and with nerves now on edge, causing anxiety, his accuracy was lacking. He wasn't drunk but bounced against the stall wall. In the excitement he struggled to get his zipper undone. At the table he had been as cool as Jason Bourne. But now, after finally getting his zipper open, his piss hit the wall behind the toilet. He quickly rallied however, zeroing in on the bowel.

"What the hell," a weak and barely audible voice confronted him from the stall to his right.

"Sorry," Virgil said, not sure how he had affected the man next to him.

"No, it's good, son," the much older voice retorted. "I fell asleep and you crashing in here woke me up. Thanks," he said then paused. "But I only wish you could have been ten minutes earlier."

"Sorry," Virgil said, apologizing again but not sure why.

"Can you do me a favor, then?" the voice queried.

"If I can," Virgil offered as he emptied, wondering what this guy might possibly want. He heard him fumbling about on the other side of the stall wall. Virgil for the second time tonight was getting a little annoyed. "Are you alright over there?"

"Yeah," the voice answered, then paused for a moment. Finally he cleared his throat and asked, "Can you come in here and help me wipe my ass?"

"Well…," Virgil elongated his stunned response while he zipped up.

The older man in the next stall started laughing. It kept on as Virgil took a deep breath and tried to relax. He had to get out of this place. "Sorry, son, I was just fucking with you," the voice informed him then laughed some more. Virgil smiled thinking this whole night had become a joke.

Hand washing was not an option. He did a quick rinse, wiped them on the towel from the dispenser. He was going to take one more left and exit the bar through the door which opened to the back parking lot. He exited the bathroom, took the left and ran into one of the two men he thought he had left at the table, but unsure which one. "Where are you headed?" the man asked.

"Back to my table," Virgil replied sternly.

"Wrong way, Virgil," another voice informed him from behind.

He turned and faced the other man. "I haven't been here that much, guess I got turned around," Virgil laughed, still confident.

The man smiled at him, "I'm Ivan and now behind you is Gus. We got you another bottle. Let's talk," Ivan said, holding his arm out pointing in the correct direction. "I believe it is this way."

Virgil would have to at least listen to what Ivan and Gus brought to the table, though in his mind he wanted to be back at his hotel room watching TV. This is not how he wanted to end this trip. Plus, he had a pump to install the next day. They walked back to the table in the far corner. The two men quickly took their original seats like someone might take the chairs away. He looked back and forth at the guys and couldn't figure out who was who. He turned to his right, taking a guess, "Alright, Gus, what is it you guys want?"

"I'm Gus," the man to his left informed him.

"Okay, Gus, what do you guys want?" he asked Gus, turning to his left.

"Actually, I'm Gus," the man to his right said. "You were right the first time and that's why we want you for a job we need done."

"Because I guessed your name?" Virgil asked, sarcastically, but confused while leaning back in his chair to just observe both of them.

"No. For your acute sense of detail," Gus said. "We know you are very good at what you do, and we want the best. You know, the right DNA."

"Not many people notice the monograms on our lapels with our initials," Ivan explained. "I'm sure you noticed that earlier at some point. Very astute, Virgil."

"Have you been investigating or following me?" Virgil asked, looking about in an effort to catch a glimpse of their lapels without making it obvious. His effort proved fruitless. He couldn't locate the initials Gus had alluded to.

"Of course we have, Virgil," Gus admitted. "Why else would we want to get in touch with you?"

"Like we said, we know you're one of the best at what you do," Ivan restated.

"So, why me specifically? "Virgil asked. "I mean there are plenty of guys in this region that can do what I do."

"The other ones we looked at are tied down to their jobs and families and couldn't do it," Ivan explained. "From what we can tell, you, not so much."

"I might not be tied down to my job, boys, but I've dedicated my life to it with the option for time off," Virgil explained, then asked, "So did you investigate or follow me?"

"We know all of this from our investigation of you," Gus leaned forward and informed Virgil.

"Okay, so what is it you want me to repair?" Virgil asked, upset that he was investigated at all and then to the lengths it seems they had gone.

"First of all, you have to know we are with the Defense Department of this country," Ivan informed him, smiling.

"Do you have ID's?" Virgil asked as Gus quickly took an envelope from his inside jacket pocket and pushed it across the table in front of him. Virgil scanned the identification cards and the paperwork with the Defense Department letterhead on it. He smiled, "Your names are Ivan and Gustav Peprov and you're from the US?"

"We are American-born, second generation," Gus reassured him, returning the smile.

"We are very good at what we do as well, Mr. Ditch," Ivan added.

"And what exactly is it that you do?"

"We recruit talented people to work on our projects. Each person has a task to achieve which in turn helps our department complete its project and meet our objective," Ivan explained.

"You will be very well compensated, Virgil," Gus added. "Your business will do very well this year."

"I've done very well the past three years, why would I want to get involved with you guys?"

"Because you will be getting paid in cash," Gus stated, sweetening the offer. "You know, tax free."

"What would my task be?" Virgil asked. He realized his government would be breaking the law by paying him in cash and further asked, "You can do that? I mean pay a person in cash?"

"Your task will come in time as long as you sign on with us," Ivan informed him. "And, yes, we can pay you in cash, we're a division of the United States Government, we can do what we see fit to obtain our objective."

"I can't sign on to something I have no idea what it will do, or have any clue as to what my part is to help you achieve any objective."

"We can assure you it is for the betterment of society," Ivan continued.

"So you can assure me nobody will die as a result of this project?"

"That is our promise to you," Ivan said, nodding toward Gus for affirmation. Gus took the cue, and they nodded in unison.

"But you can't tell me right now?" Virgil asked, stalling, in a ploy to pry anything out of the bearded duo. "Are you guys twins and from the Kremlin?"

Ivan and Gus leaned back in their chairs laughing and slapping their knees. Then together they leaned forward. "It doesn't matter," Ivan managed to give a reply first.

"Yeah, we are twins, but as we said from this country. And we still want you for the job," Gus explained.

"Can I have some time to think about it?" Virgil asked, suddenly for some reason feeling a bit more at ease. How bad could it be, he thought. "We'll give you a call in exactly one week," Ivan said, "Ten p.m. Monday night."

"Wait, it's Labor Day this weekend," Gustav interrupted. "Make it next Tuesday."

"How much money are we talking about?" Virgil asked, wanting to know but trying not to sound like he was selling out to anyone or being greedy. He was embarrassed that he had accomplished neither. He was also frustrated at this. His father had taught him greed could be sensuous and intoxicating if you let it. But ultimately it was selfish and vile. He vindicated his feelings, realizing he was only seeking the most info he could from the mystery twins.

"You stand to make as much this next year as you have made the past three," Gus explained. "We will call you in a week, Virgil. In the meantime, read this over." Gus handed him a blue envelope with the same letterhead as their paperwork. Ivan and Gus then stood.

Ivan dropped a hundred-dollar bill on the table, "Are you twins?" he mimicked Virgil, then laughed. "Enjoy."

Virgil watched them walk across the room, noticing stares from some of the patrons. He looked at the envelope, deciding to open it later, he folded it in half and put it in his shirt pocket then watched the twins exit Benny's. He finished his beer and part of his now cold burger. He waited and left half an hour after his newfound unsolicited friends had.

Back Home

Virgil arrived home from West Allis, following a quick stop in Elk Grove, Illinois, on late Thursday afternoon of that week. Earl found him in the kitchen making a sandwich, "How was your trip?" Earl asked then informed him, "Didn't hear ya come in."

"I'll throw some pots and pans around next time," Virgil joked, patting Earl on the shoulder. "The work was a pump in West Allis that went well.

But the weird thing was a visit I got from two guys at a bar."

"Wasn't one of those gay bars was it?" Earl asked, not suspecting nor wanting to know, but really joking.

"Dad, you know I don't hang in that type of bar. It's not who I am,"

Virgil answered chuckling, "These guys were from the government. The Defense Department," Virgil said. Then explained everything to his father, even the attempted escape from the bar which Earl found quite humorous. He became concerned though when Virgil couldn't explain what he had to do for the amount of money he would receive.

"Virgil, I don't like what I'm smelling," Earl said later in the living room after they had gone over the details once again.

"I have until Tuesday night at ten p.m. to give them an answer."

"I just don't like what I'm smelling."

Virgil tried to ease his father's worries, "Dad, I can just tell them no. It is an option on the table."

"I know, but something is rotten," Earl said adamantly.

"Why," Virgil finally asked, giving up on any chance of trying to appease his father on this matter.

"Cause, I think I crapped my pants over here," Earl said with a laugh as he waved his hand back and forth in the air in front of him.

"I thought my ham had gone bad," Virgil said, laughing. Finally, he pulled the folded envelope from his shirt pocket and handed it to his dad. It was still unopened. Earl stared at it then at Virgil who had been thinking the offer over from the twins. but hadn't bothered to open the envelope.

"What's this?" his dad asked.

"It was the last thing they gave me, other than the hundo they left on the table for me to enjoy. I left it for the cute waitress named Megan whom I rarely saw," his son said, completing the last part of the story. "Go ahead and open it, Dad."

Earl reached to his right and pulled the drawer open from the oak end table. He took out a metal letter opener he only used for important correspondence. Most everything else he ripped open with his index finger, but not this one. He slid the opener under the flap and moved it laterally across the envelope. He pulled out a single page folded letter then handed it to Virgil.

"Read it first, Dad, then give it to me."

"Why?"

"Because then you'll know more than I do about this whole thing," Virgil said smiling.

Earl laughed, "That guy really asked you to wipe his ass in the bathroom?" he asked, then unfolded and began reading the letter.

"Yes, for the third time, Dad, he did," Virgil answered, smiling while watching his father read. Earl's concentration reminded Virgil of the times watching him read the Sunday *Chicago Tribune* while the Cubs or Sox were playing ball on a summer afternoon. This time Earl wasn't glancing at the TV which was off anyway. Earl said nothing after reading the letter and handed it back to Virgil.

"So what did it say, what should I do, I mean what are your thoughts?" Virgil asked, wanting some of the direction Earl had always offered and provided him.

"Read it," Earl said and waited while his son did. When he was done Virgil looked at his father. Earl saw the question in his quizzical look, "I would say goodbye, see ya later, I'm good, already got a job," Earl suggested.

"It's a good offer, don't ya think, Dad?"

"Yes, it is, but think about it and we will discuss it later. Give it time to sink in while you weigh the pros and cons. It is still somewhat vague. We still going to the cabin this weekend?" Earl asked, closing the subject.

"You still up for it?" Virgil asked, knowing his dad hadn't been himself lately. He seemed fatigued, but then again, he was eighty. He also knew he was right in his approach in this matter.

"I've been kind of tired the last few days," Earl admitted. "Think I'll take a pass this time."

"That's fine. Maybe we'll get up there in October like we always do."

"Let's make sure we do that," Earl said with commitment.

The next day Virgil had to troubleshoot some machine problems locally. This was actually a blessing. He didn't have to think about The Offer. Between him and his dad it had become, The Offer, and would be referred to as such moving forward. They felt it was a good offer, yet the mystery and vagueness was gnawing at them both. They had questions. What would the government make which would benefit society, and why through the Defense Department? It was a two-part query but number one in the unanswered column. The money portion of The Offer was huge. Earl and Virgil both joked that they finally knew how their tax dollars were at work. The uncashed check included in the envelope was equal to a nice lotto ticket. Virgil realized it was more like his best five years than his past three. With what he already had saved he would become a millionaire. At his age, Virgil smiled at the chance but mulled over the ramifications. Earl mentioned he hadn't made that kind of money in his first fifteen years at his job. "Yeah, Dad, but you've been retired for some time now. These are different times," Virgil pointed out.

The next morning Virgil made the short trip to Elgin and once again to Elk Grove for some parts he needed to restock his van. He referred to it as the Bitch'n Ditch business on wheels. The company slogan had been painted on the side of the light blue vehicle by his cousin, Jimmy, who owned a sign painting business. Jimmy's payment had been a weekend at the cabin for whomever he wanted to bring. "As long as you don't burn the place down," Virgil had warned, knowing his cousin's penchant for partying. The red lettering with white accents stood out and proved to be good for Virgil's business and on one occasion he thought it was going to be the end of him.

Virgil had almost been side swiped by a woman in Michigan that had noticed his van while both were driving in the same direction. She owned a company which needed a machine repaired and was enthusiastically trying to flag Virgil over. He pulled over to the shoulder of the road to find out what the arm waving and finger pointing woman wanted. He reached for the biggest wrench he had hidden under the passenger seat of the van then exited with it to face her and defend himself if need be. The woman also exited her vehicle and immediately asked Virgil if he could fix her company's machine while quickly making up the distance between them. Her name was Dena. Virgil was shocked by her aggressiveness but more so by her beauty. He almost dropped his wrench. She was tall, slender, and athletic. Her shoulder length dark hair framed a classic face. He obliged Dena without revealing the wrench he still held but now lowered behind him. These days you never knew what could happen. She might have been packing something more powerful than his wrench. The machine fix had turned out to be a tricky one, but with tech support solved by Virgil late that afternoon. This had impressed Dena enough to initiate the whole adventure which ensued. They both laughed at his side of the story as Virgil explained it to her over dinner that night. She was grateful for the repair on the machine. She took Virgil out because she was somehow drawn to a smart rugged looking man. These chances were few and far between for Virgil, so he willingly and gratefully obliged her. It turned into a four-day weekend at her resort home in St. Joseph. They both enjoyed it but never saw each other again after.

Sunday was, as usual, a lazy restful day. Earl went to church as he most always did. Sickness or laziness being the only reasons for his absences. Holy Trinity had been his religious home for sixty-three years and counting. He had married his wife, Helen, at the wooden altar. Since then he had, mostly with Virgil in tow, attended loyally.

Over the years Earl had related stories about the goings on at the brothers and sisters in Christ establishment. Stories which seemed to be evil by nature. People backstabbing each other for petty reasons at best. Earl told him of an instance where people harassed fellow parishioners by phone late at night. Virgil stuck with him until he graduated high school. Then one Sunday morning, after experiencing stares over his choice of clothing and hair length and hearing their under-the-breath comments, Virgil made his first really grown up decision. He didn't need judgment from these people and realized his time would be better spent sleeping off a night of *I can't remember how I got home* than getting involved with people who couldn't practice what was preached to them. At least he would be honest with himself. It was a time when he needed to get out and experience a different lifestyle for a while.

He always helped people whenever he could. His dad had instilled that in him at an early age and Virgil was grateful he had. It gave him a chance to meet people, expand his business, and help society. That part of religion Virgil had taken to heart. Every time you do something good for someone it was like doing it for Jesus. Virgil tried to emulate that whenever he had the opportunity. He was not an angel by any stretch of the imagination but knew the least he could do was sponsor a little league team, host food drives, and generally help those who were in need. Like the ones who hadn't grown up with a great father like Earl, and the love and care he had provided. He swore to God and himself when he had the means to, he would help as many as he could. If anyone asked him why, he would tell them it was God's plan for him. Virgil had built his business to a point that he had been able to help many people. He was proudest of the laptops he had provided the school at the Indian community north of his cabin. The Offer would allow him to help many more people.

"You make a decision yet?" Earl asked Virgil that night in the living room as he looked up from the Sunday *Tribune* crossword puzzle.

Virgil smiled, "I think I will do it if I can pry out of them what it is we're doing."

"I doubt they will cough up any more info. I would drop it and get back to your business."

"They can only say no as I see it."

"There is just something about this whole thing I don't like. Even the letter was vague," Earl said, waving his hand.

"Did you crap your pants again?"

"No, a fucking gnat."

Virgil laughed, "Oh well, money isn't everything," he said knowing his father was probably right. "Besides, what we have is pretty good don't ya think, Dad?"

"I would say so," Earl said, always appreciative of what had come his way in life. He knew Virgil and him were blessed despite being the common sinners they were. Earl's friends described him as a humble man and that Earl and his family deserved whatever riches might come their way. But Earl was never comfortable with that praise. He always felt you devoted yourself to being the best at your job and to God. The rest of his life would take care of itself. Evolve before him so to speak.

Monday came and Virgil did burgers and brats on the grill to celebrate the holiday. Their neighbors, Ellen and Gene Kalsow, from across the street came over with some beer and they had a makeshift party. Tommy's name came up once or twice and the Kalsows only mentioned he was on a fishing trip. They enjoyed the day, and The Offer was never brought up.

Tuesday came and Virgil wished he had something to do, but the area was quiet as was his website. No companies with hot jobs that should have been fixed over the weekend calling him to help them out. A broken hydraulic hose, valve replacement, anything to forget The Offer. It bothered Virgil because it disrupted his routine and he just wanted to say, "No, thank you," and get on with his life.

Helping others was how Virgil made his living, and he was good at it. He wasn't perfect, and he could be an asshole at times, especially when it came to cutting corners on jobs. This was his biggest pet peeve, only because it was never a safe option. Nothing good ever came out of rushing through a job. You may get lucky and cut a big chunk of time off the job, but there was always that chance a big chunk could come out of you. There was always the chance within the rush and deadline that you might miss something. Something crucial where it might cost a lot of money. These days some companies didn't think twice about making sure the blame landed firmly on your shoulders. This was how he got into conflicts with them. "I want to go home at the end of the day," he would then explain his reasons why in a take it or leave it manner. Most companies took him, attitude and all.

Earl explained this side of Virgil to his son one day. It was a trait passed down from his mother, Helen. The spunk, the nerve, and the determination to be heard. She was a woman Virgil never knew. She died a week after his birth from a toxin passed somehow during his delivery. Under those rare and therefore mysterious circumstances Virgil began life with his father Earl, a reserved but firm and fair manager at the local Leath furniture company his father-in-law Harold had begun. The settlement they received from the hospital made life easier but never fuller.

Virgil's early years were graciously molded by Miss Ruth Laudy, a large but gentle middle-aged next door neighbor who had never married but was enamored with the spirit and innocence of children. She had been a nurse by day and Virgil's adopted mother the weeknights Earl was managing the furniture store. Even before this arrangement Earl had loved Ruth like a sister. Helen and her had become good friends and Ruth offered to help Earl out when Helen passed on. Ruth never had a child of her own. Having worked with the newborns at Sherman Hospital she had helped thousands. Teaching Sunday school at her church she had, over the years, cared for many other children. Together she and Earl reared his son. Like any parents they weren't perfect, but Virgil had made it. Ruth passed away before she could see Virgil graduate from high school. A sudden heart attack prevented it. She had done her best to teach her neighbor's son the right path in life, and Virgil was devastated when Ruth died three weeks before the graduation ceremony. Earl had to convince him to go and get his diploma in the auditorium, "Do it for Ruth, she would expect you to." Virgil did it for the only mother he ever knew.

Despite Earl and Ruth's efforts there were times Virgil had to forge a path on his own. This helped further build and strengthen his maturity. He had survived it all. A broken nose at age ten from a much older kid on his school's playground after classes were done for the day. His reward for sticking up for a frail classmate who was being picked on. The actual hatchet. The car at age fourteen his best friend Mark had borrowed from his brother and convinced Virgil it was okay to take it for a spin only to rear end a parked car. Earl warned him to stay away from Mark but it only, after a six-month semi-respite, made them closer. To the glory of losing his virginity at fifteen to a neighbor, Brandi, who was graduating from high school that year. For two weeks he was king of his own little world which amounted to Mark and three other freshmen he hung out with at Larkin High. After the encounter word got around but not through Virgil. Brandi denied it, but her older sister sold her out over a sweater owed to her on a different sexual adventure Brandi had perpetrated. Now at forty-seven, Virgil remembered that encounter fondly as he awaited the phone call, sitting at his desk in his bedroom. His father was right, the letter was vague. It only mentioned that he would be contracted by the government and compensated tax free. He continually looked at his phone and the time in the lower right corner of his computer. The letter went on to say the project would help eliminate a virus.

What virus is out there, he wondered again. We just had one and for that matter we have always had one. A virus, that though deadly, was not any worse than many of the prior flu strains. John Prine's first album and the gut-wrenching fate of Sam Stone played in the background as Virgil scanned his site for work. Listening to Prine he realized his hero had been taken by the Covid-19 virus. His site showed there was nothing new for the next week, but he knew his business remained strong. His buddy made sure of it. When Mark located any type of red flag in the books, he promptly notified Virgil. Earl aided the family business by keeping a bulletin board in a spare bedroom which mapped out his son's monthly schedule. When problems arose the trio would discuss it, make adjustments, and work on. This collaboration had worked for the past twenty years. There were slow and tough times, but they had fought through all of it. Now, the letter and clock weighed on his mind. Virgil hated wasting time when he could be doing something. Where was the phone call and necessary details which might change his future.

When the doorbell rang, Virgil looked at the clock on his computer then grabbed his phone, "Hello."

Confused and ashamed he swiped the phone, stood up, turned and walked out of his room and down the hall towards the front door. It rang again. He stopped and looked at the doorbell camera on his phone. It was Ivan and Gus. What the hell? They said they were going to call, not call on me, Virgil thought as he continued down the hallway to the front door. Smiling, he opened the door. "Gentlemen, so nice of you to drop by. Please come in and take a load off," he offered.

Ivan and Gus looked at each other as Virgil tried to decide who was who. Virgil looked at their lapels. There never were any monograms. Those bastards had me at hello, he thought and smirked at his own reference to the Jerry McGuire movie.

"We can wait here while you get the check, Virgil," Gus said with a stoic expression, though his eyes wandered.

"Right here," Ivan said adamantly pointing at his feet while puffing out and up his shoulders and chest. He looked like a rooster getting ready to crow, Virgil thought still smiling, especially the way Ivan did it.

"Why are you guys really here? I thought you were calling on the phone," Virgil asked, not backing up.

"Get the check, Virgil," Gus said, reaching inside his sports jacket.

"Why don't you guys come in and relax," Virgil offered, confused at their unfriendly tone and suspicious movements.

"Virgil, just get it," Ivan demanded, reaching behind his back.

Virgil was baffled as he backed away, then turned and walked back through the front room to the hallway. As a mechanic many times he had to decipher a sporadic glitch in an injection molding machine, or any machine for that matter. Finding something common to the problem was always a starting point, but this really made no sense. Why this late-night crap and why him? Above all he didn't trust his own government enough to believe he would be doing something so secretive yet help humanity. What virus could they be talking about? One coming or one invented and still coming.

Earl mentioned one time, during one of their many talks, how his dad had worked for a company which was asked by the same government to put aluminum plating on some steel parts for them. The company his grandpa Jerry worked for had the largest plating tanks in the United States and therefore met the requirements to achieve the objective. Turns out those parts went all the way to Hiroshima and Nagasaki.

He was skeptical about the lack of truth. He took out his key and opened a drawer in his desk then grabbed the check. He returned to the twins and handed it to Gus, "It was interesting doing business with you guys, but I'm going to say no to your offer."

"No was never an option Virgil," Gus said, taking the check and lighting it on fire with a matchstick he flicked under his thumbnail and lit.

"Meet us at Benny's in West Allis on Wednesday for a full explanation," Ivan instructed him with a smile.

"You guys don't get it. I'm declining," Virgil said.

"Most choose your path, but change their minds after the third meeting," Ivan explained, tapping Virgil on his right shoulder with his index finger.

"Besides, if you want the actual check you'll show up," Gus said, grinding out the ashes of the first one on the concrete porch landing.

Virgil started laughing. "Are you guys for real? I mean what could I possibly do for you that the government hasn't already figured out?"

"There is one thing," Gus informed him. "And we will let you know this a week from tomorrow."

"What part of no don't you guys understand?" Virgil asked, raising his voice, now perturbed at the whole thing.

"Ask not what your country can do for you, but ask what you can do for your country," Ivan said, puffing out his chest again and pulling an envelope from his back pocket then forcefully squeezing Virgil's shoulder with his hand. "Here is all you need to know until then." Ivan stuffed the envelope into Virgil's left hand.

"See you then," Gus said, then stuffed a wad of cash in Virgil's shirt pocket. "Here's some gas money."

They turned and walked down the five steps to the sidewalk and then to the street. They quickly hopped into a black Escalade which had just pulled up. It sped off and made a left at the next corner.

Virgil was stunned. He rubbed his shoulder and raised his arm up and down in an effort to get the tingling feeling out of his shoulder. He had declined but to no avail. "What the fuck," he said as he watched the vehicle disappear from a different angle this time. He closed the door and turned to see Earl standing in the hallway with his hunting rifle. "What the hell are you doing?" Virgil asked.

"I would've got one of them," Earl said with a sheepish grin.

"Or got us both wasted," Virgil said, shaking his head. "Whole new ball game now. What the hell."

"Told ya I didn't like what I was smelling," Earl said.

"Probably not, cause I just shit my pants," Virgil informed him. "Fuck this, I'm going to bed."

"Goodnight, son," Earl said, patting Virgil on his back. "You know sometimes God tests you," he offered.

Virgil turned and looked at his dad, "I'm not ready for this. I just want to do my job and live my life."

"He also guides us through times like these," Earl said, knowing Virgil already knew. "I will pray for you and come with you if you want."

Virgil hugged his dad around the rifle between them, "I know you would, Dad," he said, then released him. "But I have to face this one on my own. You and Mark will be involved so stay sharp," he said, patting his father on his back. "Goodnight."

To West Allis

The paperwork contained in the envelope required his signature. It linked him to the Defense Department's latest project, a virus study which wanted volunteers to literally be guinea pigs as he read it. Virgil wasn't willing to be a human lab rat. He just wanted to continue his business as usual. There was nothing in The Offer that mentioned Virgil sacrificing his life or well-being. It also referenced the building of a database. He needed guidance from a higher source than Earl, so he sat down and prayed about this situation. He had prayed for the health of people before, but it had been a long time since he had turned to God for the outcome of a situation regarding himself. He only asked God for guidance, and he was sure of the answer. He was going to decline once again. The funny thing about the government though, is that it can manipulate anything it wants, including people's lives. The next day, Wednesday, he received a frantic call from Mark, "When were you going to tell me?"

"Tell you what?" Virgil said, caught off guard.

"That you were going out of business," Mark said, breaking the news to him.

"You know damn well you would've been one of the first to know. Where did you hear this?" Virgil asked. The shock and ensuing confusion could be sensed in his tone.

"Looked at your website yet?"

Virgil opened his laptop and waited for it to load up. Little seemed to be working. Then it froze up, "What did it say exactly? My laptop just froze up."

"It said because of recent economic conditions you were shutting down Ditch Machine Repair. Then you thanked all of your loyal customers. Did you hit the lottery or something Virgil?"

"In a way I may have, but I declined their offer. Apparently though that is not an option with these guys," Virgil said, trying to get his computer to reboot.

"Now, what are you talking about?" Mark asked.

He told Mark the entire story. When he finished there was silence on the other end. "Are you still there?" Virgil asked his best friend.

"I'm here, Virgil. Sounds like something out of a spy thriller," Mark summated, then, "Did you really wipe that guy's ass?"

"I know," Virgil agreed, then, "And no, I didn't"

"So what are you going to do?"

"I guess I better meet them in West Allis a week from tonight," Virgil stated.

"You want company?"

"I better go this one alone, Mark. I'm going to get to the bottom of this once and for all. Keep alert though I may be getting in contact with you at some point during that night."

"You sure you just don't want me to come along?" Mark offered again.

"I'm sure," Virgil confirmed. "Hey, if anything happens to me take care of my dad, would you?"

"Like he was my own," Mark reassured him.

Benny's Bar

Virgil left his van as close to the front door as space allowed. He exited then walked towards the bar. Benny's on a Wednesday was not the best place to be if you were looking to meet women. For sure, Virgil wasn't. Thursday was the prime weekday night, because it was Ladies Night and women's drinks were half-priced. Tonight guys were looking for a way to blow off steam if their week was not going as planned or to just meet up with friends. Virgil's week fell into the confused category. Also, he had a different reason in that he needed to end a relationship rather than start one. He only needed to blow off steam in the sense of relinquishing a burden. He laughed to himself, pausing, then entering as he remembered the last time he had been near this doorway.

The hallway, which led to the bathrooms and his previous failed escape attempt, were on the right after he passed through the double glass entry doors. He continued beyond the next walls and into the main room where the polished solid oak bar spread across thirty feet of the hundred-foot room to his right. It was the sports and outdoors theme, punching machine, pool tables, and music that drew the guys and not surprisingly the women.

Those diversions were across the room to the left.

Virgil leaned his back against the bar and waited his turn for a beer from the hot bartender strategically placed by management to keep the men coming back for more. His buddy, Don, from his previous visit wasn't working this shift. He turned and scanned the bar looking for Ivan and Gus.

"What can I get you?" a soft and pleasant voice asked him from behind. It was his first break since the twins had come visiting his and Earl's home.

He turned and absorbed her beautiful smiling face, "I'll have a Smithwicks," he said, trying not to stare too long, then realized she looked familiar. He looked up and down the bar then at her again. There were no Ivan or Gus to be seen. He hoped they had forgotten but knew that would be impossible. He listened to the pounding music and glanced at the Brewers game on the big screen behind the bar. He realized the bartender was his waitress from his last visit. He remembered her name was Megan. A beautiful woman who had sparingly waited on him the last time he was here.

"Here's your beer," Megan said, returning and placing it on a cardboard coaster in front of Virgil.

"Thank you," he said, handing her a five-dollar bill.

"I'll bring your change."

"Keep it, Megan," Virgil said. "In fact," he said looking about the bar, "I'm in the mood to buy a round for the house."

"Wait, how did you know my name?" she asked.

"You probably don't remember me from my last time here," Virgil said.

"Sorry, I don't."

"Well I'm sure you see plenty of people in here. I had two visitors at the back of the bar that night. You were my waitress. I remember your name because someone yelled it and you responded. One of the few times I saw you."

"Sorry...," she started to say. "Wait a minute, you're the one that had the two weird visitors."

"That would be me," Virgil said, laughing.

"They followed you to the bathroom," Megan recalled her version of that night.

"How did you see all of that?" Virgil asked, then stated, "I rarely saw you."

"I was doubling in the kitchen that night, plus one of those guys put a hundred in my apron and told me to stay away and leave them alone with you. They said it was government business," Megan explained.

"I don't remember seeing you after you delivered my burger," Virgil said.

"I was earning the hundo by staying out of the way," she said, smiling.

"You actually made two hundred that night from them. They threw one on my table and I left it for you."

"Here, I thought you were impressed with my service," Megan said, laughing.

Virgil laughed as well, "Now, how about that round I was talking about."

Megan looked around the room while Virgil once again stared at her. He didn't intend anything malicious, it was just that he found her beauty riveting. Her personality was refreshing as well. She seemed down to earth, pretty much like himself. He also knew the reality of this situation, he didn't stand a chance with her. She finished her scan of the room and returned Virgil's stare. "That's about two-hundred and fifty bucks," she informed him, drawing a pause from Virgil while he turned and scanned the place again.

He laughed again remembering the twins generosity last Tuesday night, then reached in his pocket for the wad of cash Gustav had insisted he take. Without looking and not wanting to stare at her again, he put his right elbow on the bar and bent it back behind him handing Megan the money.

"This should cover it," Virgil said, twisting his head back to be heard.

Megan took a moment counting the cash below the bar top, "There's like seven hundred here," she said laughing.

Virgil turned and looked at her, "Buy the house two rounds and keep the rest for you and the waitresses who are going to be busting their butts for the next little while."

"Thank you," Megan said. "But don't expect anything but the drinks being served," she said, making sure Virgil knew she couldn't be bought in that manner.

"Thank you, but that is not my intention," he said, turning and handing her another fifty. "I believe in tipping the correct amount."

"Why are you thanking me?"

"Because I may need your help later. Besides, you are a beautiful woman," Virgil said. "Sorry, did I say that out loud?"

"If I can help, I will," she said, laughing off his compliment. Virgil was older yet rugged, and actually, to her, pretty good looking, she thought but reiterated her stance, "Remember, I'm just getting the drinks served. Besides, I don't even know your name."

"I know, I expect nothing more. And my name is Virgil Ditch," he said then paused. "Actually, if you will indulge me, one more thing. Do you have a pen and piece of paper handy?"

Megan reached under the bar, searching for a moment for the items requested then pulled them out, placing them on the bar. She studied him again as Virgil wrote down some phone numbers, tore the paper off the pad then handed it to her. "What do you want me to do with this," she asked.

"When those same two guys from last time come in here for me I would like you to call the first number there and tell the guy who answers where you're from and to have him call me in fifteen minutes."

"That's it?"

"That is all your help I will need."

"What's the other number for?"

"When this is all over, hopefully in about a month, I would like you to call it and tell me where I can take you to dinner," Virgil said, hoping and smiling. "You know, as a thank you."

Megan smiled back then put the paper in her apron, "You can count on me. At least for the first part," she said.

"Knew I could, that's why I asked," Virgil said. "And I understand the no on the dinner. I'm sure you know more guys in your age range than guys like me."

"Well actually I'm supposed to be leaving here if some plans work out. Florida is a lot warmer this time of year and I have friends in Pompano."

"Nice place, Pompano. Stopped there before I went to the Bahamas one time. Loved the beaches and the town itself was a good place to relax."

"Ever stop at the Pelican Bar?" Megan inquired.

"No, but I saw it. It's on the beach next to one of those long piers, right?"

"That's the one," she said, showing him her crossed fingers. "Hopefully I'll be working there when I leave here,"

"Well I wish you the best of luck and if that phone call comes from Florida I would still be willing to take you out for dinner," Virgil offered again. "Unless of course you're with someone. If that is the case, I apologize for being the wolf."

Megan laughed, "No worries, I'm not with anyone right now."

A few minutes later, she turned around and summoned the bar staff to the other end of the bar. There she gave them tickets to hand out to the patrons in the bar that night. "Two tickets to each person. One ticket, one drink," she explained then pointed in Virgil's direction so all knew who the benefactor was.

After about forty-five minutes, Virgil, by word of mouth, had become quite popular throughout Benny's. He smiled when Ivan and Gus finally came into the bar about a half hour later. They located him immediately upon entering the room. They nodded at him as they approached. Virgil smiled. "Welcome back to Benny's, boys," Virgil said, motioning them towards two empty bar stools.

"Let's get a table in the corner," Gus suggested.

"I like it here," Virgil said, standing his ground with a louder tone.

"Don't be stupid," Gus continued. "We can hardly hear you right here."

"I really don't care," Virgil stiffened, his voice getting louder as he leaned in so they could hear him better. "If what you guys offer is so good, maybe you could have all kinds of volunteers right here in this bar. Maybe you should offer it to them."

Ivan rammed the barrel of a pistol into Virgil's ribs through the pocket of his Washington Capitals hockey jacket. "I think we better go to the corner table."

"No, Ivan, we're staying here," Virgil said, betting he wouldn't shoot him in front of fifty to sixty witnesses, but not sure of the odds. Besides why would they need to shoot him if he was helping humanity. He was now getting pissed at and tired of the bearded twins.

"I'm not Ivan, I'm Gus."

"You know what, fuck that bullshit. You guys close my business and then just expect me to do what you say," Virgil said, turning from one to the other. Virgil had reached his limit, "Well, it's not happening."

"Would you guys like something to drink?" Megan asked, glancing at Virgil.

"Give them what I'm having," Virgil suggested.

"We're having vodka," Ivan said, slamming his fist on the bar hard enough to draw stares from everyone at the bar as the house music faded and it became quieter, "Right here," he said, slamming it down again in an effort to appear he meant it all along. The growing number of onlookers took notice.

"Yes, right here," Gus joined in tapping his left fist on the bar with a laugh.

Virgil winked a thank you at Megan, "Put it on my tab."

She threw her head back and laughed then yelled, "Two vodkas coming up."

Gus sat first, then Ivan after he pulled his hand out of his pocket. Virgil sat in the middle. With both hands Virgil motioned the twins closer to him as the music started again, "Now what exactly do you guys want?"

Ivan and Gus didn't say a word. Virgil took a sip from his bottle. The twins remained close to their target as Megan returned with their drinks. "Enjoy gentlemen," she said, placing the drinks far enough away the twins had to break their pose to retrieve them. She winked at Virgil, holding her hand to her ear like she was talking on a phone. She had called Mark. She now turned to help serve the second round the twins had given him money to buy.

Ivan and Gus leaned back on their bar stools and looked behind Virgil. They were, for the first time in this scenario, confused. They leaned forward again. "Virgil, we want you to take a shot," Ivan offered.

"A shot of what, Stoli?" Virgil asked.

"No, a shot of whatever you want on the back of that bar," Ivan said pointing at the variety.

For the first time in Benny's, Virgil realized the vastness of the mirror built into the bar. It made the room appear larger. Distorted things. Deception could work on these guys he thought, staring at his and the twins' reflections. That's when he noticed the GP and IP stitched initials on their lapels. The red initials on the blue background were backwards, but initials for sure. When they grabbed their drinks, he once again motioned them in close. He pulled their heads in with his left and then right hand. Gus from the left, Ivan from the right, "Gentlemen, what exactly do you want?" Virgil asked again when their temples finally rested against him from each side.

"We want what we have always wanted," Gus said, sipping his drink.

"And what is that?"

"Take a shot and help us out," Ivan said, switching glasses with his brother. "They never get our order right here, do they Gustav?"

"Told ya, I don't want a shot of Stoli"

"Remember the virus we informed you about in the letter we presented you?" Ivan asked.

"Yeah, what about it?"

"We want you to take the shot and let our people record your symptoms and more importantly, the final results," Ivan said, finally coming to the point of all the cloak and dagger bullshit.

"I thought I was supposed to build something for you," Virgil said, referring to the prior meetings.

"You are," Gus said. "You're building a database for this strain of virus."

"And all the other people are doing the same thing?"

"Yes," Gus assured him. "We wanted a diverse group and that is why we handpicked everyone."

"You are not going to die from this, Virgil," Ivan said, patting him on his left shoulder.

"You're right, I won't die, because I'm not taking it."

"You will be fine," Gus assured him, patting him on the other shoulder.

"Did you guys take it?" Virgil asked, smiling at one then the other. He downed his beer and motioned to Megan for another.

"Early results tell us that you will get sick with flu-like symptoms, and it might last three to five days," Gus informed him, ignoring Virgil's question.

"So why the big money offer?"

"Because we want to follow up to see if antibodies are created. Then we can create a vaccine. We feel the money is an incentive as well as compensation for time missed from your job," Ivan explained.

"This could take some time to happen, and we don't want you working," Gus said.

"Or spreading it. Is that why you shut down my business?" Virgil added and asked, raising his voice just as the music calmed again. People looked in their direction, nodding at Virgil and raising their drinks to salute him. "Is that why you are trying to ruin me?" he asked even louder. Now some of the bigger male patrons moved closer in concern for their newest drinking buddy.

"Look here, you ungrateful little prick," Ivan said, rising from his barstool.

"Hey, dickhead," a voice came from behind them. "Leave our buddy alone."

Gus and Ivan turned to see most of the guys and some women in the bar crowding around them in grateful interest, like another drink might be forthcoming. "Yeah, leave Virgil alone," another man joined in. The twins hadn't researched this scenario.

"Hey, this is none of your business," Gus said, knowing it was probably a mistake as the words rolled off his lips. He stood and faced the group with his brother.

Virgil's ringtone of Santanna's "Europa" sounded. He pulled the phone out of his pocket and swiped it. It was Mark, "Excuse me, boys, I gotta take this," he said and walked towards the bathroom hallway where he would be able to hear. Ivan and Gus started to follow but the crowd closed in around them as Virgil had passed through it. Virgil heard someone suggest to the twins it would be a good idea to let him take the call and an even better idea if they sat back down and finished their drinks.

The Cabin

"Virgil," Earl yelled again when he had reached the Adirondack chairs they had purchased together the previous summer at a local flea market. He remembered the day and the argument which ensued about the transportation of the heavy, awkward but comfortable and beautifully crafted chairs back to here. Tied to the top of Virgil's van they had made it to where Earl now let his body fall into the nearest, the red one. He stared at the stone encased fire pit at his feet then the blue sky above and back again. "Where the hell are you," he said to himself. He wanted to know his son was safe. In the years he and Miss Laudy had raised Virgil it was their main objective. That, and that Virgil was to make smart decisions. The latter was now in question.

The phone call he had received last Wednesday evening was reassuring but did not answer all the questions Earl had running through his mind as he leaned back in his chair. He wanted the answers face to face from his son. Not the anxiety it caused then and now. He knew the flight from Benny's Bar in West Allis was going to be a necessity when Virgil had left earlier that Wednesday afternoon from their home. He didn't believe the cabin would be empty when he arrived here though. While resting he ran Wednesday's conversation through his mind wondering if he had forgotten or missed something.

"Dad, Dad," he recalled Virgil yelling into the phone. He could tell his son had gained an edge in this mystery by the excited tone of his voice.

"I'm here, Virgil," Earl yelled back.

"First of all, I'm alright. Second, call Mark and tell him I'm headed to the cabin. Third, tell him to look at a new email. Tell him it might show up under spam. Can you do that?"

"Wait a minute," Earl had answered excitedly, stumbling for a pad of paper and pen. "Are you okay?"

"I'm fine, Dad. I'm going to the cabin. I don't think they'll find me there or if they even made it out of the bar alive."

"I'm coming up there," his dad instinctively said, then paused. "Why? What did you guys do to them?"

"No Dad. Stay there. I, or should I say we, turned the tables on them," he explained. "I need you there, so stay. Lock the doors and stay put or go to Ernie's place if you feel safer there."

"Okay, I might do that," Earl relented. "Be careful and stay safe."

"Dad, I love you, please just do as I ask. I should be home by Friday," Virgil said, knowing his dad's determination and perseverance.

"I will," Earl reluctantly agreed. "Told you I didn't like what I was smelling."

"I'll be okay. I have places to hide, so don't worry."

"Love you, son."

"Love you too, Dad," Virgil said, realizing at the time he probably had not told his father that nearly enough in his lifetime.

Upon arrival Earl had searched the entire cabin after he had looked through Virgil's van parked in front of the cabin which faced the lake. It was usually parked behind the structure but if it were in front, or lake side, it couldn't possibly be seen from the road even at the hundred-yard distance. Earl knew first hand Virgil was no dummy and had seen him prove it many times. Now Earl rose from the chair and walked past the van. He was just past it when he noticed a dark spot on the ground along with what appeared to be another set of tire tracks next to it. He examined the tread on the van's tires and the imprint left in the mud from a rain sometime before he had arrived. It didn't match. The spot he noticed had been left on some leaves which had already migrated to the earth and stood out against the white gravel. The leaves were in a flat but thick clump. There was some hair stuck to it and it appeared to Earl to be human. He looked at the black spots on the leaves and though dry, he knew it was blood, not mud. He smiled knowing Virgil didn't have black hair and nothing this thick. But where the hell was he and did Ivan and Gus follow him here and grab him? Earl's vision wasn't what it was ten years ago, and he missed things. Knowing that, he surveyed the area again, bending over in an effort to possibly uncover more clues. The six-hour drive to the cabin, the excited instant search when he had arrived and now the new evidence, though promising, was beginning to wear Earl down. He knew his age. He knew his limits, though he would never admit it. He pressed on, albeit at a slower pace.

That's when he noticed some broken twigs and a spot on the earth that looked like an imprint of something that had hit the softened ground. Getting down to his hands and knees he found more dark thick hair and some blue shirt material. Then crawling about like he used to when he was Virgil's living room horsey, he noticed a footprint that was definitely not his son's Asiacs. It was next to another tire track that matched the first. The heel mark was large and left enough letters in the mud next to it to know it was a Wolverine brand boot. There were more black dried blood stains on the crushed gravel that made up the driveway. That's when he noticed another footprint a few feet away. This one was Virgil's, and it was pointed in the direction of the woods.

He didn't know exactly where Virgil was, but he sensed his son was safe because Virgil's tracks led to the edge of the woods. He smiled and walked to the cabin to have a bite to eat. A sandwich and a beer would do. Virgil always had peanut butter and some jelly in stock and there was a six pack of Old Potosi in the refrigerator. He ate and drank quickly, noticing the daylight was beginning to wane. He grabbed a battery-powered lantern, took one last sip from the bottle, set it on the counter, and exited the cabin. He followed the last footstep he had seen in the damp gravel. He found two more of Virgil's prints just off the gravel which led him to a path heading North into the woods. He followed the path at least fifty yards into the woods. If he was hiding in here he was doing an excellent job, Earl thought, as he could no longer find any more signs of his son. He called out Virgil's name every ten yards down the path. No answer.

Fit for a man his age, Earl could go on for a long time in this quest, but he knew he had to be practical. So far he had found nothing that made his search seem futile, but he was a majority of one. He smiled, sometimes you just had to call it a day. Live to fight another day, he thought, hoping and praying his son would be able to do that as well. It was dusk and he turned on the lantern. It was dim, but hopefully it would last long enough to light the passage over the uneven, rocky ground back to the cabin. At this point, on this particular day, he just wanted to have the bed he knew awaited him in the cabin. He trudged on with the meager light thinking of the upper loft and the security of the shotgun underneath the king-size bed. He prayed to God his son was alright as he reached what they both considered the front door. It didn't face in the direction of the road that brought you here, but rather towards Booth Lake about forty yards below it. Virgil and Earl had felt they wanted the house to welcome in the serenity first thing every morning. It was why the cabin faced east. Two and a half hours later, Earl was asleep two minutes after his head hit the pillow. It was a restless sleep however, as he constantly awoke to any slight sound, thinking Virgil was coming home late at night from a job. Each time he was mistaken and he finally succumbed to the veil of weariness which hung over him.

A shotgun blast startled him awake the next morning. With arms flailing about he threw off the covers and grabbed his pants while reaching under the bed for the twelve-gauge shotgun. He had assumed it would be there, but it wasn't. The last line of defense he and Virgil had agreed upon was gone. It was always there before, but Earl was now worried as to who possessed it. Virgil had to have it, he thought, nobody else knew it was there. Three more volleys sounded. Earl came to his senses, then laughed, realizing it was duck hunting season this time of year. He sat back down on the bed hard. He was sore from the previous day. Two more errant volleys resonated through the air. He dressed slowly and at the same pace made his way down to the kitchen. The eggs left from previous tenants were questionable, but the expiration date gave Earl enough confidence to fry up the remaining three. He was smart enough to not use the milk and made them over hard. He looked out the large front window that faced Booth Lake. The rain had returned in the form of a light mist blowing across his view, occasionally gusting, then plucking seasoned leaves from the moors of its branches. Where the hell is my son, he thought, as he returned and scooped the eggs from the frying pan onto his plate. His toast popped up as another duck hunter's shot echoed about the expanse of the small lake. Two more immediately followed, and Earl chuckled at the inaccuracy of the hunters. Hopefully the defense department twins were equally as bad, Earl thought. He then remembered an earthen berm that matched the natural contour of the landscape on the slope to the lake. It was the perfect hiding place for Virgil. Earl recalled some fallen trees resting against it which made it virtually undetectable if a person was hiding from someone. "I have some hiding places," Virgil had said to Earl that Wednesday night on his route to here.

Earl wiped his mouth with a napkin and threw it with the paper plate into the garbage. That's when he noticed a spot next to the trash can and two higher up on the wall. The spots were not affected by any weather and were more definitive as blood but minus the dark hair. Earl couldn't believe he had missed it. He put on his hiking boots and rain jacket, exited the cabin and went to his Impala on the driveway. He popped the trunk with his fob and grabbed the rifle he was ready to use on the twins when they had visited their home in Illinois. It was a thirty ought six deer rifle. Even though he no longer hunted and hadn't for some time, Earl liked to take it out and fire off some rounds from time to time, usually at old water jugs or more challenging a coffee can lid nailed to a tree at a hundred yards. Virgil was always amazed his father could consistently nail both objects at that range. Earl threw the strap over his shoulder and turned to head down the path towards the lake. Why he hadn't thought of this direction yesterday made him mad at himself and the entire situation. People shouldn't be put in situations like these, he thought, then started towards the berm and fallen trees.

On the route he slipped a few times but finally made his way around a large rock at the edge of the trail which led to the berm and fallen trees. He slowly approached the area not wanting to receive a shotgun blast to any part of his body. He looked about for any sign of his son. He rolled over a log, hip first, swinging his legs as he twisted his torso and landed on the other side of the fallen Aspen. Another tree had fallen atop that one to form a V-shaped barrier. He slipped again, grabbing a branch to balance himself. He looked down and saw Virgil's running shoe and then his pant leg. There were leaves and branches stuck over the length of his body. "Virgil, you okay," Earl whispered as he looked around. He nudged his son gently with his boot still not wanting to receive a blast of buckshot. The misty rain was now amplified by more gusts of wind and the leaves above finally relented to the forces of nature. Maple and Aspen leaves rained down like a flock of birds fleeing in fear but ending the flight by sticking to anything across the forest floor. With his arm shielding him Earl deflected as many as he could while scanning the immediate area.

Virgil moved from side to side. He was half buried with debris, some pulled on by himself the rest nature had graciously provided. He sat up on his elbow. "Dad, what are you doing with your rifle?" was the first thing he asked his father, noticing it against his shoulder and aiming in the other direction.

"Do you have the shotgun?" Earl asked, wanting to know which side that weapon might be on.

"Right here," Virgil said, pulling it from under more debris in front of him. Leaves blew off the barrel as he raised it and rested the twelve-gauge on its stock. He pulled himself up with the barrel then leaned against the other fallen tree behind him. The wind gusts blew leaves, wood chips, and bits of mud off of Virgil as he wiped down his sleeves then pant legs.

"Are you okay, are you hurt?" Earl asked, still scanning the area and not facing his son.

"I think they did a number on my leg."

"Was that your blood I saw in the cabin?" Earl asked, still making sure they were safe, surveying the landscape uphill from them. He smiled, knowing they were together again. That his son was alive.

"No, it was one of them."

"Are they still in the area?" Earl asked.

"I don't think so," Virgil answered. "I think they finally got what they paid for."

Earl wasn't sure he wanted to face his son, but knew he had to. He was afraid what the twins might have done. "What do you mean by that?" he asked, finally turning.

Virgil set his gun against the tree then leaned back against a branch and spread his arms and legs apart, revealing to Earl the damage from the confrontation with his government employers. The wind blew more debris off his body. His left sleeve was torn and bloodied. Earl noticed a makeshift bandage from another part of his brown flannel shirt wrapped around his forearm. Virgil's left pant leg looked like a bobcat had torn at him. Shredded and also bloodied, Earl saw more of his son's shirt knotted around his shin and calf. Earl turned and scanned the area again, then once again looked Virgil over, trying not to show his fear or pity for his son. He looked past Virgil towards Booth Lake. The mist and shower of leaves now subsided, and he could see the duck hunter's boat. Virgil was quiet as Earl collected and calmed his feelings. Earl looked at his son and smiled. "Are you cut?" His emotions hit him then, and he stammered as the smile faded. "I'm so sorry this happened, Virgil."

Virgil accepted his father's hug and love, wrapping his arms around the man who had come to help him. "Screw it, Dad, sometimes shit happens," he whispered into his dad's left ear. They held the embrace until a shotgun blast a minute later shook them both back to the task at hand. "We better get back to the cabin and get you cleaned up," Earl said.

"Are you okay to walk?"

"Yeah, I can make it," Virgil informed his dad.

"Come on then, this weather sucks," Earl said, wanting to get them back to the shelter and safety. "Tell me what happened on the way back."

Virgil pushed away from the branch he was now holding on to, took two steps forward, slid his right hip over the fallen tree and out of the berm like his father had entered. Earl followed after looking around one more time. Another hunter's attempt echoed across the lake, and he shook his head, turning to follow his son. "I swear Ray Charles is hunting today," Earl said, catching up to his hobbling but upright son. "So what happened?" Earl asked, putting his right arm under Virgil's left and bracing him as they continued up the wet incline towards the cabin.

"You know those guys were not very good shots for our country's defense department," Virgil started. "In fact, they were pretty bad."

"So they didn't hit you?" Earl asked, wanting confirmation.

"One graze to the left calf and another to my left arm," his son answered, laughing. "It was at close range and not the caliber gun I would expect them to carry. It was like they were using birdshot."

"What did it feel like?"

"I remember getting hit in the same leg when you gave me that BB gun for my birthday. I was shooting some tin cans in the backyard one afternoon and I caught a ricochet at close range. This felt like that but both hits broke skin and burned."

"Did they leave right after it happened?"

"No. I knew they were still out there but not sure exactly where," Virgil said. "That's how they originally caught me off guard. I heard them get out of their car when they got here. I was looking out the back bedroom window when I saw one of them walking around the cabin. I didn't know it was a diversion until I walked back to the kitchen and one of them was waiting on the other side of the fridge," he continued, "I never could tell those fuckers apart with or without initials on their lapels."

"How did you end up buried in the berm?"

"When that guy jumped me in the kitchen, I hit him with the butt of this gun, and he went down. I got him good too. I'm pretty sure he was hurting for sure no matter which one it was."

"Explains the blood on the wall."

"Remember that trap door under the bed of the back bedroom?"

"Yeah."

"I heard the other one shutting their car trunk. I figured my best bet was to get to the berm and hide. I used the trap door and crawled under the cabin."

"Good choice, son," Earl said, guiding his son towards their destination.

"I got to the north end of the cabin, you know right where they were parked. I made a break for it, but he heard me and opened up on me. The other one came around the end of the cabin firing as well. That's when I got hit, but that's also when I returned fire, got one of them for sure. It was Ivan."

"Thought you couldn't tell them apart," Earl asked.

"I heard him say, damn it, Gus, the bastard nailed me."

"When was that, I mean was it today?"

"I believe it was Thursday late afternoon," Virgil guessed.

"That's when you went to the berm?"

"Yeah."

They neared the end of the path at the east end of Virgil's property.

"You're sure they're gone," Earl asked, stopping with his son and scanning the property again.

"They left after having lunch by the fire pit, and I know Ivan was hurting because he was moving slowly."

"Why didn't you come up to the cabin then?" Earl asked, confused.

"I couldn't move."

"You mean it hurt that bad?"

"It still burned a bit, but I just couldn't pull myself up. I had no strength and was so tired I just laid down and took a nap for a while. Actually, I think I just passed out."

"Virgil, you know it's Sunday morning, don't you?"

"Really? That was one hell of a nap."

Back Home

They waited until Monday morning to leave the cabin. It took Earl some time to clean and bandage the wounds on Virgil's left arm and calf, even after his shower the wounds looked like he had been stabbed with an awl. The skin was torn on the surface but narrowed at an inch of its depth. The oddity was the blackish skin at the point of entry. Like it had burned in the area. Earl used the extensive first aid kit required by law for the rental cabin and patched his son up. The antibiotic cream applied to the wounds seemed to ease any discomfort his son was feeling.

"Let's stay the night and go to Galena in the morning," Virgil suggested while his dad tended to his injuries.

"You mean go home."

"That's what I said. Go home to Galena."

Earl grabbed Virgil by the shoulders and stood him up from the chair he had been sitting in for the past two hours. He gently shook him then slapped him lightly on his cheek then a second time but harder. "We live in South Elgin, Illinois. Remember," he said, emphasizing the word remember.

"Yeah, I know, but don't we always go to Galena?"

"We do," Earl said, hugging his son and now grasping what he had been through. "But not this time. We need to get home. We'll come back for your van later."

"Okay."

They had stopped at an intermediate care facility in Elgin so a professional could look at his wounds. They made up a story about the wounds so the police would not be involved. They stopped to pick up an antibiotic then arrived home late in the afternoon. Their home had been built by Grandpa Jerry atop the foundation of an old bar. It was a solid three-bedroom house which had withstood the wear and tear of five boys and anything nature decided to throw at it. Earl was the youngest and had bought out his brothers to stay at the A-framed home with an upstairs dormer in back and a large kitchen addition his father had built on in the rear. Earl gladly remained to care for the home he had grown up in. He harvested the apples off the tree behind the garage and tended to the double lot of grass, hydrangea, and now modest garden.

"Know where you're at," Earl asked his son as they entered through the back door.

He weakly smiled at his father, "Home sweet home," he whispered.

Virgil was not a dumb person. He proved early on he had something to offer the show we call life. At ten years old he stopped one of his dad's faux pas by opening the door of his Ford Falcon as it rolled down the driveway, climbed in, and stepped on the brake, stopping the small blue sedan from going out into the street and hitting any oncoming traffic. Though he felt like a fool himself it assured Earl he had a child to be proud of. He knew his wife Helen would have accomplished the same, but Earl, with Ruth's help had taken good care of Virgil and brought him this far.

During Covid-19, however, it was Virgil not the mentor who had done the heavy lifting, guiding him through the confusing and introverted society they had to deal with. Earl hated all of it, but Virgil got him through it with their sanity intact. Earl now stood with his somewhat unresponsive son waiting for an answer. He shook him again. "Do you know where you're at?" Earl asked again. He sat him back down in a blue high-backed upholstered chair and went to the kitchen. He heard his son grunt as Virgil adjusted himself in the chair. Earl knew his boy was ailing but not only from his wounds. There was something else going on inside. He knew it was an illness for sure, but to what extent. He needed to guide him through this sickness the twins seemed to have made sure he had partaken of. He was sure Virgil's wounds were the source of inoculation.

"Dad, I'm glad we're home," Virgil informed his dad. "But I don't feel all that well."

Earl returned, noticing Virgil's face was pale and he was leaning on the end table next to his chair shivering. "Are you cold or are you going to puke?"

"Both."

Earl scrambled back to the kitchen, retrieved a pan, and quickly put it in Virgil's hands. He grabbed the well-worn afghan blanket Helen had made off the back of the sofa and wrapped it about Virgil's shivering shoulders massaging them as he did. He took the Blackhawks blanket off his Lazy-Boy recliner and added another layer, straightening Virgil in the chair. He went to the kitchen and returned with a glass of water and aspirins along with the antibiotic. Breaking the fever would be a start at getting whatever this was under better control. The other pill was for any infection. "Keep the pan in front of you and take these when you can," Earl said, handing the glass and pills to him.

Virgil set the pan on the end table then took the glass and pills from his dad. His hands shook and he dropped the pills followed by the glass of water onto the carpet. "I'm sorry, Dad," Virgil said, slumping forward in an effort to help clean up the water and find the errant white oblong shaped medicine.

"Sit back, I'll take care of it," Earl said gently, pushing Virgil back and upright into the chair, steadying him there. "Don't move, I'll get it." He found the pills under Virgil's chair and returned to the kitchen for a refill on the water and a dish towel, "Open your mouth," Earl said, directing his son then placed the dose on his tongue. "Here's the water," Earl said, holding Virgil's chin in the palm of his hand and softly setting the rim of the glass on his lips. "Drink and swallow the pills."

Virgil did as told. "I think I'll just lay down now, Dad," Virgil said, slowly rising. He stood for a minute to steady himself and let his senses clear. Standing there he laughed a little. "Remember when you had Covid, Dad, and I took care of you?"

"Yes, I do. What about it?" Earl asked.

Virgil shuffled towards the plush tan sofa. "Guess the tables are turned now, and I'm the old man." He sat, then rolled into the best sleeping couch they had ever owned, grabbing the pillows and sinking his head into them. Right now he just wanted to stretch out and sleep. When he was working he had weeks where he put in seventy to eighty hours in a week and was tired for a reason then, he thought. That was the last awake thought he had that night.

Earl bent down and patted the carpet to mop up the water. He looked over at Virgil motionless on the couch. "Goodnight, Virgil," he wished his son out loud. There was no response. It was eight in the evening.

Tuesday

Earl woke up in his recliner, like he had been awakened by another shotgun blast. He was startled by his sleep location. Disoriented in the silence, he thought it was just the first light of the day. In reality it was eight-thirty. He looked at the couch. It was empty, as was the pan on the end table. This made him feel better, at least Virgil hadn't vomited he thought. "Virgil," he called out. There was no response. He pulled the lever on the side of the chair and released the footrest. It lowered and he rose.

He looked about the room, steading himself against the arm of the chair. Virgil was not there. Earl went into every room at least three times, including the basement as well as the walk-in attic. He looked out the kitchen window and surveyed the yard then went to the front room. Virgil was not there or in the front yard.

The wind had trailed them home from the north and continued to blow, sending leaves flying about their yard. Earl quickly put on a sweatshirt, then before he exited the backdoor, donned his jacket. He searched that yard then the front. He went back and forth calling Virgil's name. He entered the garage by its side door, the closest to the house. "Virgil," he called out.

"Yeah," a voice said, but Earl saw no one.

"Virgil," he asked again, raising his volume.

"I'm over here," the jumbled voice responded. A man rose up next to the workbench at the rear of the one and a half car structure. He stumbled a bit and leaned against the bench.

Earl wasn't sure it was his son. The light pouring through the east side window washed out the features of the figure's face. A hood pulled over the person's head aided the deception. Earl was in total defensive mode. Too much had happened since Wednesday, and he hated all of it while trusting none of it. He looked to his right. He saw a pitchfork and grabbed it, holding it in front of him.

"What the hell you doing, old man?" the man asked with a slur.

"Is that you, Gustav?" Earl asked, speculating who this stumbling fool actually was. "Or is it Ivan?"

"Of course, it's me."

This confused Earl. "What was my wife's name?" Earl asked.

"Why do you ask me that?" the man countered, seemingly annoyed.

"Are you feeling better?" Earl asked. "Last night you said you were gonna be sick right before you crashed on the sofa," he explained, trying to establish if this man was his son.

"What the hell are you talking about, Earl? By the way, your wife's name is Helen."

"How old were you when your mother died?" Earl asked the man across the garage he knew was not his son. His size was wrong. Too bulky and taller than Virgil. The voice didn't match as well. Since Virgil had gotten ill or inoculated he didn't sound the same. But he knew this man wasn't his son. He was upset that he hadn't seen it right away. Where the hell was he anyway, Earl thought as the man made his way alongside the workbench towards him. He lifted the pitchfork over his head with the intent to strike. The sound, just a plink, of breaking glass, caught Earl's attention. He turned to his right and back in time to see the figure grab his head and fall to the floor of the garage. A red mist lingered in the air. Earl heard the person hit the floor on the other side of his car. "Virgil," Earl yelled as loud as he could. He repeated it. Then he slammed the pitchfork down hard enough that sparks flew about his feet. He slid down the long handle to the tines that had chipped the floor. The blood of his pursuer was running over the floor, under his car, and towards him.

"Dad."

He heard Virgil's voice coming towards him. He knew it was him. The matter-of-fact tone. The resonance and the octave in that tone when he was excited. "I'm over here, Virgil," he called out, pulling himself up from his side of the car.

"Dad," Virgil said again, walking on the same side of the car his father was now trying to pull himself up at.

"What are you doing with that?" Earl asked, nodding towards the rifle in Virgil's hands.

"I heard something outside and went out to take a look, besides I would have got one of them right, Dad," Virgil said with a smile, referring to Earl's quip from the Tuesday night Ivan and Gustav had surprised them by showing up at their front door.

"Well, you nailed the one lying on the other side of the car."

"What are you talking about?" Virgil asked.

"Didn't think you were that good of a shot. Direct hit to the head."

"What are you talking about?" Virgil asked, now standing next to his dad. "I didn't shoot the rifle."

Earl slowly wrapped his fingers around the barrel of the rifle, finding it cold to the touch. He looked at his son and asked, "If you didn't shoot him then who did?"

"Get back down and stay there," Virgil said, holding his father's arm as Earl lowered himself back down, sliding down the handle of the pitchfork. Virgil moved past his dad, the rear of the car, and the closed garage door. He saw the broken glass from the small window in the door scattered about the floor. He lowered himself down to the floor and turned to his left to look down the side of the car. There was a body just as Earl had said. He crawled over the broken glass to the body and saw a bullet hole in the forehead of the bearded man and a pool of blood next to it on the floor. The victim's arms were raised above his head and spread out on the floor. It was one of the twins. He never was sure who was who with these guys and he trusted none of what they said, did, or how they appeared. It definitely seemed to be one of them though and that he felt sure of. He stayed down and searched the body after looking about the room from his vantage point one more time. Virgil had entered through the back door of the garage just after this had happened. Thinking he had heard something break inside the garage he quickly fumbled for his keys to open the always locked rear door. Then he thought he had heard someone yell his name. His hearing was muffled from whatever had gone through or was still in his body. He was still weak, but he had finally managed to get the door opened. Now this.

He found the man's wallet and unfolded it. It belonged to Tom Kalsow. He wiped his eyes and looked at the victim again. It was Tommy.

The driver's license picture was before he had grown a beard. He knew Tom had been away on a fishing trip and now wondered how he ended up in their garage. He slowly rose and looked around again. He took the rifle off his shoulder and made sure it was loaded. He held it out from his chest as he walked past the front of his dad's Impala to the back door. He opened it and looked out quickly. "Dad, you okay?" he asked, leaning back into the garage and relocking it.

Earl was already standing. "What the hell is going on, Virgil?" he asked, then, "Are you feeling any better."

"What?"

"You feeling better?" Earl asked again but louder.

"Yeah, I'm okay, but I can't hear for shit."

"What the fuck just happened, Virgil?" Earl asked again even louder.

"I'm not sure. It appears that Tom Kalsow is lying over there."

"What the hell would he be doing in here?"

"They borrow any tools lately?" Virgil asked.

"No, but I got my car keys on me, let's get the hell out of here."

"And go where, Dad?"

"Maybe they thought Tom was you, Virgil," Earl reasoned. "We can go to Ernie and Sylvia's."

"Everything we want is in the house, but we can't risk going in there that's for sure."

"Or we can do what we probably should have done before it went this far."

"I'm not calling the police, Dad. They said at our last meeting not to even try."

"Of all the shit they have possibly spewed, you buy not calling the police?" Earl asked, then, "What are we going to do with Tommy?"

"Guess I was intimidated at the time. Besides, I tried, and it didn't work. Nobody showed up. It's like they have my phone tapped," Virgil explained. "Or the power to make the cops back off."

"Then they are definitely after us, Virgil."

"Get in the backseat and get down, I'll drive," Virgil said, opening the driver's side door.

"You feel up to driving?" Earl asked.

"I can do it."

Earl stared at him.

"I feel better than I did last night, alright. I can do it," Virgil assured him.

Earl tossed the keys over the car to Virgil then got in the front passenger's side door. "Let's go," he said, putting on his seatbelt.

Virgil handed him the rifle then got in the car. He put the key in the ignition. He knew they should do this quickly, but he was concerned about his dad. "You okay, Dad?" he asked, reaching across the seat and grabbing him by the shoulder.

"I'll be okay once we get done with this shit."

Virgil regretted ever bringing this problem home, "I know, Dad. I should have never gotten you involved."

"As I see it, Virgil, you didn't have much of a choice. These assholes came after you. Not like you were looking for this."

He massaged his dad's shoulder, "I should have used better judgment, that's all."

"I would have been pissed if you didn't get me involved," Earl said, grabbing Virgil's arm and pushing it towards the steering wheel. "Let's get the hell out of here."

"You're right," Virgil said, starting the car and pressing the button above him to open the garage door, "We're a team, right?"

"Always have been," Earl said making sure there was a bullet in the chamber of the rifle, then pushed the safety button to the off position.

When the door was clear, Virgil slammed on the gas backing up faster than he ever had in any vehicle. Earl held tight to the rifle, ready to use it as he might need, but unsure where to aim. The house was alongside at their right, remarkably they missed it. They went downhill to the apron of the driveway and then into the street. A black Escalade was parked halfway up the block, facing them to their left. The vehicle lurched forward then began picking up speed, heading towards them. Virgil was sure it was the same Escalade from the Monday night the annoying duo had come to visit, then he suddenly felt faint. Whatever had entered his system hit him again and he slumped forward over the steering wheel.

"VIRGIL," Earl yelled, looking straight ahead seeing the black square missile coming towards them. He pointed the rifle in its direction but not sure he could make an accurate shot or wanting to shoot his son. "VIRGIL," Earl screamed.

Virgil snapped to and suddenly stepped on the gas again just as the Escalade was honing in on them. The Impala shot backwards into the Kalsow's driveway which was aligned with theirs on the west side of the street. The projectile flew past, screeching to a halt at the end of the block. "LET'S GO," Earl yelled again knowing his son was having a problem. "LET'S GO."

Virgil shifted to drive and hit the gas again, turning the car to the right as he did. Earl opened his window and put the rifle out the window aiming at the Escalade which was trying to perform a three-point turn to get turned around.

"Shoot!" Virgil yelled.

Earl fired once then quickly reloaded the bolt action rifle and squeezed off another round at the now stationary Escalade as they passed by. "I think I hit it," he proclaimed.

Virgil sped by the idle Escalade. He knew his way around his hometown and had no problem getting to a spot where he felt it was unlikely those who were after them could follow and find them.

"We have to keep moving, Virgil. Let me drive if you're not feeling well," Earl said.

"You have your cell phone with you?"

"Yes, I do."

"Call Gene Kalsow and ask him if the Escalade is still sitting there. I'll be right back," Virgil said, getting out of the car then stopping and turning around. "Don't say anything about Tommy." He ran as best he could to the woods next to the building they were hiding behind. It was a small machine shop named Armin Tool after the husband and wife that had taken a chance and given it birth. It had been there before Virgil was born. He had even worked there one summer. Earl found Gene's name in his contacts and called.

Virgil slowly went to the edge of the stand of trees, a cluster of Maple and Oak that had prospered through the years. Underbrush had kept most people away from the area. He wrapped his cell phone in a Farm and Fleet bag he found in the back of his dad's car then walked it as far back into the woods as his body would allow him to. He bent over in pain, covering the bag and contents under fallen branches and leaves. His body ached again from the invading inoculation. He slowly made his way back to the car. He took a deep breath and leaned against the car.

"You okay, Virgil? You want me to drive?" Earl asked.

"What did Gene say?" Virgil asked in return.

"Talked to Ellen, she happened to pick up," Earl explained.

"What did she say?" Virgil blurted out, only wanting to know the answer to his query.

"It was there, she said, and it was smoking from the engine then someone came and picked the guy up. Then ten minutes later a tow truck came and took the Escalade away."

"What kind of vehicle are they in now?"

"Ellen, do you remember what type of car the guy picked him up in," Earl asked, still on the line with their scout.

Virgil scanned the area again, looking for anything out of the ordinary. In his state though, everything seemed out of the ordinary. He was paranoid and not trusting what he was seeing. The rooftop of Armin was occupied by three snipers when in reality two guys were cleaning a rooftop air conditioning unit. He laughed to himself, how the hell did they make it this far, feeling like this, he wondered. Suddenly, his ears popped. It hurt at first then faded as he sat back down in the driver's seat.

"She says it was another black Escalade."

"Imagine that," Virgil replied. "Probably have a fleet of them."

"What's our next move then, Virgil?" Earl asked.

"Did anyone go into our house or garage?" Virgil asked his dad to ask Ellen.

"Gene took the phone and said when the tow truck came two other vehicles pulled up to the garage and removed something in a large black bag. The house was never entered."

Virgil got out of the car, shutting the door hard. The slam coincided with another sudden pop in his ears. This one, louder than the first. He leaned against the Impala, looked around and in that moment didn't really care what happened from here forward. He had been through enough. Oddly, after his ears popped though, he started feeling better. He pushed away from the car and walked around, his balance getting stronger with each step. He opened the door and hopped in the Impala. Virgil started it, put it in drive, and pulled out from behind the red bricked building.

"You okay, Virgil?" Earl asked, looking at his son while scanning the area as they pulled out onto Collins St. He held the rifle in his lap, below the car windows. No need to draw undue attention. "You okay?" he asked again when Virgil said nothing for a block.

Virgil laughed, "Whatever they shot into me sure is weird, Dad. It knocks the shit out of you. Then your ears pop and you feel better."

"So right now you're feeling better?"

"The best I've felt today."

"Great," Earl said, now looking at Virgil. "Now, where are we going?"

"I'm not sure, but I got rid of my phone in those woods back there. I'm pretty sure they were following us by the signal."

"Now what do we do?"

"I'm thinking," Virgil said as he drove them in a westward direction towards a more rural area. To remain safe Virgil felt it was the best direction. He hoped it would be better than his last encounter with the great outdoors. This job for the government was the worst job he had ever had, he thought. Then wondered, how do we get rid of a company that will not accept no as an answer.

Old Pal Ernie's House

Ernie O'Grady was a lifelong friend of Earl's. The strong stout red head and Earl had grown up together in South Elgin two houses apart from each other. They joked one day, when they were playing, that they could have had the biggest sandbox in town if they had lived next to each other. Together they ventured much further than their sandboxes. They explored their neighborhood, always looking for something to do and someone to do it with. Baseball with other kids, swimming, fishing, making a dirt course to ride and crash their bikes. Trouble seldom followed them, mostly adventure. Imagined or achieved. Like the most times sledding down Kenyon's hill without crashing Or the distance from the bump at the bottom which sent you airborne until landing flat on the cow pasture. If enough kids were involved you could combine both events and have witnesses. The distances always increased with their ages. The thrill and challenge never got old. The amenities of today were not yet invented in those times and even into their high school years they enjoyed that challenge. Of course they had other thrills and intentions on their minds then when they invited girls to the hill for an evening of sledding and a campfire the property's owner, Bud Kenyon, had allowed.

They drifted apart during their final year in high school though. Both sought the affections of the same girl and treated each other with disdain for several months leading up to graduation. Earl took Helen to prom that senior year and the battle between the best friends had ended, however the ill feelings towards one another remained until after they graduated Elgin High.

It was the day of their graduation parties that Earl and Ernie both surmised and agreed they had been fools to act the way they did. Ernie's parents and Earl had planned to hold one big party at a pavilion down the street at Lion's Park. The families had been tight throughout the boy's friendship so most of the people that would attend knew both graduates. It was on the route to the park two blocks away that Earl and Ernie, still trying to avoid each other, came face to face. They surprised each other near a large oak tree they once had built a treehouse in. They stared at each other for a moment. Then smiled, both feeling any ill will evaporate into the sunshine of that early June Saturday.

"We're too good of friends to let this stand between us," Ernie had proclaimed, holding out his right hand.

"You're right," Earl agreed, then shook his hand. They hugged then started laughing.

"Time to have a party," they said in unison, heading towards the park.

"Why are we sitting in front of Ernie O'Grady's house, Virgil?" Earl asked.

"Because you suggested it," Virgil mentioned, scanning the area for a black Escalade. Or, for any movement he considered abnormal.

Ernie's ranch-style home rested on four and a half acres. There was a stand of oaks, maples, and elms which made up about an acre. This paralleled a forest of oaks and elms two or three acres beyond that to the west. Only a grass covered old farm lane separated the two properties. Flower gardens, a vegetable garden, and a half acre of lawn made up the rest of Ernie's property. He had lived here ever since O'Grady Construction became popular throughout the region. It was a business he began after taking classes at the local junior college while working for Peterson Construction Company. He had sacrificed a lot. He had gone out on a limb and had become successful. He had lost Helen to Earl, but had found Sylvia, a client, wanting an addition built on to her father's home she had inherited.

"You feeling okay, Virgil?" Earl asked, scanning the property for his own peace of mind. His phone rang. He looked at it and laughed, "It's Ernie."

"Before you answer," Virgil said, grabbing Earl's hand holding the phone. "Do you recognize the number?"

Earl looked at the number on his screen, "That's Ernie, I'm sure of it."

"Answer it then. What are you waiting for," Virgil said, laughing and releasing his grasp.

Earl shook his head, "Sometimes you have a weird sense of humor."

Virgil laughed again, still scanning the area, but starting to feel a bit at ease. Their neighbor's son's body was in their garage. He couldn't totally explain the unknown virus in his body. They were constantly being followed, but for some reason he felt at ease here.

"Hello," he heard his dad say into his phone.

"He wants to know if we are going to sit out here all day or come in."

"Dad, ask him if anyone else has come around here lately that he doesn't know."

Earl relayed the question to Ernie then put the phone on speaker. It took a minute for him to think over the past week. They could hear Ernie asking Sylvia the same question. "No, we only had her younger brother stop by on Monday," came the reply.

"Can we park our car in the storage barn?" Virgil asked.

"For sure, it's about empty," Ernie replied.

A minute later Earl exited the front door and waved them towards the barn. It was down the driveway and just beyond the garage at the edge of the woods. Virgil put the Impala in drive and entered the driveway. Earl grasped the rifle in his lap. They were quickly in the barn with Ernie shutting the door behind them. Virgil stopped the car and turned off the ignition. He opened his door and hopped out, walking around while looking around. It took Earl a little longer but he walked around to meet Ernie and give him a hug.

"Thanks, buddy," Earl said, patting him on the back.

"No problem, what's going on?" Ernie asked. "You guys aren't in any trouble, are you?" Virgil laughed and Ernie let go of Earl. He looked at his best friend's son. "What's with him?" came a third question.

"He's had his ass kicked and has a ton of shit to figure out. Actually, we both do," Earl said, then started explaining the past week's events to Ernie as they walked back in the direction of the house.

"I'll be back in a minute," Virgil yelled to the old chums, as he headed towards the woods, waving his right arm in an attempt to get their attention. He needed some time alone to think about this situation. Earl waved back in acknowledgement without turning around.

"He okay?" Ernie asked looking over his left shoulder.

"Like I said, he had his ass kicked," Earl said. "And, no, I am not sure he's okay."

Virgil came to the end of Ernie's property. He continued across the overgrown lane and into the next stand of trees. They were in a safe place at last, he thought and hoped for a respite from any more crap like what had just happened. He walked around the elms, oaks, and soft maples which shaded and hid him at the same time. The last time he had been here he was in his thirties. It was on a fall day much like this. He had been given an open invitation from Ernie to hunt squirrels here anytime he wanted and had taken advantage of it. He had a couple days off work and needed some relaxation and time to himself. It had been cool and windy but with a bright blue sky overhead. He could have been the great hunter that day but instead became enamored with the many frolicking squirrels and didn't have the heart, want, or need to pull the trigger. Now, he was hoping nobody else felt that need either. While looking up at the trees he debated what his next step would be. The mighty oaks withstood a sudden gust of wind while the limber elms and maples swayed and gave up leaves, but no answers came Virgil's way. He leaned against an oak tree and waited for anything the rhythmic wind and his inner thoughts might blow in his direction.

He realized at this moment how fortunate he was to have his father and the connections Earl had made in his life. He was actually glad he didn't have a wife and kids. Though maybe if he had the twins would have left him alone. "Others are tied down, you not so much," he could still hear Ivan saying. It was something he had always wanted but had never worked out. The one chance he had was with a girl named Cheryl. They had been living and enjoying each other's company for about a year. He was in his early twenties then. He was naive and thought he would spend the rest of his life with her. His conundrum was how to pop the question. He came home early from work one day and found her in bed with a coworker of his that had called in sick that day. The conundrum was solved. He packed his things and moved back in with his dad. He had been there ever since. The burden of a family of his own in this situation would have been unconscionable. He was confident he might have his dad taken care of now. But he now needed a way out of this job opportunity imposed upon him. His dad had been right. The smell of the entire situation was offensive. Virgil took a deep breath. The twins wanted results from whatever they shot him up with and, in this case, literally with whatever they hit him with when they shot.

It was a virus, God's check on life. Call it Covid or whatever other name fits the ten o'clock news, Twitter, Facebook, or any other sound bite dished out. It had been an event, worthy of Noah's ark in comparison. But did it matter? If this one didn't have its effect would there be one more needed to accomplish what the powers to be sought? The one thing Virgil and his dad had agreed on from the outset, about all of it, was that it pitted two forms of thought against each other. Politics had everything to do with it and each side played it to their favor. They had been vaccinated. Earl for health and Virgil for work. The problem they also agreed with was, what was the truth? They knew life as they knew it would never be the same. There would always be a virus to conquer, and the media would never let us forget it. But who did you believe? The media always made many news items sound like Armageddon and the sad thing was many believed them. Even minor weather fronts had been sensationalized. Earl and Virgil had given up on watching the news on a regular basis. If a tornado siren went off they tuned in on the TV in their basement and prayed for the best outcome.

He knew he needed to give the Defense Department what they wanted so he could get back to his life and the job he loved to do. He now knew they were capable of anything and wanted to oblige them. Virgil knew he had been inoculated with something and would eventually have to meet the twins again. Most of all he wanted his father to be safe no matter what he had to do. A small branch fell from a limb above him and struck him in the face. Virgil dove to the ground in defense. He looked in each direction and foolishly waited. He hadn't heard a gunshot but somehow felt he was under attack. He laughed out loud, slowly at first, then louder, ending with a loud, "Screw you." He rose and leaned back against the tree, looking up to see if he should expect any more wooden gravity laden surprises.

He pulled his wallet out and found the card given to him by Ivan and Gustav the first time he had met them at Benny's. He saw the telephone number and reached in his pocket for his phone. "Damn it," he cussed under his breath. His phone was somewhere in the woods behind Armin Tool in

Elgin. He started back towards Ernie's house. His head felt like it was spinning. He stopped, leaned against a young sapling small enough he could secure his hand almost around it. He heaved forward and vomited two times. He picked up some leaves and wiped his mouth. The virus had returned. He forced himself to continue towards the house, stopping two more times to let the effects of the virus wretch from his body. He finally reached the back door of Ernie's about forty-five minutes later. Once again, he was exhausted.

Wednesday Night

Virgil opened his eyes. He lay on a bed in the guest bedroom at the rear of the sprawling ranch. How he got there and exactly where he was before eluded his memory. A man wearing a mask stood over him. He started to reach for a gun that wasn't there. "It's okay, Virgil," he heard his father's voice say. "This is Dr. Harmon, an acquaintance of Sylvia's."

"What's he doing here?" Virgil asked weakly while wiping his eyes. "And where are we?"

"We're at Ernie's, remember," Earl explained.

"He's taking a look at you to see if there is something we can do to help your illness," Sylvia, also masked, explained further.

"You have a new type of flu, Virgil," Dr. Harmon's deep voice informed him. John Harmon was a large man with graying hair. He had large hands for a surgeon but locally was known as one of the best. Sylvia knew him through her work on the board at Grant Hospital in Elgin.

"That's what they told me it was, doctor," Virgil said, sitting up and resting against the headboard.

"The results of your blood work haven't come back yet," the doctor said.

That's when Virgil noticed the IV drip hanging from a stand behind him. "What's this for?" he asked, holding up his right hand the needle was stuck in.

"Just keeping you hydrated for now," Harmon explained. "I've seen this before, but we want to know exactly what we're up against. It's a virus for sure though."

"How long ago was it that you saw these symptoms, doctor?" Virgil asked.

"About three weeks ago we saw the first case and a week later two more. Symptoms just like yours."

"What happened to those people?" Virgil asked. His mind was beginning to race.

"Don't worry about that, son," Earl said.

"I want to know, Dad."

"Let's just get you better," Harmon encouraged.

"Now, I really want to know," Virgil said, leaning forward towards the doctor. Virgil waited in silence while all of his visitors looked at each other then Earl.

"Go ahead and tell him, doc," Earl finally said.

Dr. Harmon stood silently for a moment looking at his phone. He looked at Earl then Virgil and back at Earl. "Yeah, c'mon doctor," Virgil said. "I have the right to know."

Harmon slowly turned and faced Virgil, "The first two died, but were much older than you and one of them had a bad heart," He looked at his watch then around the room. His phone rang. "Harmon here," he answered. "I see. What about that panel I asked you to check," there was silence then, "Okay, thank you." He ended the call.

"What were the results, doctor?" Earl asked.

"He has what the other three had," he confirmed to them and again faced Virgil.

"What did you do for the others?" Virgil asked.

"We have a drug on the way over here. We've had good results with it when dealing with the other cases."

Virgil rolled his eyes, "You mean the two who died."

"It was helping them," Harmon explained. "You are in much better shape than they were, Virgil."

"But they're dead," Virgil reiterated.

"You're going to have to trust me if we are going to get through this," Harmon boomed loudly.

The room remained silent for a few minutes. Everyone except Sylvia and Ernie avoided eye contact with each other. Virgil tried to make eye contact with Earl, but his dad exited the room for the bathroom. "Dad," he called to him.

"Trust the doctor, Virgil, just trust him," Earl called back.

Virgil stared at Dr. Harmon but couldn't get him to leave his phone alone. Harmon was texting someone and was involved with an intense information swap. He didn't want to interrupt him; it might help the doctor save his life. He did have another question though.

Ernie and Sylvia left the room as Earl returned. Then the doctor left. Earl continued in and sat on the bed next to Virgil softly grabbing his son's left hand. "You okay?" he asked. "I mean are you feeling any better?"

"Yeah, my head is not spinning anymore and I'm not as nauseous."

"That's good," Earl encouraged him.

"Dad, I want the truth, what happened to the three cases he talked about?"

"You heard him, those guys weren't in as good of shape as you. They couldn't handle it."

"That was the first two. What about the third case?"

Earl looked towards the door, then again at his son. He stared at the IV drip now not wanting to make eye contact with Virgil. "The whole truth, Dad. I can handle it." Earl looked back at the door.

"Dad," Virgil said, grabbing his father by his shoulder, "I can handle it."

Earl turned and faced Virgil, "The third guy disappeared."

"What do you mean disappeared?"

"He left the hospital or was taken from the hospital somehow."

"By who?"

"They are not sure."

"They're not sure or aren't saying?" Virgil asked.

"I'm not sure which," Earl confessed. "I can't get it out of them."

"Sounds like my twin buddies," Virgil offered an explanation.

"Maybe so, at least we would know who we were dealing with," Earl surmised.

"Yeah, and we know there is most likely a third party involved," Virgil said, adding to the summation.

"And who might that be?" Earl said, throwing out another question then, "But you know what Virgil?"

"What, Dad?"

"It's time we started answering some of the questions we're posing."

"I would agree with that," Virgil said.

Dr. Harmon returned with a syringe and another IV bag. "I need to give you a shot, Virgil."

"What will it do to me?"

"Make you drowsy, but fight the virus that's in you," he explained.

"I need to get some things done. I need to get out of here. I can't be lying in bed," Virgil countered.

"It wouldn't be a good idea to leave this room for a few days. Five at the least."

"Sorry, doc. I need to find out what they're after."

"In five days," Harmon said, raising his voice. "Everyone here is getting this shot."

"I'll give him the shot doctor," Sylvia said, taking the syringe out of his hand. "I'll give all the shots."

"We need to do this, Virgil," Earl said. "I can look into things."

"I'll help him," Ernie offered.

Sylvia rolled up Virgil's sleeve, swabbed his shoulder with an alcohol cotton ball, and administered the shot without any more protest from him. "You're in good hands with the doctor, Virgil," she said. "We are here to help you."

Virgil sat back against the headboard as Sylvia adjusted the pillows behind him. She patted him on the shoulder then backed away from the bed. He looked at her then around the room. He was safe now. He knew they weren't invincible, but he felt better about their chances. He rested his head on the tops of the goose down pillows Sylvia had arranged. He was fading fast, not to death, but much needed sleep to hopefully eradicate this illness. Virgil slept while Ernie and Earl discussed strategy.

He awoke the next morning feeling much better. He felt strong enough to get up and go to the bathroom by himself, IV in tow. He didn't hear anybody in the other rooms. Where were they, he wondered as he exited the bathroom, turning towards the kitchen. Slowly he reached the large kitchen, but nobody greeted him. He leaned against the marble island equipped with a stove top. Where did they go, he wondered again as he sat down on one of the stools on the counter side of the island. He looked out the back sliding patio door at the woods he had traversed the day before. He stood, opened the door and stepped out onto the tan-bricked patio, lifting his IV stand out with him. The air felt great. The fall winds had died down and some leaves now gently floated towards the ground. Almost like a welcomed journey. Virgil looked at his hand, trying to figure out how to get rid of the needle in it. The sun was directly above him, warming him and giving him the time of day. Virgil was restless. He wanted answers to questions he and Earl had conjured up, but his resources were limited to acquire any explanation. He grabbed the arm of an Adirondack chair Earl had insisted they bring back as an anniversary present for Sylvia and Ernie.

It was one of two.

"How are you doing, Virgil?" Sylvia asked, coming outside and taking a seat in the other chair.

"I feel much better," he informed her. "What are the chances of getting rid of this?" he asked, holding up his right hand and wiggling it back and forth.

"The doctor will be back either later today or tomorrow morning," she informed him. "He is the one to decide that."

"Can't you call him?" Virgil suggested.

"For your safety, Dr. Harmon asked that we just let him come out here, or text him."

"What is it that you guys aren't telling me?" he asked. "And where are my dad and Ernie?"

"The boys went to get some food, we are running low on a few things," she explained.

"And?" Virgil let the question hang in the comfortable air.

Sylvia rose from her chair. "Are you hungry Virgil?" Sylvia asked, trying to change the subject. She stopped and took Virgil's wrist in her hand and took his pulse.

"Come on, Sylvia," Virgil pleaded, rising slowly from his chair when she was done. He followed her into the kitchen, nearly knocking the IV stand over as he entered. "Did that third guy with the virus leave the hospital or was he kidnapped?"

"I don't know the details, Virgil," Sylvia said. "Let me take your blood pressure."

"But you know something," Virgil said, probing.

"I know the guy was at the hospital for two days then left," Sylvia said. "And that's all I know."

"You're on the board there. Why don't you know more?"

Sylvia almost shouted, raising her usually soft calm voice. "Because I don't! Now, let me take your blood pressure."

Virgil sat down on one of the four stools in front of the island and cooking station. He let his nurse take his pressure which was stable as was his pulse. Sylvia set the cuff out of the way at the end of the counter. She took bacon out of the refrigerator and started frying four slices in a frying pan. She sliced up a tomato and shredded some lettuce for her planned BLT sandwiches. She put four pieces of bread in the toaster, two wheat and two white, and pushed the lever down, making each duo disappear. "If I tell you it cannot leave these four walls," Sylvia finally said. Virgil leaned on the counter in anticipation of Sylvia's revelation. Then, Earl and Ernie came through the door leading to the attached three-car garage.

"How you feeling?" Earl and Ernie almost asked in unison. Laughing as they entered the kitchen.

Virgil looked at the two buddies, "I'm fine. You guys sound too happy for what we're going through here."

"You're going to be fine, Virgil," Earl said. "Isn't that right Ernie?"

"That's right, buddy," Ernie confirmed. "We talked to Harmon, and he said in a couple of days you should be fine."

"That's great, but how can he be sure? Did the third patient survive?"

Sylvia looked at the old friends then at Virgil. "Yes he did Virgil," she told him. "He was found the other day near your house with a rifle on him. That's when you guys ended up here."

"He killed Tom?"

"It wasn't Tom, Virgil," Earl chimed in. "It was Ivan."

Virgil stared at his father in disbelief, "But I saw his driver's license."

"All planted on him, Virgil," Earl explained.

"He had a beard, but I know it was Tom," Virgil insisted.

"It was Ivan though," Ernie confirmed.

"Who told you?" Virgil asked, still not believing what he was hearing.

"Dr. Harmon confirmed it," Ernie said with Earl nodding in affirmation.

"Who shot him then?"

"He's with the CIA. His name is Chung," Sylvia said.

Virgil was almost leaning on the counter. He still wasn't sure about what he was being told. Finally he laughed out loud.

"What could be funny, Virgil?" Earl asked, chuckling with him.

"Chung! Does our government have anyone with an American name working for it?"

Though caught off guard by the comment, they all laughed at the irony of what Virgil had brought up. Virgil sat up still laughing. His laughter suddenly stopped, "Wait, why did Chung kill Tom?" he asked. "What was the purpose of that?"

"It was Ivan, Virgil," Earl reiterated with Ernie nodding his approval this time.

"But I saw him, you never did," he explained to them.

"You were sicker then, Virgil," Earl said. "You weren't yourself."

"Maybe, but I'm sure it was Tom."

"Chung was sent to get them off your back," Sylvia said. "Our government didn't like what those two were up to."

"Wait a minute, the twins worked for the Defense Department."

"They said they did, but it wasn't true," Sylvia went on. "They were a couple of Russian hacks working for scientists looking to make a buck."

"So where is Gustav?" Virgil asked.

She looked at her husband then Earl and back at Virgil. "That, we don't know and that's why it's a good idea for you and Earl to stick around a few days."

"Are we safe?" Virgil said, staring directly at the tall dark-haired woman.

"They'll find him, don't worry," she said, putting his sandwich together.

He looked at his dad, then Ernie, "And what do you guys have to add?"

"Harmon said the shot he gave us will take care of any more symptoms," Ernie answered, sitting down on another one of the stools.

"It's a lock to do the job," Earl said, backing up his old friend.

Virgil bowed his head. He felt bad for hounding his dad and friends.

Sensing this Sylvia said, "Here's your sandwich, Virgil. Eat up and relax, we're in this together."

"If we wanted to hurt you we already had the opportunity," Ernie said, laughing and Earl did as well.

"Sorry guys," Virgil said, then took a bite out of the BLT. "This tastes great, Sylvia. Thank you."

"Hey, where's ours?" Ernie asked. "I could eat," Earl mentioned.

Sylvia handed her sandwich to Earl and rolled her eyes in Ernie's direction. She started the process again for her and her spouse.

Friday Morning

Doctor Harmon lightly tapped on the front door at five that gray Friday morning. He had already texted Ernie. The day awaited the sunrise as he entered. Ernie showed the sixty-five-year-old doctor to the kitchen where a pot of coffee brewed and a dim sink light was the only illumination. "Where we at with all this doctor?" Ernie asked. He would give his life for Earl and Virgil, but he didn't want his wife to give hers as well.

"The medicine we gave you is what you needed," he reaffirmed. "Remember that coyote flu a few years back that also turned out to be nothing?"

"I remember that," Virgil said entering the room. Harmon and Ernie turned to look at him. "It was nothing, but I don't remember anyone having the symptoms I had."

"That's because this is a variant of that and the Covid-19," Harmon explained. "Fortunately, since all of these variants have been kept up with, we have the shot we need right now."

"You mean science is ahead of this?" Ernie asked.

"Not ahead, just keeping pace," Harmon said. "The production end is being worked on."

"Then my biggest question is, why me? Or what do they want from me," Virgil asked. There was silence. Ernie filled two cups and set them on the island. Harmon grabbed one and added some sugar. Ernie poured cream in his and offered the tiny pitcher to Harmon who declined it.

"Is there a chance we're reading too much into this?" Ernie asked.

"I've thought about that, but why would the government care about what happened to me? As I see it I'm expendable in all of this," Virgil said, realizing nobody was going to answer his original questions.

"Wish I could answer that," Harmon said. "I'm just a doctor."

"Virgil, remember when the twins came to our house that Tuesday night?" Earl said, entering the room.

"Morning, Dad. Yes, I do remember,"

"There was a third guy then."

"No, Dad, it was just the two of them," Virgil replied.

"You told me two guys came to your house that night, Earl," Ernie said, hoping to refresh both their memories.

"Who picked them up then?" Earl asked.

"I would think, their driver," Virgil said.

"And would his name be Chung?" Earl asked, sitting down on a stool by the island. They all sat down. Four stools, four minds trying to figure out what the hell was going on with one more still sleeping in the master bedroom.

He was just the doctor. He knew the shot Sylvia had given everyone would fight off what Virgil had, but he had his theory as well. "Chung is definitely CIA," he started. "Those Russian goofs were just trying to make a buck off of you, Virgil, and all they achieved was somehow inoculating you. We know Chung eliminated one of them and maybe he has gotten both of them. But that we can't be sure of," Harmon further explained his ideas on the subject.

"I'm just throwing this out here, doctor, but who scares you the most in this scenario? Sylvia asked Harmon as she came into the room, though the question was there for everyone to take a crack at. She entered the kitchen fully dressed in black slacks and a white sweater. The hospital she was a board member of was taking a hit in the PR department and she wanted to end the negativity.

"I'm really not sure," Harmon confessed, but wanted to offer more. He, being connected to the hospital, wanted answers as well. When he had patients in the fourteen-story building he was there sometimes seven days a week. His caring, warm, and gentle bedside manner expanded his great reputation. No matter how tired he was or what time of day it was, he cared and would show up for those depending on him. He was somewhat frustrated by these events but kept calm.

"For me it's Chung," Sylvia offered. "By now Gustav has shit his pants and run back to Russia if someone hasn't hid him somewhere. But for what purpose?" She said then paused. "What would he have to offer anyone now?"

"Morning, dear," Ernie said, giving his wife a cup of black coffee.

"Morning, love," Sylvia replied, smiling at her husband of forty-four years. She and Ernie had a ten-year age difference when they were married. She was in her mid-twenties at the time. It was the second time around for Sylvia whose first husband, Don, had collapsed and died while working on his car in their two-car detached garage. She found him after wondering why he hadn't come in for lunch. Don had made it to the back door of the garage but had never opened it. Sylvia performed CPR promptly but too late. Solemnly she walked back to the kitchen and called an ambulance. The autopsy showed her first husband had a heart defect doctors had never detected and actually might not have mattered if they had.

Two years later Sylvia sought a contractor to connect the garage to the house with an addition. She had contacted Ernie's company seeking a design which would blend the two structures together. Ernie returned with the plans he and his team had come up with about a month later. He had not met Sylvia Burns prior to the meeting since his front men had taken all the measurements required. Ernie, being the owner, preferred to take care of design matters and let the men and women in his company do the actual building. He presented the plan to Sylvia who loved it, and during the course of the actual work and Ernie's supervision fell in love with Ernie.

Ernie was treating it like any other job but cognizant of the widow's beauty. He was there throughout the project when in the final week, Marci, one of his laborers, finally suggested he ask her out.

"Boss, this woman is into you," Marci informed Ernie on a Monday afternoon lunch hour.

"She is a beautiful woman and I do like her company," Ernie had responded.

"Then ask her out, Ernie," Marci coaxed. "You'll regret it if you don't."

It took another week. While they made the final inspection with the building inspector Ernie finally asked Sylvia out. The inspector was checking Sylvia out more than the construction and Earl was getting tired of it. He took Sylvia's hand and pulled her into the kitchen as the inspector continued his inspection without realizing they were gone. His back was to them when Ernie had made his move. "Would you like to have dinner this Saturday?" he blurted out.

"Yes," she said with a stipulation. "If we pass the inspection."

"Fair enough, I'll pick you up at seven," Ernie confidently agreed.

A year later they were married. Ernie moved into her house and while his business expanded. They planned and built the house which they now resided in. Sylvia eventually gave up the nursing profession and helped her husband run his business. She eventually was asked onto the hospital board due to their philanthropy within the community.

And now here they were helping friends look for answers in a situation they both hoped would soon come to an end. "I would really like to know where Chung is at," Sylvia bolstered her point.

"Let me out of here and I'll go find out," Virgil said, sensing their concern.

"I'm not sure you're ready, Virgil," Sylvia mentioned.

"I'm ready," Virgil said standing. "Get rid of this crap and I'm good to go," he said motioning to the IV stand.

"We can take that out now," Harmon offered. "But you may want to wait a few days and make sure you're alright."

"Wait," Virgil said, raising his voice then quickly calming. "It seems to me that's all we've been doing since we got here."

"Relax, Virgil," Earl said rising from his stool. "They have only been helping us."

"I'm sorry," Virgil said, repeating it to each person with a less stressful voice. "But think about it. Haven't we all been waiting on our government or the medical profession, or test results for what seems forever?"

"There is a purpose for all of that," Harmon said, defending his profession. He walked over to Virgil and calmly removed the IV. "There you go, son. I still think it would be a good idea if you stuck around, but that is your decision."

"Dad, can I have the keys for the car?" Virgil asked, turning to face Earl.

"We're staying the night, Virgil," Earl proclaimed, then turned and went back to his bedroom.

Virgil stood there like a scolded boy. "Yes, sir," he called after him.

"And we are going to have a plan," Earl yelled from the doorway of the room. "It's not going to be another play it by ear journey," he further stipulated.

"Yes, sir."

Saturday

Sylvia and Ernie had served a great brunch. Earl and Virgil had agreed the night before they needed to let the O'Gradys have their home back. They would have to figure out how to repay them later. They packed slowly, following the meal of ham, eggs, bacon, and pancakes. "That meal was like a sedative," Earl mentioned to Virgil as they packed their meager belongings into one suitcase Sylvia had brought out of their attic.

"You up for this, Dad?" Virgil asked his dad.

"Hey, let's stick to our plan then figure the rest out later."

They said their goodbyes at the back door of the large ranch home, thanking their friends for the hideout and recuperation. The host couple smiled and laughed, saying they would do it anytime. Ernie tapped his phone and the garage door opened to the machine shed where Earl's Impala awaited.

Once inside the garage Virgil walked around the car, looking over and under it for anything unusual. He opened the trunk, lifted the suitcase and examined it before placing it in. He realized he might be overzealous in his behavior, but he also knew it was just him and his father now. His dad was responsible for getting him to this point and he wanted nothing less than Earl's safety. He felt he owed it to him. Virgil had tried to convince Earl to stay at Ernie and Sylvia's, but he wouldn't hear of it. He opened the hood of the car and looked at the engine.

"What are you doing?" Earl asked.

"We haven't run this car since we've been here have we?"

"No, we haven't."

"That's what I'm doing, then," Virgil said. "Making sure it's how we left it."

Earl opened the passenger side door and slid onto the front seat. He looked over the seat at a blanket covering the rifle resting on the backseat. He lifted the blanket and made sure their one defense was still there. He looked over further to see if there was anything or anyone on the floor in the backseat. Everything looked good. "You gonna get in?" Earl shouted to his son. There was no response. "Virgil!" he yelled.

Virgil closed the hood of the car. "What?" he yelled back to his dad.

"This isn't a crank start car, Virgil," Earl joked.

"I know, Dad."

"What the hell are you doing, then?"

"Making sure there are no bombs, cut brake lines, or empty reservoirs before we take off," Virgil replied, opening the driver's side door and sitting down. He looked at his dad, leaned over, then kissed him on the forehead. Virgil put the key in the ignition then crossed his fingers. "Should we light this candle, Dad?"

"Let's do it," Earl said.

Virgil turned the key. The car started immediately. He hit the button to open the windows then put the car in gear. They exited the thirty foot by forty foot shed.

They waved to the O'Gradys as they passed by the house. Earl had made no phone calls and had received none since they had come to this hideout twelve days ago. He now called their neighbors across the street, the Kalsows. Nobody was answering, so he left a message for Gene or his wife Ellen.

"Wish they would pick up," Earl mentioned to Virgil. "Like to know a little more before we stop home."

"Call Mark, I should let him in on what's going on," Virgil suggested.

Earl did and handed his phone to him. "Hello, Earl. What the hell is going on?" his best friend asked.

"Mark, it's me," Virgil replied. "We've been hiding out for a while at some friends' house. We didn't think it was wise to make contact with anyone until we were ready."

"So I'm out of the loop now," Mark shot back a little perturbed.

"For your safety, pal," Virgil quickly replied. "Your call to Benny's that night worked, but the assholes hunted me down at the cabin," he explained further.

"You alright?" Mark now asked, his tone turning to concern.

"Think we have gotten through the worst of the illness. Now we want to try and reclaim our home and lives."

"You can come here if you need to, Diane won't mind," Mark offered.

"By chance did you go by our house this past week?"

"Actually, I saw your place on the local cable news over a week ago Tuesday night," Mark informed him. "I actually tried to call you, but you didn't pick up."

Virgil relayed the info to Earl. His dad shrugged his shoulders, "I don't have my phone. I ditched it for a while. What were they showing?"

"Quick video of a crash down the block from your house. Some of the neighbors were concerned as to who was involved, because everything was cleaned up within fifteen minutes," Mark explained.

Virgil put the phone on speaker while they retraced their route towards home.

"Cleaned it up that quick," Earl said.

"Yeah, some of them questioned the fact that it was a government vehicle in the crash," Mark explained.

"Has anyone contacted you?" Virgil asked. "And have you been by our house?"

"Nobody has bothered me. I drove through your neighborhood the day after the story was on the news, but I didn't see anything that was odd."

"Did you stop at our house?" Earl asked.

"Matter of fact I did, Earl. And it looked alright."

"Was the garage door shut?" Virgil asked.

"It was," Mark confirmed. "I knocked on your door and looked through the garage door window. Saw your car was gone and that's when I started calling you."

"I ditched my phone in some woods. I thought they were following us through it," Virgil told him.

"When you looked through the window in our garage, was it the side window?" Earl asked.

"No, the entry door window," Mark said.

The puzzled look on Earl's face prompted Virgil. "Mark, we need to take care of a few things. When we get home and things check out, I'll call you."

"Okay, but if you need to stay somewhere Diane and I will put you up," Mark offered.

"Thanks," Earl and Virgil both said. Earl took the phone from Virgil and hung it up.

They had made it back to Armin Tool. This late on a Saturday meant it was closed and Virgil parked the car towards the back of the parking lot closest to the woods sprawling behind it. He went looking for his phone. He had wrapped it in a bag left in Earl's car when he disposed of it. He traversed the woods looking for a little piece of the bag peeking out from under the leaves that had dropped from just about every tree in the area. About half an hour later Virgil stumbled over a hidden branch and the bag appeared with the branch. He grabbed the bag and opened it to make sure of the contents. The phone was there, barely wet, but he wasn't sure if it would work until he was able to charge it. He returned to the car.

"Did you find it?" Earl asked when his son opened the driver's side door.

"Yes, I did," Virgil said, getting in. "Let's go home."

"We're going to stop at Gene and Ellen Kalsow's house first," Earl informed him.

"Why?"

"I got hold of them while you were screwing around in the woods," Earl kidded his son.

"I wasn't exactly screwing around," Virgil defended himself. "What did they say?"

"They are inviting us to dinner for one thing," Earl said. "They have some info for us."

"They couldn't tell you over the phone?"

"They wanted to see us," Earl said. "You know, make sure we're alright."

"Okay, I guess," Virgil relented. "But our plan was to get home."

"I know, but I figure we can observe our house for ourselves from right across the street."

Virgil laughed. "That is actually a good idea. I'm surprised you thought of it," Virgil said straight faced.

"You're a dick without even trying sometimes," Earl stated then chuckled.

They left the parking lot, continuing the same route they had fled on from their home by. Their return pace was much slower than when they fled.

Twenty minutes later Virgil pulled into a Bucky's gas station five blocks from their home.

"Why are we stopping here?" Earl asked.

"You're going to wait here for ten minutes then drive the car to Gene's house. Sit in their driveway for a few minutes to see what happens. Go to his door and ring the bell," Virgil said, laying out a plan not part of the original one they had agreed upon just the night before.

"What do I tell them when they ask where you're at?"

"Tell them I wasn't feeling well and just wanted to get home. Keep an eye on our place and don't tell them what we have gone through. Tell them we were up at the cabin doing our fall trip."

"Where and what are you going to be doing?"

"I want to go look at our place, starting with the garage then the house."

"You better take the rifle," Earl suggested, reaching over the back seat and pulling it to the front.

"Not sure I can conceal it for that long."

"Just leave it wrapped in the blanket," Earl suggested.

Virgil did as told while Earl slid across the front seat, struggling up and over the console. He finally got behind the wheel. "I'll turn my bedroom light on and off three times for the all clear signal," Virgil said, holding the blanket and weapon over his right shoulder.

"What if you're in trouble?"

"If you see a flashing light, then I'm in trouble," Virgil said, turning and walking away.

Earl waited the ten minutes he and his son agreed upon then slowly drove off.

Kalsow's House

Earl sat in Gene and Ellen's driveway, scanning the area. He used the rearview mirror to observe his own home for any sign of Virgil, or for that matter, anything. He looked at the Kalsow ranch-style T-shaped home, wondering how all of these events would eventually play out. He saw a light come on in the Kalsows' kitchen so he knew they were home.

He and Virgil had almost always gotten along with the Kalsows. Earl and Gene had run a boy scout troop together for a couple years, enjoying each other's company while raising their sons. Tom was three years younger than Virgil, but the older scout helped the tenderfoot find his way within the troop. They had their differences as well. Gene once accused Earl of borrowing a hoe and not returning it. Earl in turn accused Gene of borrowing a rake and not returning it. The accusations and inquiries went on for two weeks until the next time they needed the tools they found them in their respective garages. They then thanked each other for returning the tools to the proper place. Neither knew what was going on. They confessed neither had returned the tools in question.

Two weeks later Virgil overheard Gene and Earl verbally jabbing each other on the topic of the garden tools. "You shouldn't be arguing about that rake and hoe," Virgil intervened.

They looked at Virgil wondering what he could possibly add to their conversation. "What are you talking about?" Earl asked.

"Ellen came over here about a month ago carrying a hoe. She asked if we had a rake. I told her if she was done with her hoe I would give her a rake in trade."

Gene and Earl looked at each other then at Virgil. "Why didn't you tell us?" Gene asked.

"We both forgot. When we saw you guys arguing about it we decided to let it go on for a while," Virgil explained with a smirk, while Earl and Gene stewed over the revelation. "Of course, we put the tools back before you guys decided on a duel at dawn," Virgil said with a broader smile then walked away.

Earl perked up after seeing the all-clear signal from Virgil and exited the car. He was now standing at Gene's front door pressing the glowing button of the doorbell. After a brief wait Ellen opened the door. Earl noticed Ellen appeared tense, not her usual happy to see you self. "How, you doing?" she asked Earl blandly.

"I'm fine," Earl told her. "How about you?"

"Seen better days," she replied, stepping back and opening the door further. "Come on in."

Earl was skeptical as to what he was walking into. He had never seen Ellen in this mood. She usually had an I'll pick you up attitude during any situation you might be involved in or confronting together. But now she stumbled. "You alright?" Virgil asked, grabbing her by the right elbow.

Ellen was barely five foot, had dark hair, and was usually a spark plug of a woman. She was wearing black slacks with a tan long sleeve sweater covered with the dark blue smock she always wore when she was involved with a craft project, "Yeah, I'm working on Christmas cards," she said with little conviction.

"It's getting to be that time of year," Earl said, then, "Sure you're alright?"

Ellen pulled her elbow away from Earl's grasp. She gently took his left wrist and guided it to the right pocket of her smock. "Use those if you need to," she said, looking Earl in the eyes.

"What?" Earl asked, confused.

"Go with the flow, Earl," she said, leading him towards a bedroom.

"Where we going?" Earl asked.

"Trust me for now."

Virgil had been peering through the slats of the beige colored blinds covering the front window of the living room. He had signaled his dad then watched him enter the Kalsow home. He continued exploring their home like he hadn't been there in years. It seemed like he hadn't. The absence of evidence throughout the house, the repaired garage entry door, the body left within the garage gone, put Virgil on edge. He paced in the kitchen while his phone, lying on the counter, was charging. He went to his bedroom, sat down at his desk and opened his laptop. He Googled his business and was amazed that his site was alive and well. He emailed Mark to inform him of those facts.

Mark replied: What the hell do you think I was doing while you were ignoring me.

Virgil: Thanks. I'll see ya later.

Mark: Kiss my entire ass.

Virgil: I don't have that much time.

He was on edge but felt safe enough to place the rifle under his bed. He saw a flashing light outside his window. He pulled it back out lifting the bed up two feet in the process. He grasped it again with both hands, letting the bed slam on the hardwood floor. He looked out his window at the rear of the house, trying to see where the light was coming from. He walked about the house looking out every window, using all angles available. He reached the front door then the front room, again peering through the slats of the blind. He waited for another flashing light, wondering where it had come from. He stared at the Kalsow home, a T-shaped ranch structure with a pool in the backyard. A pool he had used by invitation many times, and a few adventures when they weren't home.

Virgil and Mark had been with fellow freshmen one night when they needed something beyond their usual stoic nerdy behavior. The pool would be perfect, they thought. His neighbor, Brandi from a block over, had the same idea. They had their fun in the pool, dunking, cannonballing, splashing, and trying to tear the suits off each other. Then Brandi showed up in her red and white checkered bikini. Virgil knew her and therefore had the advantage over the others who only knew of her. She seemed unimpressed with her underclassmen and mentioned she might have to tell the Kalsows about their trespassing. She mentioned she had an open invitation from Kalsows' son, Tom. The boys, not wanting any trouble, reluctantly agreed to leave and let her enjoy her swim. Brandi motioned Virgil over while the others retrieved their suits underwater then exited by the wooden gate.

Virgil and his friends returned to his house where they parted ways shortly after. Virgil waited for Mark's car to go around the block then ran across the street, nearly knocking over a person out for an evening stroll to get back at the pool per Brandi's previous request. She was there, now in the water and only wearing her bikini bottoms. Virgil, though not in her clique of friends at school, somehow knew this night might be special. At least that's what another part of his body felt at the moment. Now, he stared out the front window and smiled at just how special that night turned out.

He saw a flashing light again. This time he pinpointed the source. It was coming from the side window of the Kalsows' house. Virgil tried to remember the layout of the house he had been in several times, but not for a while. He and Brandi had only used a chaise lounge chair outside the night they had awkwardly explored each other. The awkwardness mostly being from Virgil's inexperience.

The light could be from a TV showing an action flick, he thought, then realized that the single window was for the bathroom off the kitchen of the house. They were signaling him, Virgil surmised, then quickly exited his house through the back door. He walked down the block with the rifle over his shoulder but tucked behind him. He crossed the street and walked north. He entered the Prestons' backyard. They were two lots from Ellen and Gene's. He pressed his way through a trimmed pine hedge. He was now in the Cooper's backyard and he quickly crossed it to the wooden fence hiding the Kalsows' pool. He rose up and looked over the fence. The bedrooms were to the rear of the house, and he noticed the light on in the one nearest to him. He saw Gene sitting in what appeared to be a kitchen chair. His hands were behind him. Earl entered the room with Ellen and a man following them. Virgil ducked back down behind the fence. He waited a few minutes then slowly rose to look over the cedar planks once again. He surveyed what he could see from his limited vantage point. It appeared Gene was tied to the chair and Earl was now sitting opposite him in another kitchen chair. It appeared his hands were free. He was talking to someone to his left but not in Virgil's sight line. He couldn't see Ellen or anyone else. He knew he had to get in there and see for himself what was going on. He lowered down again and rested with his back against the cedar fence. It still smelled fresh, having been erected earlier that summer.

Virgil walked to the back of Cooper's yard. An outside light came on to the right of their backdoor. He picked up his pace and grabbed a low branch on the McIntosh apple tree in the corner of the yard by the fence and hoisted himself up, then over Gene's security fence. He lowered the rifle as far as he could then dropped it on the grass. He used the same procedure to get himself on the Kalsow property. He went to the opposite side of the yard and stayed against the fence until he reached the back of the house.

"Who's out there?" he heard Bill Cooper yell.

Virgil kept below the windows as he made his way around the pool to the backdoor.

"I've called the police," he heard Cooper inform the area.

Virgil grabbed the doorknob he knew led to an area used for wet swimsuits and towels. A back porch, so to speak. It was open and he let himself in. He knew the inside door would open to the hallway that led to bedrooms on both sides and continued to the bathroom, then the kitchen if he remembered correctly. He knew they were all in the first bedroom on the left, but who was the guy holding court.

He tried the door handle. It was not locked. He slowly opened the door, entered then leaned against the wall just inside the door he now closed. He turned and pointed the rifle in the direction of the doorway of the bedroom. The safety was off. He took a step towards the doorway when he noticed another flashing light. It was from the police Cooper had called next door. He must have told them his home was being invaded for them to show up that quickly and in that manner. It was then a man Virgil knew was not Earl or Gene quickly came out into the hallway. Virgil gave him a shot to the side of his jaw with the butt of the rifle. The large man went down in the hallway as a pistol fell out of his hand. Virgil grabbed the pistol, put it in the waistband of his jeans then looked for a light switch. He turned one on, but it was for the outside lights by the pool. He quickly turned it off. He flicked the next one and the hallway lit up as Ellen came out of the bedroom. "Took you long enough," she said, scolding Virgil.

"You alright, Ellen?" he asked as the man on the floor writhed in pain.

"He didn't hurt us. He was waiting for you," she informed him.

The man rolled over and sat up. There was blood trickling down the right side of his jaw and clotting in his beard. He wiped it off with his sleeve. Virgil stared at him and kept the rifle ready. "Are Earl and Gene okay?" Virgil asked Ellen.

"Oh yeah," Ellen laughed. "Guess I should untie them." She turned and went back into the bedroom.

"What do you want from us?" Virgil asked the man on the floor.

He wiped more blood off his neck and applied pressure to the wound on his bearded jaw as he looked up. "Virgil, you don't recognize your old friend?"

Virgil then realized it was Gustav. The last person he would have suspected to be anywhere near here. With Ivan gone he had agreed with Sylvia that Gustav was on his way back to Russia with his tail between his legs. "Gustav, what are you doing here?"

"Just trying to finish the job," he said with his right forearm pressed to his jaw. "With Ivan gone someone has to do it."

"So for the last time what do you want from me?" Virgil asked, then informed his opponent, "Remember Gustav, I'm the one with the upper hand now."

Gustav laughed, "Can I get up?"

"Slowly," Virgil said, backing up with the rifle still at the ready.

There were flashlights reflecting about the back wet room now as the police investigated Cooper's backyard, shining their lights over the fence. They then made their way to the front yard where they informed the Coopers they hadn't found anything.

Gustav slowly stood, leaning against the wall. Gene came out of the bedroom first followed by Ellen then Earl. Gene walked over to Gustav and punched him on the right jaw. It wasn't much of a punch because of Gene's diminished strength. Ellen followed, reaching into her pocket bent on some revenge of her own, Earl, knowing her intentions, yelled, "Don't, Ellen, there's no need for it now."

She turned and went in the opposite direction, "I'll make some coffee, I think we're in for a long night."

"Gene, Dad, are you guys alright?" Virgil asked.

"We'll be okay," Earl answered for both of them. Gene had followed his wife, but Earl walked to Gustav and kneed him in his left thigh. "That's for all of us."

"Dad," Virgil scolded, but not too loud. The police were still next door, discussing the unsubstantiated invasion with the neighbors.

"Hey, you already got your shot in," Earl said, looking at his son then back at Gustav.

Virgil almost felt sorry for Gustav. Almost.

He and his alleged brother were the ones who had started all of this with their visit to West Allis, installing a glitch into Virgil's week, computer and as it turned out, his life. Virgil had been doing just fine before all of this. Business had been good again, as was life, post pandemic of whatever was now out there. Virgil's business had taken a hit for three weeks, no work. It had returned pretty much back to normal when another panic, or variant, took hold of society. Nobody took it well except the pharmaceutical companies. Then six months later the twins showed up at Benny's. Virgil hadn't been pissed off in a long time so the butt of the rifle had relieved a lot of frustration. Gustav deserved it, Virgil felt and now hoped his nemesis had ascertained that meaning.

"Thanks for not shooting me too," Gustav said.

"The night is still young," Ellen called from the kitchen.

Virgil remembered the woman could hear a pin drop two blocks away and he lowered the volume of his reply. "Gustav, you must know I will do it if necessary."

Gustav looked over his shoulder then nodded the affirmative. "I believe you."

"It's not that I want to, it's that I might have to," Virgil explained further, still in a soft tone.

Gustav nodded again, staring at Virgil. "So how do you feel?" he asked in a whisper.

"I'm good. A doctor gave my dad and I a shot that stopped your shot's effects.

"What about the others?" he asked.

"What others?" Virgil returned the question.

"The house you were staying at," Gustav said.

Virgil was stunned for a minute. How did they know he and Earl were at Sylvia and Ernie's home. He played dumb. "What house?"

"Ernie's place out in the country," Gustav informed him.

"We weren't there," Virgil countered.

"Only watched people leave and return five or six times," Gustav said. "Harmon was a regular."

Virgil wanted to use the butt of the rifle again just to cease the suddenly invasive information. He now realized that he and Earl had gotten away with nothing. Can't fool the government these days or whoever was responsible, he thought. "So who killed Ivan?" Virgil asked in an effort to counter punch his way out of this corner.

Gustav looked down then up again, "You tell me. I thought you guys got in a lucky shot."

"You expect me to believe you don't know?" Virgil asked, raising his voice. "If you guys have been following us then you should know that."

"You want anything to drink, Virgil? Maybe hot coffee to pour on him?" Ellen yelled, leaning into the hallway. Gene laughed in the background.

"I'm good," Virgil said, waving his hand at her. "Come on Gustav," he now whispered, "What the hell is going on now. Why are you still here?"

Gustav wiped his sleeve on his jaw as he moved up the hallway towards the kitchen. Virgil reached into the bathroom and grabbed the nearest towel. He had the gun trained on Gustav but wanted to keep his distance while still aiding his captive. He threw a tan bath towel at him. "Here, use that on your jaw. We'll get you some ice," he said motioning towards the kitchen with the rifle.

"Did the police leave next door?" Virgil asked as they walked into the kitchen.

Earl, Gene, and Ellen were seated at the table drinking coffee. "I watched them drive away," Ellen told Virgil. "Either of you need something to drink?" she asked, getting up.

Virgil was taken back by her sudden change of heart. "An ice pack will do. So much for our plan, right, Dad?"

"Yeah, not working out so well right now, Virgil," Earl replied.

"So what is it that you want from me?" Virgil asked Gustav, giving him the ice pack Ellen had pulled from the freezer. "Here."

"Thank you, Ellen," Gustav said. "I'm sorry about all of this. I do mean that," he apologized, looking at Ellen then the men at the table.

Virgil was all over this. He poked Gustav in the ribs with the barrel of the rifle. "We don't believe your sincerity," He said shoving the barrel deep enough to make his captive pull the ice pack down in defense, "Now, what do you need from me that will cause you to disappear?"

Gustav looked at Virgil then at the others. "Answer him, son," Earl and Gene commanded almost in unison.

"I need a couple of vials of blood from you and your father," Gustav stated like he still held the winning cards.

Earl and Gene laughed. "I guess it's my one time to defy the government," Earl said, looking at Gene, then Virgil.

"What would you do with it if you had it?" Virgil asked.

"Figure out what they shot you up with and find the antibodies."

"You mean what you and your brother shot into my son," Earl corrected. "And, I mean literally, they shot it into him," he explained to Ellen and Gene, standing like he was pointing a rifle.

"No, I mean what doctor Harmon injected you with," Gustav informed Earl and his son, looking at both with the ice pack once again pressed against his jaw.

Earl and Virgil looked at each other.

"Not possible," Earl said, raising his voice.

"I don't think so, Gustav," Virgil said, backing his dad with equal volume.

"Why do you think we let you get this far?" Gustav asked with a spitballing tone.

"Wait a minute," Virgil countered the confusing question. "Why would you do to me what you did then let me escape and follow me around?"

"You knocked Ivan pretty well at the cabin, Virgil. But we accomplished our objective. We just needed time to recoup, rest and watch. We knew you weren't going anywhere and knew where you might visit. We knew your options," Gustav said, presenting his version of the events.

"Should I just end this?" Ellen asked like she had the option.

"Earl, you and Virgil need to get this unwanted guest out of here," Gene stated loudly as he pushed his chair back hard enough against the chair rail that it returned under his legs, forcing him to sit once again. It surprised everyone, including Gene. The starch of the request dissipated as he now gathered himself. Ellen laughed with her left hand over her mouth while pulling the scissors out of her pocket, turning away and placing them on top of the refrigerator.

"I agree with my flailing husband," she concurred, still chuckling, but under her breath.

"What do you mean you let us get this far?" Earl asked, leaning forward in his chair, his elbows resting on the table.

"We could have brought you in anytime we wanted," Gustav informed them. "I told Virgil we were with the Defense Department when we first met. You knew from the start."

"What do you mean all of us?" Ellen asked, grabbing the scissors and returning them to her smock pocket.

"You and Gene are all good," Gustav assured her. "We only need Virgil and his father," he said, staring at Earl.

"I will give you what you want," Virgil said. "Just leave my dad out of it."

"Oh, he's in it for sure," Gustav said, dropping the now warm ice pack into the sink behind him. "I think we should go across the street to your house."

Gene stood again, this time with control, "I think that would be a good idea for all of us," he said.

Virgil and Earl looked at Ellen. She returned the stare but agreed with her husband, "Yeah, if ya don't mind."

"Let's get outta here, then," Virgil said, poking Gustav with the rifle again this time in the ass and towards the direction of the front door. The prisoner didn't like it but followed orders. They marched across the streetlight illuminated street. Earl followed with the car.

The Living Room

Gustav sat on the sofa Virgil had slept on before he and Earl had made their escape from the garage. Virgil perched himself on an ottoman that was paired with a chair from another room. The rifle was resting on his left thigh and still at the ready while Gustav got comfortable and seemed to relax. Earl came through the same back door they had entered.

"Guess we better have some supper," Earl said from the kitchen,

"What would you like, Virgil?"

"Just pop in a frozen pizza, Dad," Virgil replied, looking at Gustav.

"Better make it two, Dad."

"Thank you," Gustav said, nodding at Virgil.

"Fuck you, Gustav. I'm just hungry," Virgil shot back, but with no intent to deprive his captive of food.

Gustav smiled as his shrugging shoulders hid some internal laughter. "I understand."

"Glad you do, because we don't understand any of this," Virgil confessed. "I don't know why you chose me, why you included my father, or why you chased me to my cabin and shot me with some drug."

"Ivan and I tried to explain that to you at Benny's," Gustav reminded him. "I thought we made it clear the last time you left us trapped in the bar."

Virgil smiled, hiding a laugh under his shrugging shoulders. The rifle was still aimed at one of the two men he had left surrounded by enough supporting patrons that night. Two free drinks had convinced most of them. "But you came to our house and demanded the check back, then burnt it on our porch. Why did you come to our house?"

"We wanted to surprise you and let you know we meant business."

"But you included my father and I don't like that," Virgil said, messing with the safety on the gun to make sure it was off.

"He helps you with your business and that is the only reason we included him," Gustav said.

"But you didn't need to, is what I'm saying," Virgil explained.

"He was friends with Ernie and Sylvia, and we needed that access as well."

Virgil was stunned. It seemed like our government was in control all along, but he didn't want to believe it. He didn't want to admit he had been played, or that he had lost. He still wanted the feeling of control for a change, no matter how long it would last. "Who picked you up that night you came to our house?"

"You know of these cars that can drive themselves?"

"I've actually seen delivery vehicles used like that," Virgil admitted.

"The black Escalade picked us up, then Ivan drove it off."

"Someone had to control it to get it there," Virgil suggested.

"An address is all you need."

"You both got in the backseat, though," Earl recalled, entering the room.

"You are correct," Gustav said looking at Earl. "Ivan climbed over the seat and drove."

"How did you guys get out of the bar and why did you follow me to the cabin?" Virgil asked.

"We finished our drinks then told everyone we would buy two more rounds for the house. They backed off after that."

"Why the cabin?" Earl asked.

"Because we hadn't given him the shot yet," Gustav explained. "We never wanted any of this to get out of hand, but you panicked, Virgil."

Virgil stood. He pointed the rifle at Gustav's head. Earl looked at his son but didn't interfere. Gustav cowered, pressing his shoulders against the back of the sofa, but not covering his face. "You come hunting me at a place I should be safe at, and you say I panicked," Virgil yelled at his captive. "What the hell did you expect me to do?"

"Take the shot in the interest of science," Gustav calmly replied. "Like all the others."

"How long has this been going on?" Earl asked.

"Actually, before the first pandemic began."

"What? Why?" Earl asked.

"Our government knew something was out there. We were trying to find out what and from where," Gustav explained. "Now that the first pandemic is over, we are trying to get ready for the next one."

"Dad," Virgil said.

"Yes, son."

"Come and take this rifle."

"Why, I don't want to shoot him," Earl stated.

"Good, because I do right now. And I don't trust myself not to," Virgil said, handing the gun to his father.

Earl took it from his son and clicked the safety back on. He looked at the man on the sofa. "What do you mean the next one?" Earl asked.

"These viruses have always been around and there will always be variants. We are always trying to stay a step ahead of them so it doesn't cause widespread panic when it hits."

"Can't you stop them before it goes too far?" Virgil asked.

"Yes, we can if we have a database and that is why we contacted you and many others," Gustav informed them.

"But when Virgil declined you wouldn't leave it be," Earl mentioned. "You persisted. I would have panicked too."

"People hear about something, and they talk about it," Gustav said. "With the media we have today we can't take a chance of someone making up stories about what we are doing. How do you think the original pandemic got out of hand?"

"You were right about that then, Dad," Virgil said patting him on the back. "Our government did fuck up."

"In a sense, yes," Gustav agreed. "We fucked up as you say because the wrong information was given out and people panicked."

"You mean it wasn't from Wuhan?" Virgil asked.

"It was definitely from there."

"Then what information was wrong?" Earl asked.

"They said it could kill many people," Gustav said. "When in fact it could, but only the most vulnerable. You know the people with underlying conditions."

"Then why were the large numbers being reported as being the cause of death?" Virgil asked.

"Part of it was politics," Gustav admitted. "The other, well...it was the government not wanting to admit such a grievous error."

Earl looked at Virgil, "You better take this gun, son."

Virgil slowly took it from his father's hands and clicked the safety off. "I didn't believe what you were telling me about getting the shot. I didn't want to die because of another person's screw up," Virgil said, sitting once again on the ottoman across from Gustav.

Gustav sat in silence for a moment, looking up at Earl and over at Virgil then down at the floor. A beep from the kitchen informed them the pizzas were done. Earl left the room without saying anything. His son kept his eyes fixed on the Defense Department employee. Earl opening the stove, getting dishes from the cupboard, and cutting the pies were the only noises to be heard in the now silent living room. Earl returned, "Everything is ready, let's eat."

Virgil motioned Gustav to the kitchen with the rifle barrel. He slowly rose and headed in that direction with Virgil following. Earl and Gustav sat at each end of the table while Virgil sat by the counter with the rifle in his lap. "Water good enough for you?" Earl asked his son.

"That's fine, Dad."

Gustav ate four slices of the sausage, mushroom, and green pepper pizzas. He wiped his mouth on the napkin provided after downing the rest of his tumbler full of water. "Thank you for the dinner, that was good."

"You never could guarantee that I would be safe could you," Virgil asked, resuming the questioning.

Gustav wiped his mouth again with the napkin.

"Answer him, damn it," Earl demanded, pounding his fist on the oak table.

"No, we could not, but we had only two fatalities in the one thousand we had recruited, and that was because the guy had a heart attack."

"Caused by your shot no doubt," Earl suggested.

"The doctor said it was a possibility, but they would have to do more testing," Gustav explained.

"Then I had the right to be afraid. I had the right to panic," Virgil stated.

"Where did this guy die?" Earl asked.

"I'm not sure Gustav replied, looking about the room.

"Was it locally, or in another state?"

"What does it matter?" Gustav asked. "You guys are fine and with no after effects."

"What about the effects I had until I got the shot from Doctor Harmon?"

"What did you experience?" Gustav asked.

Virgil explained the lack of strength, dizziness, fever, nausea, and plugged ears. Earl filled in the fact that Gustav and Ivan had left him to die in the woods and that the symptoms would come and go over the course of the days until they saw Harmon.

"Very much like many of the others," Gustav informed them.

"Did you guys leave the others to die in some woods somewhere?" Earl asked, rising from his chair and collecting the plates.

"Honestly, we could not find you and we looked for most of the following day," Gustav explained. "We assumed you had gone to another cabin in the area."

"So you just left him out there without knowing or caring?" Earl asked.

"Like I said, Ivan was hurting and needed medical attention. We needed to leave," Gustav explained.

"And you knew where we might go," Virgil asked, wanting confirmation. He could hear his phone ringing in his bedroom. "Dad, keep an eye on our friend."

Earl turned from the kitchen sink and received the rifle from his son then leaned against the counter. "I'll be right back," Virgil said, then headed to the bedroom.

Earl could hear Virgil talking to someone but could not make out what was being said. "So, the one guy who died from your shot, where was it he died?" Earl re-asked a previously unanswered question.

"You mean the heart attack?" Gustav said. "I think it was at the local hospital now that I think of it."

"Grant hospital, the one where Harmon works?"

"Yes, I believe that's the name of it," Gustav said.

"I was told another patient with the same symptoms was there as well and left the hospital without anyone's knowledge. Would you know anything about that?"

Gustav looked about the room then at Earl, "I wasn't at the hospital so I don't know anything about that."

"Do you know Doctor Harmon?"

"He knows him," Virgil answered as he returned to the room, "And Sylvia as well."

Earl looked at his son like he had just been slapped across the face. He handed the gun back to Virgil and then started pacing from the kitchen to the living room and back.

"It appears they had help with all of this," Virgil informed his father.

"I can't believe Ernie would do anything like this," Earl yelled from the living room, then began pacing again.

"He wasn't aware what his wife and Harmon were up to, but he does now."

"Who were you talking to?" Earl asked.

"Ernie," Virgil answered. "Sylvia finally told him what she and Harmon were doing and who they were helping."

Earl stopped in the kitchen and looked at Gustav, then his son. "I can't believe it," he said.

"Call Ernie when we're done here, he'll explain it to you," Virgil told his dad. "All we have to do is give a couple vials of blood each and this guy should be on his way."

Gustav slowly stood up, "I'll get my bag. It's in my car around the block."

"I'll go with you," Virgil informed him, grabbing a blanket to cover the rifle.

"Leave the rifle and take this, Virgil," Earl said, reaching in his pocket and handing his son a snub nose .38 pistol. "It's a little easier to conceal."

"When did you get this?" Virgil asked, taking it and handing Earl the rifle.

"When this asshole showed up at our house with his brother," Earl explained. Virgil looked at his dad but kept an eye on Gus. Earl could tell Virgil wanted to know from where, "I phoned a friend," he answered the quizzical look.

"Come on Gustav, let's get this over with," Virgil instructed his prisoner turned blood drawer. They started down the backstairs.

"You only have to pull the trigger on that one," Earl called out to Virgil as they opened the back door. He then started cleaning up the kitchen from dinner as Virgil directed Gustav. Earl quickly put the dishes in the dishwasher and wiped the table then threw the used napkins into the trash. He took his cellphone out of his left back pocket and called Ernie. He was pissed at his longtime friend but not sure what for. Ernie and Sylvia had taken care of them while they stayed there. No harm came to them and now they were home again. However, why hadn't they been truthful? What were they hiding and for God's sakes what was this all about?

"Earl, how are you?" Ernie's voice boomed from his phone.

"How do you think I am, Ernie?" Earl sarcastically asked.

"Virgil said you might be pissed."

"I'm sorry, Ernie. Do I sound pissed?" Earl said, upping the volume and attitude.

"Come on, Earl, we've been friends too long for this to come between us," Ernie pleaded.

"That is exactly why I'm pissed," Earl explained. "Friends for that long don't confide with the enemy."

"Doctor Harmon has been friends with me and Sylvia for a long time," Ernie shouted back in defense.

A long time back they had both happened upon each other on their way to their combined graduations. That day they resolved their issues, but today Earl was more cautious. "I know, but why didn't you guys just tell us the truth? Why, didn't you just tell us all of this instead of the Defense Department?"

"Our hands were tied."

"How so?"

"They were going to make my business go away and Harmon could've lost his license," Ernie informed Earl.

"Just like they did to Virgil and me."

"See, so we are in this together," Ernie explained further.

"Yeah, because you guys helped them get to us," Earl responded then hung up when Virgil and Gustav returned.

"So why did they need to involve Harmon and Sylvia in this?" Earl asked Virgil and Gustav as they entered the kitchen.

Virgil handed the pistol to Earl and left the rifle leaning against the end of the counter. "Because they came to them before us and made them the same offer," Virgil informed Earl, "They had the same choices as us. Lose your business for a while and we'll take care of ya."

"That's pure bullshit," Earl yelled at Gustav, waving the gun at him as they continued into the living room. Gustav sat on the sofa again and set a small black leather bag on the coffee table.

"Why are you getting so upset, Dad?" Virgil said, smiling at his irate father. "One vial of blood each and we're done with this shit."

Gustav opened the bag and pulled out two syringes along with two vials. "I'm not going to harm you, Mr. Ditch," Gustave reassured the older Ditch.

"You've already done something to us," Earl stated the facts. "You're just not telling us what it is exactly."

"You will be fine, I assure you," Gustav said again.

Virgil was looking at his dad and wondering why he just couldn't agree to this simple task. It was then he realized that indeed, Gustav and the others had done something to him and possibly his father. Before and at Ernie and Sylvia's place they were questioning everything. They had left that house with a plan to find out what had happened to them and why. The plan had been altered by the altercation at the Kalsows' house. Now, Virgil looked at Gustav, wondering why he was caving into the will of people he had no idea of what they were really doing.

Earl stepped back into the kitchen and returned with the rifle. He made sure it was loaded and the safety was off. He pointed it at Gustav with his finger on the trigger. "Put it back in the bag," Earl demanded, pointing the rifle barrel at the syringes and vials and then again at Gustav.

Gustav did as told with a smile on his face. He looked at Virgil then back to Earl, "Why's everything a big deal with you guys?" Gustav asked.

"Because you have not answered the questions we've been asking." Earl verbally took a shot. "We still don't know the truth."

"You asshole," Virgil shouted, standing over Gustav while still allowing his father a clear shot. Earl was right. The questions they asked had never been answered. "Question number one. Why did you use Doctor Harmon, Sylvia, and Ernie?"

Gustav looked at his duffel bag then at Virgil. "To get to you guys. They agreed to help us contact you."

"Question two. Why us? Why not, just about anyone else?"

"You were the healthiest in your categories."

Earl waved the rifle up and down. He wanted to pull the trigger at almost anything at this point. Once again he and his son were being stifled.

"Categories of what?"

"It's all about how healthy you are," Gustav said.

"For what reason?" Virgil asked.

"They told us they only wanted the healthiest people in their age groups for this project."

"Again. For what reason?"

"That category would last the longest and give us the best chance of propagating the population of the world to survive the next virus."

Earl didn't lower the rifle but stared at Virgil for only a moment. His son returned the stare. It was the first, what the fuck stare, they had exchanged during the course of these events. Personally, both had thought about it many times. Virgil more than his dad.

"You mean the earth could come to an end because of this next one?" Virgil asked.

"Yes, but just the people. You thought Covid and the variants were bad. Wait until winter hits."

"Then what?"

"All hell is going to break loose."

Earl pulled the trigger. The oak coffee table splintered, and the duffel bag slid towards the end of the table from the impact. Virgil was startled, but somehow expected it, and barely flinched. Gustav grabbed his bag and pulled it into his lap. Earl grabbed the bolt action lever and completed the motions to reload without taking his eyes off the target.

"Who's starting this one?" Virgil asked, holding up his left hand towards his dad in a stop motion.

Gustav sat upright, "It doesn't matter."

"To me it does," Earl said. "Who is it?"

"Answer my dad, Gustav."

Gustav set the bag back on the coffee table with the hole in it. "Let's just finish this so I can go home and you can stay here."

"You need to tell us or, the next one doesn't go through the coffee table," Earl replied, leveling the rifle for his best shot.

"Just answer, then you can go and we can stay home," Virgil suggested.

"You know Putin never got over the Ukraine, so this is his revenge."

"And you and Ivan are from Russia to make sure everything gets off to a rousing start," Virgil asked.

"No, we have always been from the Defense Department. That is a fact."

"Ours," Earl asked.

"The severity of what is going to happen requires us to do what we are doing," Gustav calmly stated, ignoring Earl.

"Once again, you are from our country?" Earl asked.

"Yes. Ivan and I were born here. Our grandparents immigrated from the Ukraine after World War Two."

Earl lowered the rifle a bit and looked at Virgil who had backed up a few steps. "That's nice, but how bad is the next virus," Virgil asked.

"There isn't much that will stop it," Gustav explained. "Doctor Harmon gave you one of the best options we have found, so far."

What the fuck, Earl and Virgil mouthed to each other so Gustav couldn't see. Virgil shuffled about the living room knowing they had avoided nothing. Earl backed away from Gustav a few feet. The rifle remained on target. Earl nodded at his son. "How did you know about that?" Virgil finally asked, bumping into an end table.

"If only you had believed us from the beginning," Gustav said, rising to his feet.

"You're not leaving just yet," Virgil informed his, once again, employer.

"Believe in you, from the beginning, '' Earl said, annoyed, "Sit down."

"Sorry, I needed to stretch," Gustav said, pushing his arms up in the air and rotating them. Earl followed the arm movement, while keeping the rifle aimed at the exerciser's chest.

"That's fine," Virgil said, granting his approval with a nod as well.

"Who shot your brother?" He asked, still facing Gustav and nodding.

"You are not in danger," Gustav said, lowering his arms to his side with both index fingers and each hand pointing at his captors.

"Why do you always avoid that question?" Earl asked, lowering the rifle and pulling the trigger again. A piece of carpet and underlayment flew into the air. Gustav sat down, grabbing at his right foot. "Told ya it wouldn't be the table."

Gustav knew they could kill him if they wanted but they could never get away with it like he could. "You have to realize, if I get a blood sample from both of you, I'll be gone and you will not be harassed. And that you will help us save lives, possibly thousands of lives, maybe millions," Gustav offered as a distraction.

"Gustav, for the last time, who shot your brother and why?" Virgil asked, slamming his fist down on the fractured coffee table.

"The why comes first," Gustav countered. "Remember the other guy at Grant hospital? You know when the first person that died from the soon to be new virus?" Gustav waited for a response that was not going to come. Earl waved the rifle in a motion that must have invoked the idea to continue, because Gustav did. "There was a second patient admitted as well. It was Ivan. He was infected with the new strain. It had to be stopped. This strain can be transmitted easily, airborne or on contact. They filled him up with whatever they could to fight his lack of resistance to it. The first guy didn't stand a chance with his bad heart, but they kept him alive as long as they could. They wanted data on what worked and what didn't."

Virgil sat on the ottoman. He felt Gustav was finally giving the truth. Their nemesis had never talked this long or to this extent. Still, he remained cautious. As did Earl.

"Can I get a glass of water?" Gustav asked, lowering his head.

"Give me the rifle, Dad," Virgil asked.

"Go get it for him, son," Earl replied. "Why was Ivan shot in our garage?"

"Because the strain had to be stopped," Gustav said. "It was the only way to stop him. He would have begun the whole epidemic right here."

"Wait, did he escape from the hospital?" Earl asked.

"Yes."

"But why did he have to be killed?" Earl asked.

"This new strain can be controlled for a week or so but that is it."

Virgil returned with glasses of water for everyone, setting one on the end table closest to Earl and one on the coffee table for Gustav. He sat back down on the ottoman, taking a sip from his glass before setting it on the same table as Gustav's. "Then what?"

"It goes out of control in a hurry," Gustav said, grabbing his glass and downing half the volume. "That's when it is time to stop it at any cost."

"How do you know this?" Earl asked.

"Harmon and the others have been testing all the samples we have accumulated as well as poring over the data," Gustav said, finishing the rest of the glass and setting it back down.

"I've known of Doctor Harmon for many years and have met him several times, hell, he removed my gallbladder," Earl said. "Has he always been involved with our government?"

"He was one of our first recruits for this project," Gustav said. "So he's been with us about a year before the first pandemic."

"So you're saying the new virus is already here," Virgil asked, standing up again and instinctively backing away.

"Yes, but don't worry. I don't have it and I'm vaccinated against it."

"So there is a vaccine?" Earl asked.

"Yes, for the virus coming out of Russia. The one we believe they are trying to spread," Gustav explained.

"Then what is the worry?" Virgil asked.

"That we can produce enough vaccines fast enough, and that it is definitely the correct one for this strain."

"What will this new strain be called?" Earl asked.

"55N37E is what scientists use for labels," Gustav explained.

"And the significance of that?" Virgil inquired.

"It's the longitude and latitude of Moscow," Earl answered before Gustav had the chance. He lowered the rifle as Virgil and Gustav stared at him awaiting an explanation. Earl stood there shaking his head.

"What is it, Dad?"

"I heard them talking about it at Ernie and Sylvia's place," Earl explained. "They were talking loud enough the one evening after they thought I was asleep. I heard them say 55N37E so I Googled it and Moscow was the answer."

Virgil looked at Gustav. "Is it true?"

"Yes."

"Damn it," Virgil shouted at Gustav. "You shot me up with that?"

"You were never in any harm, Virgil," Gustav said. "It's why we wanted you, remember."

"But what if I had something wrong with me you didn't know about?" Virgil suggested, "What if I was the one who died?"

"We knew you wouldn't. We made sure of it."

"How?"

"Remember the last physical you had," Gustav asked.

"Yeah, but it wasn't with Harmon," Virgil answered. "It was with Doctor

Lentz."

"Remember we knew everything about you," Gustav said. "He did extra blood work for us, and remember the scan he requested you get?"

"The CT scan you mean?" Virgil asked.

"Yes."

"He said it was a good idea to get one at my age because it would detect anything that might be going on."

"And, he was right," Gustav said. "You had a clean bill of health."

Virgil felt like taking the rifle from his father and putting a bullet in Gustav's forehead, or at least punching him, "Stand up," Virgil demanded of Gustav.

Gustav slowly stood up, stretching his arms out in front of him as he rose. "Thanks, I need to move around. I get stiff from sitting around too much." He paced back and forth between the sofa and length of the damaged coffee table, stumbling once on the torn carpet and floor. He stopped a few minutes later and stood facing Virgil.

He wanted to deck him, but Virgil realized it would accomplish nothing at this point. "So my dad and I are going to survive this 55N37E, or whatever you call it?"

"Yes. Your dad never had it, just you, Virgil," Gustav said, hoping to put his captors at ease once again.

"The shot Doctor Harmon brought and Sylvia gave us was the vaccine?" Earl asked.

"Yes, it was, and we will contact you both if there is a booster shot recommended."

"How was it that I wasn't contagious?" Virgil asked. "How did my dad not get it?"

"When you were infected..."

"You mean shot," Virgil corrected Gustav.

"Yes, when you received the shot and your dad came in contact with you it was in its earliest stages. If you had it for several weeks then you would have had to be disposed of."

Virgil let this last bit of information mull over and stir within his mind.

"Why the bar again then?" Virgil asked, referring to Benny's.

"You left us no choice," Gustav replied.

Virgil quickly nailed Gustav with a left jab to his nose followed by a right overhand that caught the left cheek of his intended target.

Gustav didn't land on the sofa as Virgil expected but shook his head back and forth then smiled back at his attacker. "I deserved that, I suppose," he said, rubbing his cheek.

"You're lucky we don't put a bullet in you like your brother got," Earl said, raising the rifle once again.

"But you didn't put the bullet in him," Gustav said, rubbing his cheek while checking his nose for blood, "I did."

Virgil instantly felt remorse and guilt course through his mind. This thing must be so bad that a guy would kill his own brother to prevent the spread, he thought. "I'm sorry, Gustav," Virgil offered leaning towards him. "It's just that it was mentioned that a guy by the name of Chung killed your brother."

"In many ways that is correct," Gustav said. "That is the common name for this virus."

"Wait, why would they call a Russian virus by a Chinese name?"

"Why take the blame if you can pin it on someone else," Gustav said. "All this stuff started in Wuhan, why change the brand name."

Earl lowered the rifle and walked into the kitchen. He returned a moment later without the gun and holding three cans of Stella Artois beer. He set one down in front of Virgil and Gustav each and opened the one in his hand. He raised his can towards them both. "Cheers," he said then took a healthy swig. "I'm ready for my blood draw now Gustav."

Virgil opened his can then nodded to Gustav to do likewise, "I'm ready as well," he said, raising his can as if he were toasting the admission. "Sorry about the punch a minute ago."

"You certainly have regained your strength, Virgil," Gustav said, opening his can of Stella and raising it towards him and then Earl. He pressed it against his cheek for a minute then set it down on the table. He leaned forward and pulled the syringes back out of the duffle bag. "Who's first?"

Two Weeks Later

They started to live again. At first they looked over their shoulders everywhere they went, but the paranoia eventually faded. They agreed you didn't go through what they had gone through and not remain cautious. Virgil joined his father at church the next Sunday. He wanted to thank God for looking over them during all that had happened since the Saturday Gustav had got what he wanted and left.

Virgil contacted Mark and his business was ready to go. He had sent out emails to all former contacts explaining the status of the business. He was over his illness and ready to resume working. Now he would have to wait. Fortunately, it was only a matter of a few days before he got his first call. It was local and a minor repair, but it was a start.

Earl worked on investing half the money they had received from the government into vaccine producing companies and PPE products. They tithed a portion of the money to Earl's church and local charities as well as the Indian reservation by the cabin.

It was the second Monday following his church visit when Virgil got a call to go back to West Allis. It was welcomed business, but he couldn't help thinking about what had started there and what he and his father had gone through. He had the parts needed for the repair in his van and would drive up there in the morning.

"You want to go with me, Dad?" Virgil asked Earl as he walked into the living room. The coffee table and carpet still needed to be replaced, but by moving furniture and a strategically placed large book the effects of recent events were hidden.

"No, I'm going to stay here. Ernie and Sylvia are stopping by."

"And what are you guys up to?" Virgil quizzed his dad.

"They are just checking up on us and we are setting things straight between us."

"That's good to hear. Am I needed here?"

"No, son. You go to Wisconsin."

He left the next morning at five-thirty am wanting to get ahead of traffic. He made it to West Allis in little over an hour. The best travel time he could remember. He waited in the parking lot for the Maintenance Manager to finish his morning meeting and come out and let him in.

As he sat there he thought about his dad, Sylvia, and Ernie. What were they up to, he wondered. He couldn't help it but realized by doing so he was not trusting his father who would never harm him. He felt ashamed of himself for this, but still contemplated if there was more to their visit than a checkup. Sylvia and Ernie hadn't exactly told the whole truth through the time at their home. How could he not feel this way after all that had happened to him and

Earl. Above all he wanted his father to be safe and live out his life on his terms, not looking over his shoulder for what may be coming.

Therein was the problem, they knew what was coming to a certain extent, but what could they actually do about it. "Don't create a panic," Gustav suggested. "Or give the government a reason to take a closer look at you." They could only tell those involved with them personally and they better use discretion.

Virgil's cell phone rang. It was Earl. "You in West Allis?" he asked.

"Yes, I am."

"Didn't hear ya leave," Earl said.

"I'll bang some pots and pans around next time," Virgil joked.

"Just didn't realize you were leaving so early."

"Sorry. I woke up at four-thirty this morning and I just kinda went with it," Virgil explained. "Realized I could beat traffic and did."

"Good for you," Earl said. "I just wanted to let you know that I'm going to take a vacation with Sylvia and Ernie."

Virgil didn't expect this. He was stunned in fact. His dad had not taken a vacation anywhere that hadn't included him. They had seen Denali and the Grand Canyon together and wanted to make Pearl Harbor someday. But they mostly went to the cabin in the spring and fall, including Galena. "Where are you going? Wait, I thought you guys were burying the hatchet?"

"We've already buried the hatchet," Earl said. "They're coming by today to plan the trip."

"When are you going?" Virgil inquired.

"We haven't decided that either."

"Then why are you calling me?" Virgil asked, laughing to himself.

"Because I didn't tell you last night," Earl explained. "I didn't want you to be left out of the loop."

"Thank you for that," Virgil said. "Right now I have John the Maintenance Manager waving at me from the backdoor of the place I'm at."

"I'll let you go then. I'll keep you informed."

"Thanks, Dad," Virgil said, getting out of the van and waving back at John as he ended the call.

"Glad you are available again," John greeted him at the steel door.

"Glad to be back in business," Virgil admitted. "How's your business?"

"We just got a government contract for a bunch of PPE products," John informed him.

"That's great, my dad and I have invested in companies that are doing that and I think yours is on the list."

"Good idea then we'll all be ready for the next virus," John said, smiling. "How are you feeling?"

"What do you mean the next one?" Virgil asked.

"There is always another one that arrives around this time of year, and we need to get this line up and running to keep ahead of it," John explained.

"How do you know that?" Virgil asked.

"Our VP, Mr. Holmgren, is on the board of Grant Hospital and he is pressuring me to get this line running, you know, like yesterday."

"There's a Grant hospital up here," Virgil asked.

"Actually, it's down by you, but there is St. Marks here and the two are part of a group. Grant is the main hospital and where he received the heads up about the new virus."

"I thought Grant hospital was only connected with Illinois hospitals," Virgil said, surprised at the coincidence.

"The mergers that go on these days are hard to keep up with," John said, shaking his head. "So how are you feeling?"

"Good now." Virgil said then added a lie for his absence, "I had hernia surgery and had to take some time off."

"Thought you had closed your doors for good by the last post on your website last month," John said.

"Yeah the guy didn't word it the way I had wished," Virgil expanded the falsehood. "Then I was so out of it that I just let it ride and hoped for the best."

"Glad it worked out."

"Me, too."

They arrived at the machine the company was counting on to make syringe bodies for a company supplying the government with the new vaccine. John explained the problem and what he thought was causing it. Virgil performed some tests of his own and concurred with John's diagnosis. He had the valve in his van and it would take a couple hours to replace it. Virgil got right to work.

"I can have one of my guys do the heavy lifting for you if you would like," John offered.

"For what?" Virgil said, forgetting his story.

"I don't want you getting another hernia, Virgil," John said, concerned and somewhat baffled at Virgil's nonchalance about his injury.

"If you have somebody available that would be fine," Virgil said, realizing he had to play the story out.

The job was completed by eleven that morning, but Virgil stuck around and tuned the press for optimal performance. John was happy the parts were popping out of the mold by noon and the line it fed was running shortly thereafter. Virgil felt a renewed sense of accomplishment. He knew he was helping humanity in another way now. He knew what was coming but couldn't let on about it. "That press is humming right along," he said proudly.

"Yes, it is," John said, smiling. "The best it has run in a while. What else did you do to it?"

"Remember that diagnostics page on this one? Screen 49 I believe it was," Virgil asked.

John nodded, "Yes, I've messed with that a little."

"You can tune the valve we just put on, but you can also tune the pumps and that's where I got the extra speed," Virgil explained, then showed John the screen and which values he had altered.

They returned to John's office and sat down. "Ever think of settling down in one place?" John asked.

Virgil smiled, knowing this time would come eventually, "You offering me a job, John?"

"Mr. Holmgren, the VP of manufacturing, said if you get us up and running to make you a lucrative job offer. He wants someone available that is close by," John explained.

"I've got my dad back home to keep an eye on," Virgil explained. "He's in good health, but won't be forever. Besides, it's home for both of us."

"Take this with you and look it over is all I ask," John said, sliding a large yellow interoffice envelope across his desk to Virgil.

Virgil laughed, thinking here we go again. Then laughed as he stood up, thinking at least John isn't from the government. "Thank you, John. I will do that and let you know."

"It's a great place to work," John said, shaking Virgil's hand. He followed him to the steel door and let him out. "Let me know as soon as you can, Virgil."

"I'll do that," Virgil assured John, but was wondering how and in what way all that happened was somehow related.

Virgil was going to find a different route home that afternoon just to break the mojo of feelings now feeding his anxiety. Ten minutes after he left Chase Products, John called. He was probing for a phone conference. "Sorry to bother you, Virgil, but I was wondering if we could tune the press to get a little better cycle time."

"You can go to the page I showed you and tweak a few things," Virgil responded. "Wait, is it still at 12.4 seconds?"

"Yes."

"Then why would you mess with it?" Virgil asked.

"Holmgren wants the cycle at 11."

"With all due respect, you told me the standard was 15," Virgil sarcastically replied.

John laughed like he did when lacking a plausible reason for his interruption. "He wants us to squeeze everything out we can get," John offered with little conviction or desire.

"Smells like greed to me," Virgil said.

"Just give me some ideas and consequences."

"Consequence is that if you go to a 11-second cycle I will be up there in two days replacing the pump and possibly the motor if it gets bound," Virgil informed his client.

"That's what I thought you would say."

"Ideas," Virgil shot back. "I have one. Leave it the fuck alone."

John laughed, "I'll word it differently when I tell Holmgren."

Benny's Again

Virgil decided to stay in the area in case he was needed again. He now had a windfall of money, and was working again, so he treated himself to better accommodations. The usual Hampton, though comfortable, didn't quite have the feel of the king-sized bed he now stretched out in at his room on the fourth floor of the Ambassador. He was the most comfortable and relaxed he had been in the past few turbulent months.

He called Earl to let him know of his change in plans and questioned him about his plans with Ernie and Sylvia. His dad informed him of a trip to Vicksburg, Mississippi, to see the Civil War battlefield. It would still be warm there into November and the hotel prices were a bargain.

"So how long are you staying for?" Virgil asked. "It's only the middle of October."

"We haven't decided," his father nervously replied.

"Is everything okay, Dad?"

"I'm, I mean, dammit."

"Dad, are you okay?" There were some nondescript noises in the background of their conversation and Virgil needed to know his dad was safe.

"I'm fine, Virgil, I just knocked some pans into the sink," Earl finally said, defusing the situation. "I just need some time away from here. Ernie and Sylvia are the best friends I have," Earl said now laughing, "Sorry, I mean second and third best friends."

Virgil laughed, "I understand either way. When are you leaving?"

"This next Saturday," Earl said.

"Those were quick plans you guys made."

"Like Gustav said, you have to stay ahead of it."

"What the hell are you talking about, Dad?"

"The virus, dummy. If it's going to take us all out eventually then I'm going to see all I want to see."

"What the hell are you talking about?" Virgil asked, not getting any of what his father seemed to be blabbering about. "What do you guys know that I don't?"

"Virgil, we're going to the south. They tell us it's the best place to be and watch all that is going to happen in the north."

"Are you telling me it has already started?"

"Soon," Earl said. "So you still have time to join us before it takes hold there and wipes almost everyone out."

Earl's nonchalant manner heightened Virgil's concerns. Now what was going on, he contemplated, rising from his bed and walking to the window. He took in the view to the east and could see the not too distant lights of Milwaukee. "What if I stay here and ride it out?" Virgil asked.

"You will probably be alright, because of Harmon's vaccine, but from what we have talked about here, the south is the best option for us to fight against it."

"You mean a better survival rate?"

"Yeah."

"Who is telling you all of this," Virgil asked, wanting something more substantial.

"Doctor Harmon mostly."

"Come on, Dad, who else?"

"Gustav has had some contact with us."

This caught Virgil by surprise. He quickly pulled the drapes closed then backed away from the window and to his right. He couldn't respond to his father for a moment. He was ashamed of the manner in which he had just reacted. He dejectedly sat down on a captain's chair at the desk against the wall still further from the window. "Why would he contact you guys?" Virgil finally asked.

"He told us he would let us know if there were any updates we might need to survive."

"So what did he say?" Virgil asked.

"We're all in good shape with the shot. And, that the virus will start to the north, head south, but then will die out at the Mason-Dixon line."

That sounded corny to Virgil, like the south will rise again or something in that tone. He understood the fact they wanted to get away, but it didn't sound like they were coming home anytime soon, or maybe ever.

"How much time do I have up here?"

"Two, possibly three months," Earl simply stated.

"That's it," Virgil quizzed his father. "They can't say where it will begin?"

"Not with any certainty," Earl said. "Just get down here when you can, son."

"I think I may head to the cabin for a week," Virgil told his father. "You know, just to see it one more time."

"I understand, just don't lollygag up there," Earl said. "And remember just tell who you have to, we don't want to start a panic."

"I will see you in a month, or sooner," Virgil informed Earl, though his dad's panic comment bothered him a bit.

"Love you, son."

"Love you too, Dad."

Virgil rose from the chair, walked to the window and quickly pulled the drapes back in the same way he had closed them. At this particular moment he didn't give a shit about anything that had happened or was about to. He stood there, once again taking in the view for five minutes. Then he felt a need to go somewhere. He turned, grabbed his room key off the dresser the TV stood on and stuffed it in his front pocket. He was heading to Benny's, it was three blocks to the east, and though a cool evening, the walk was just what he needed. He pulled his heavy red Blackhawks hooded sweatshirt on during the elevator ride down to the main floor. He started through the elegant but sparsely populated lobby.

The night manager stopped Virgil before he reached the front door, "Is everything alright with your room, Mr. Ditch?"

"How do you know who I am?" Virgil asked, not remembering the mid-twenties manager, Ken.

"I registered you earlier today, sir."

"I'm sorry it's been a long day," Virgil said, collecting himself. "Yes, everything is fine. The best I've ever had."

"That is always good to hear. Is there somewhere you need a ride to?" Ken quickly asked then as quickly explained. "We have a van that takes people to the city if you would like, Mr. Ditch."

Virgil laughed. He had never been treated this way when staying at a hotel. Ken's enthusiasm for his job only amplified the atmosphere of goodwill. "Will they run me to Benny's just down the street?"

"Yes, we can," Ken offered.

"Appreciate it, but it's a nice night for a walk."

"Call the number on this card and we will pick you up. That is until midnight," Ken offered another option.

"That, I might take you up on," Virgil said, taking the card and giving Ken a fist bump. He exited the hotel into the well-lit covered driveway and beyond onto a sidewalk. He turned and looked up at his room. He knew it was his because the light was on and the left drape was resting on the sill. He looked around to get his bearings then started off towards the bar where this adventure had all begun.

During his walk Virgil relaxed in a different way than the afternoon nap he had enjoyed on the king-sized bed. He was alive and apparently somewhat protected from the new gloom and doom virus, but most of all, his dad was safe. That alone tempered any fears of the unknown. After all that he and his father had been through he knew he could handle almost anything.

As he continued on he laughed, remembering the first night he met Ivan and Gustav. Then laughed even harder, thinking about his failed escape attempt. A siren blared from an ambulance down the street to his right. Startled, he backed away from the intersection he was about to step into. He was one block away from Benny's and didn't need to be run over. The emergency vehicle passed by him and beyond his destination then made a left turn three blocks farther down the street.

A black Escalade then passed through the intersection just after Virgil made it to the other side. The vehicle reminded Virgil of the one in the middle of his street when he and Earl had escaped their home. He hoped he wasn't walking into a repeat performance inside the bar. He stopped and watched as the Cadillac stopped in front of Benny's. The front passenger's door opened. A large man, in a black leather jacket and hat, jumped out and opened the rear door on the curb side. A much smaller man in a red leather jacket with white leather pants and blue shoes jumped out. He was followed by two long-trussed, brunette-haired women dressed in dark blue leather with a white star pattern splattered about their ensemble.

Virgil wasn't exactly sure who they were or what was happening. The large man led the others past a small but growing crowd to and through the front doors of Benny's. They disappeared inside as the crowd surged forward. The Escalade slowly pulled around the corner into the parking lot behind the building. He smiled at his imagined fright as he followed their path in, calmly but gently pushing his way through the younger crowd to the second entry door. A large bouncer scanning tickets was sitting on a tall bar stool letting people through the double doors into the bar.

"Hey, you can't cut in line," a male voice sounded its disapproval from behind him. "Yeah, go to the back," a woman's voice allied with the first.

Virgil turned, expecting to confront the younger sounding couple. He was surprised at how young. They looked barely eighteen and were spindly in build. In fact of the two, the girl with the red, white, and blue hair was the most intimidating. "Sorry kids, but I need to get in there. I need to meet someone."

"Yeah, and so do we," the girl said, trying to make herself look as intimidating as one can be with the look she was presenting.

"Let the man through," the bouncer said, moving forward and directing the couple to step back with his large hand and forearm.

Virgil turned his back on the kids while recognizing the bouncer/doorman. "Thank you, Jeff."

"They can be annoying at these events," Jeff replied. "Enjoy your evening."

"Thanks again," Virgil said, wondering what the event might be.

There was no music blasting through the bar as usual when Virgil entered, just softer background tunes. You could hear people shouting at random. There was an anxiety fluttering in the air, but he couldn't recognize or confirm its source. He glanced to his left and saw the overhead stage lights pouring red, white, and blue rays down upon it. Yes, live entertainment, he thought. Even better, he found a barstool near the same spot he had been when Ivan and Gustav had firmly requested he meet them after the meeting on his and Earl's front porch. He leaned forward and scanned up and down the bar in each direction. He saw men with beards, but none which looked like the man he thought he was looking for or somewhat expected.

"Ladies and gentlemen, boys and girls," a cute blond with shoulder length hair nervously spoke into the microphone in front of her. "Are you ready for this West Allis?" she asked, laughing as the place erupted with cheering, shouting, and whistling while some booed the "boys and girls" comment.

Virgil leaned back against the bar. He was ready to be impressed by the three people he had seen rushed into this place twenty minutes earlier. "What would you like to drink?" a female voice asked from behind him. The rest of the people in the inner entrance had made it inside and the volume and excitement grew. "What would you like to drink?" the bartender asked again to no avail. Virgil was people watching and was riveted to the actions of the crowd. He then thought about the coming virus and how many of these people might not be here in a year. He wanted to jump up on the stage and tell everyone what was going to happen but knew he couldn't. He could only sit there not hearing the bartender and feeling somewhat remorseful.

The drummer came out along with two guitarists, both capable, as it turned out, of playing lead. The room cheered the band's entrance then quieted in anticipation of what was going to happen next. The guitar player to the left of the stage played the opening song's beginning chords. "Here is Virus," the thirtyish looking athletic blond yelled into the mic, no longer afraid but relieved at the same time.

After a minute the place erupted again as the trio danced on to the stage from the left. The blast of enthusiasm excited Virgil. The costumes they had arrived in were alike but different in the style shown and portrayed. As the lead singer fumbled with the microphone and its stand the two beautiful women backup singers took their positions behind their mics. Virgil recognized the first few chords of Led Zeppelin's "Whole Lotta Love." This could be good, he thought. It was. They mixed in some Reggae with the use of the keyboard played by one of the women. Their fans and new fans loved it. Virgil felt his phone vibrate and immediately thought of his father. He pulled his cell out of his jacket and answered. "Hello," he said, holding his left index finger in his left ear and not recognizing the number.

"What do you want to drink?"

Virgil thought he had heard someone asking him something earlier, but wasn't sure. "I could enjoy a Smithwick, but only if it is cold," he replied, recognizing the voice. He turned to face the bar and saw Megan standing behind the bar with her phone to her right ear. "What happened to Florida and the beach?" Virgil asked her still over the phone, because it was now the only way to be heard.

"I might still be going but just not now. Besides, you owe me dinner, remember," she explained to Virgil while chiding him as well.

"Where would you like to go?" Virgil asked, smiling.

Megan put her phone in her back pocket then turned and walked away. Virgil thought it was a little odd. Turned out she was messing with him some more, returning a few minutes later with a cold bottle of Smithwicks. "Here's your beer, Virgil," she shouted over the music while setting the bottle on the bar.

"Thought you left," Virgil joked.

"Had to get your beer. It was in a cooler in the back."

"When did they start live entertainment here?" Virgil asked. "Hey, wait a minute, how did you know my name?

"About a month after I last saw you. The new owners said they wouldn't change the name of the place, just how some things were done. So they built the stage. For the other, I just remembered your name," she confessed.

"For a Tuesday night this is a pretty good crowd," Virgil mentioned, laughing at her nonchalance to her memory reference.

"Yeah, the owners know somebody that could get this band here for one night before they do a concert in the city this coming Friday."

"Sounds like they must have some money to get an act like this."

"They're still paying me," Megan said, laughing. "So I guess I better get to work."

"You still haven't told me where you want to go for dinner," Virgil asked.

Megan smiled, "I'll let you know before the night is over."

Virgil turned and faced the stage and the cheering crowd of people now waiting for the second song to begin. More people had joined the party, but they were not wall to wall. He noticed the red, white, and blue hair of the girl he had cut in front of at the entrance with her boyfriend in tow. They came in dancing and didn't stop until this first pause in the show. He had leaned back against the bar with his bottle of red Irish ale and enjoyed the music as well. He had heard the reggae sound in the opening song, but also noticed various genres throughout the group's first set. Back home he had always tried to get out and see local talent in small venues, sometimes catching stars that happened to stop by and try out some new material. However, this had an entirely different feel. It was an excitement he could get used to despite what was about to spread throughout this country. The now slower beat and bluesy sound gave him time to think about it again.

He must have looked dejected, because Megan returned during the intermission and tapped him on the shoulder with a full bottle of his favorite brew. "What's going on, you look like you just lost your best friend?"

"I have a lot on my mind, sorry," Virgil explained and smiled back at Megan. "Thanks for the beer," he said, handing her a twenty.

"It's on the house," she said, pushing Virgil's hand back at him.

"Tip, then," he asked, setting it on the bar.

Megan shoved it back at Virgil, "Keep it."

"Okay, then you see those two kids over there?"

"The one with the patriotic hair?"

"Yes, her and the boyfriend. Give them what they want for twenty bucks."

Megan looked at Virgil, remembering the last time he was here he had bought two rounds and only asked her to make a phone call. "Okay, but do you shit money or something?"

"No, why?"

"The last time you were here you spent a ton of money and now you're here buying two kids drinks they're not even old enough to have."

Virgil laughed, "Make sure they're legal and the rest I'll explain over dinner when you decide where we are going."

Megan smiled back at Virgil. She moved up the bar to the left of Virgil, rinsing glasses in the sink. She left the twenty on the bar top.

"Hey, you're the asshole that cut in front of us," a voice shouted from behind Virgil.

He turned back to see the kids standing two feet in front of him. They were now looking eye to eye, but only because he was sitting on the barstool.

He smiled at them, reaching behind him to grab the twenty. He held it out in front of him as a peace offering. "Here, your drinks are on me. But only if you're of age," Virgil negotiated.

"Thank you, but we don't take charity from assholes," the young man said, hanging with his attitude.

Virgil stood up. The kid was taller than he thought, but still spindly. He must have played basketball or some sport but didn't pose any threat as Virgil saw it. "Relax, Choppy," Virgil replied with a name his grandfather and Earl had used in referring to some people they wanted to change a subject with. Nobody ever knew what it referenced, or meant, but would just confusedly comply with them for some reason.

"Don't tell us to relax, line cutter," the female wigged partner joined in, but with little verve, apparently caught off guard at the name Choppy.

"You two are having a good time, right," Virgil asked leadingly. The kids looked at each other and nodded, still confused but with the smiles only intended for each other. "And so am I," Virgil continued, noticing the interaction. "So let's have one together and accept my offer."

The kids, Billy and Barb, slowly turned their smiles in Virgil's direction.

"Who the hell is Choppy?" Barb asked now laughing.

"Something my dad and his dad used to say to diffuse a situation."

"Well, I guess it worked," Billy said, laughing while hugging Barb.

"What are you guys drinking?" Megan's voice then grabbed their attention. They turned and faced the bar. "It's on this guy," she said, grabbing the green Jefferson from between Virgil's fingers, smacking him on the nose with it then putting it in a cash drawer below the bar.

"Where are we going for dinner?" Virgil asked, laughing.

"So what will you guys have?" Megan asked the kids as she pushed Virgil's forehead out of her sightline.

"You guys a couple?" Barb asked, noticing the playfulness.

"Couple of what?" Virgil asked.

"You know, like we are," Barb said, pulling Billy in closer and putting her patriotic head on his shoulder.

"We barely know each other," Virgil replied. "But I would like to change that if she would ever go out to dinner with me," he explained further.

"What do you guys want to drink?" Megan asked, ignoring Virgil. "I have other customers," she explained.

"Two of what he's having," Billy said, pointing at the bottle of Smithwicks Virgil was holding.

"I need some ID," Megan requested.

"We left our IDs in the car," Billy offered.

"You had to get in here with them," Megan countered.

"We are both twenty-one I can assure you," Barb leaned on the bar top in an effort to emphasize her point.

Megan looked at Virgil, smiling, "What do you think Virgil, go to Culver's down the street?"

"Works for me," he replied.

Megan untied her apron and put it under the bar. She grabbed her black leather purse then walked up the bar to talk with the manager. He was a big, bearded man that reminded Virgil of both Ivan and Gustav. He instinctively stared at his collar for any indication. The manager was nodding at her every word, whatever those were. Virgil couldn't hear any of it though, because Billy and Barb were hounding him about their underage drinks.

"You guys have to prove your age," Virgil said, not wanting to be an accomplice to anything tonight. He turned to see Megan walking towards them.

"Don't worry, guys," Megan said to the kids. "Herron here will get you your drinks." she said, patting the big bartender on the right shoulder. She reached under the bar for something she now stuffed in her back pocket. She lifted up the hinged bar top and exited from behind the bar. She grabbed Virgil's left hand. "Come on," she yelled, pulling him off his barstool towards the exit.

The blond emcee calmly walked to the center mic, "Once again people, Virus," she yelled as the band ran on stage.

"Enjoy the rest of the show," Virgil called back to the kids as he quickly stood to keep up with Megan and her determined flight towards the front door. They bumped into several people on their way out, but Megan laughed all the way while Virgil kept saying, "Excuse us," to anyone they may have offended. He laughed as he followed, not sure where, or what this was leading to.

"Good night, Megan," Jeff called out.

"Later, Jeff," Megan replied.

"Thanks again, Jeff," Virgil added.

They ended their flight down the wall from the side exit of the building which faced the east parking lot. They moved in silence until they found a more dimly lit area and stopped. Both looked around, and at each other. It was like they had just found this spot and were meeting for the first time. In reality, they were. They had never really talked, only barroom banter. Their previous time together had been more of a collusion for his escape than anything else and that had mostly involved instructions.

As he looked at Megan, Virgil realized he had only been in love with a woman once before. He felt many of the same feelings right now. But he thought about how it hadn't worked out before. And of the infidelity and his flaw. His flaw in those times being his naive youth. Though Megan seemed to be a trustworthy person, he couldn't bring himself to entirely buy into her actions. "What exactly are we doing here?" Virgil asked, not wanting it to end but only seeking clarification.

Megan looked up at Virgil, and with both hands, adjusted his Blackhawks sweatshirt so the shoulders were even then ran her fingers through her shoulder length blonde hair. She smiled then said, "Weren't we going to Culver's?"

He stopped her before she could push away from the wall and pass by him. "We can, but we could also have some great steaks in my room," Virgil suggested, looking directly into her blue eyes.

Megan smiled, the playfulness and energy from their escape fading. She dropped her forehead into Virgil's chest not wanting to run blindly anywhere or into anything as well. "No expectations," she requested.

Virgil stepped back so Megan would lift her head up and face him.

When she kept it down he gently lifted her chin with his right forefinger. "Expectations," Virgil repeated her phrase softly. "I never thought I would meet someone like you. How's that for expectations," he confessed.

"What do you mean?"

"I live in another state, I mean, what are the chances?"

"You FIBs come up here all the time," Megan explained.

"FIBs?" Virgil questioned.

"Yeah, fucking Illinois bastards," Megan answered.

"You gotta be kidding me," Virgil shot back, laughing.

"Why," Megan asked, smiling. "What?"

"I've rarely heard a woman use that term. Usually it's more of a guy to guy thing."

"Really," she countered, laughing. "My dad once told me it's been used round here forever and by whomever."

Virgil laughed, looking around the quiet parking lot. You could hear the beat of the music from a small, opened window towards the top of the wall. "Then, there is the other thing," Virgil mentioned after a few more moments of scanning their surroundings.

Megan leaned back against the wall of Benny's, looking at Virgil.

"What's that?" she asked.

"The age difference," Virgil said, then asked, "Isn't it obvious?"

"Oh, you mean the fact I'm probably twelve years younger than you," Megan asked with a matter-of-fact tone.

"Wait, how old are you?" Virgil asked.

"What does it matter?" Megan countered. "Weren't we just going for dinner?"

"That was the plan," Virgil responded. His heart sank a bit from the realization she seemed to be sticking with his original offer. "What will it be then, Culver's or my room?"

Megan stepped forward lightly slapping Virgil on his left cheek, "Why would I eat burgers when I could have steak," she said then grabbed his left hand once again.

Virgil's heart jumped at the revelation, "This way then," he said, taking a large first step towards the Ambassador Hotel.

The Room

They entered Virgil's suite after receiving stares from two older couples that had joined them on the elevator at the lobby. During the ride up to the same floor destination, the wives stared at Megan and Virgil. The men only stared at Megan. "Is there a problem?" Megan finally asked.

"I just told our friends here that you are nice looking like your father."

Megan couldn't resist. "We're on our honeymoon."

"That's disgusting," the elderly woman replied, stepping back into her husband.

Virgil was encouraged by the way Megan clung to him on the short walk from Benny's to this moment. He looked at Megan then directly at the couples,

"Not the way I see it."

The elevator door opened to the fourth floor and Virgil and Megan waited as the appalled couples exited, turned to the left and walked down the hallway towards their adjoining suites. "Don't do anything we wouldn't do," Megan yelled to the couples.

Virgil pulled her hand in the opposite direction she was leaning towards, "Let it be," he suggested.

"I doubt they even heard me," Megan said, laughing as she followed.

"If you want, take a look at the room service menu on the dresser and decide what you want to eat," Virgil suggested as they entered, and he turned on more lights. "I have to take care of a bladder issue," he said, then disappeared into the bathroom.

Megan grabbed the menu, turned on a black metal lamp that stood atop the nightstand. At the corner of the room she turned around and sat down, nestling into a high back brown leather chair. She pulled off her shoes and put her feet up on the ottoman matched with the chair. She studied the menu, noted what she wanted then, tossed it on the bed. She leaned back into the chair raising her hands above her head stretching as Virgil came out of the bathroom.

"You comfortable?" Virgil asked her, standing next to the dresser watching her for a moment.

She looked up, smiling back at him while stretching her legs out across the ottoman. "Nice place you have here, Virgil."

"I like it even better now," Virgil said. "Even without expectations."

"Should we order before it's too late?" Megan asked. "The menu said no orders after eleven."

Virgil grabbed the desk phone and tapped the button for seven. He ordered two filet mignon tenderloins, a bottle of Pinot Noir wine and a six pack of Smithwick's. "It will be forty-five minutes," Virgil said. "Is that okay, Megan?"

"I'm not going anywhere for a while," she answered, stretching her arms and legs once again.

Virgil completed the order then opened the mini fridge next to the dresser and pulled out two bottles of Smithwick's, "Would you like one?"

"Sure."

Virgil looked around for his bottle opener which he suddenly realized he had left in the van. "Damn."

"What's wrong?" Megan asked.

"Forgot my opener," Virgil said. "I don't want to use the handles on the dresser, it's too nice."

Megan laughed at Virgil. "You forget I'm a bartender," she sarcastically asked. Then reached into her jean pocket and threw her pearl handle opener across the room at Virgil.

He caught it then dropped it, bending over to pick it up he said, "I didn't think you would carry one with you at all times."

"It's my job, besides the corkscrew makes a good weapon," she explained.

Virgil admired the handle and craftsmanship on the opener. He opened the bottles and walked across the room, handing Megan her bottle and the opener which she placed on the floor. He turned away and grabbed the swivel desk chair with casters on each foot and sat down hard enough that some beer spilled out of his bottle onto the crotch of his jeans. He brushed off the suds while Megan laughed. He stood, set his bottle on the desk, then walked to the bathroom and grabbed the hotel provided hair dryer. Megan laughed harder when he turned the dryer on, knowing what he was using it on. A couple minutes later Virgil returned, shaking his head back and forth, taking his spot in the desk chair again. He grabbed the bottle off the desk and took a healthy swig. Then shook his head back and forth again. "Nervous as a sixteen-year-old on his first date," Virgil said laughing.

Megan took a sip on her brew and reached down to set it on the floor. "Are you married, Virgil?" she asked, leaning back into the leather chair again.

"No," he answered, stunned a bit by the question, but understanding why. "Came close one time, but she found someone better and told me by letting me walk in on them."

"Had that happened to me too," Megan confessed. "Some people always think they can do better."

In the forty-five minutes they waited for their steaks the two jilted people shared a synopsis of their lives. Megan had worked at Benny's for six years and as a hair salon stylist prior to that. She still styled hair out of the basement of her mom and dad's modest home two or three times a week. She hadn't gone to Florida because her brother wasn't ready for her to come down just yet. He was still working through the transition of running the bar. She had not married yet because she hadn't found a man she would trust. And though she had only dipped her toe into the pool of prospects, hadn't found anyone of her own sex any more stable. The conversation finally evolved to the last time Virgil had been at her place of employment.

"Who owns the bar right now?" Virgil asked.

"Some guy by the name of Igor Peprov," Megan answered.

Virgil knew the name Peprov for sure. "Had you ever seen the two guys that approached me at the bar that night?" he asked Megan.

"Yes, they had been there the first night you were there and three or four times before your last time."

"Were there three guys any of the other times they came?"

"Two of the times they came in, yes."

"Same guy each time?"

"No, there were two different people with them."

Virgil was stunned. He recalled Earl's theory of a third person being involved with Ivan and Gustav, but he let it go for now. "You remembered me from the first time I was there," Virgil asked, changing the subject.

"Well, it was only about two months ago. You left me a hundred-dollar tip and the two guys handed me another hundred to stay away from your table. I remember that stuff."

"So you're in it for the money?" Virgil asked, probing in an effort to know where this might end.

"Believe me, I didn't want to stay away from your table. Remember how I helped you out the last time you were there," Megan explained and asked.

"You really didn't want to stay away from my table?"

"Hey, I don't know what it was, but I thought you might need my help that first time too."

"I'm sorry, Megan. I'm being an idiot. Of course you helped me. What am I thinking," Virgil said, apologizing and scolding himself at the same time.

"I understand, Virgil. After all the shit you've been through I would be skeptical too."

"But right now I'm being an asshole to someone who helped me out of a jam."

"What are friends for," Megan said, shrugging her shoulders then grabbing her beer and finishing it.

Virgil noticed and offered her another which she accepted. "The two guys that came in with Ivan and Gustav were not the same people?"

"Right, but what's so important about that," Megan countered with another question.

There was a knock on the door. Virgil stood, walked to the door, and opened it. A short but stout dark-haired man from the hotel kitchen presented a chrome cart to Virgil then pushed it into the room and up to the desk. He accepted Virgil's generous tip, nodded, then left the room. "Let's eat," Virgil said, holding both hands out to aid Megan up from her chair.

Megan took Virgil's hands and stood, pushing the ottoman with her shins in front of her to the cart. She adjusted its position with her legs then sat down, releasing herself from Virgil's grasp. "Thank you, but you didn't answer me," she challenged Virgil as she took the lid off her plate. She put the white cloth napkin in her lap while Virgil opened the white wine.

"What did the guys that were with them look like," Virgil asked, pouring a taste of the wine into her glass. "I'm just trying to figure out something," Virgil said and finally admitted, "To answer your first question."

"The second guy was the one who now owns the place," Megan said, cutting into her steak and savoring a piece of the succulent fare.

"And the other?"

She chewed on the piece for a minute, "Damn, that's good," she said and cut another slice from the filet mignon, looking at the juice dripping off it. "This is a great cut of beef."

"And the other," Virgil asked again.

She looked at Virgil. To get past the questions, she tried to seductively take the meat off the fork. It ended up in her lap. She quickly picked it up off her napkin and placed it into her mouth. "That is so good, Virgil, thank you."

Virgil tossed her an extra napkin. "It is good, isn't it," he replied, taking a small bite of his cut.

"They called the other guy 'doc,'" Megan said, wiping her chin with the napkin in the palm of her hand..

"Was he a big guy and older?"

"Yes, he was. And a handsome man for his age."

That had to be Harmon, Virgil thought. But for what purpose he then considered. They enjoyed their late dinner. The Pinot Noir was a perfect fit for Megan and her steak with baked potato while Virgil enjoyed another red ale with his. Virgil, despite trying to think of reasons Harmon might be at Benny's still enjoyed his medium rare steak like he imagined when he made the order for them.

"Did you talk to any of them?" Virgil asked, wiping juice off of his chin and lip with only the palm of his hand. "I agree, this is really good steak."

"Damn good wine as well," Megan said, laughing as she sipped from her glass. "Is this a new type of date?"

"What do you mean?" Virgil asked, knowing he was asking too many questions.

"You can call it dinner and an interrogation," she stated, laughing in a way which softened the blow of her intended sarcasm.

Virgil was embarrassed. He looked at Megan, took a swig from his bottle and rolled his eyes in self-deprecation. "I'm sorry, but there are a lot of things that have happened to me and my father. I'm still trying to make sense of all of it. You know, get it straight in my head and what my next move might be."

Megan leaned forward and cupped her hands under Virgil's jaw making him look up at her. "It will be alright, Virgil," she said, smiling at him and lightly slapping him on his cheeks with both hands. "You survived till now." Virgil weakly smiled at her, and she sensed more questions. "Forget about it for the night, Virgil. We can talk about it in the morning."

The steaks and drinks consumed, Virgil's and her next moves lasted until three in the morning. He fell asleep by three forty-five. When he woke later that morning about seven-thirty, Megan was gone. There was only an empty lipstick-stained wineglass to prove she had really been there with a note that directed him to read his text messages. He fumbled for his phone as he climbed out of bed, wiping his eyes with his left hand. He hadn't realized he had slept naked until he stood in the middle of the room and felt a chill. A morning urge hit him, and he quickly walked to the bathroom. He sat while he searched for Megan's text.

Her message read: Thank you for last night. I am up for doing it again sometime soon. I woke at 4am and looked at my phone to find my mom needed me at home. She is ill with some new type of virus. That's what the doctor told us anyway. When we finally saw him in the hospital. She and I are there now. I think she will be okay. Thanks again. You are a kind, loving person.

Virgil set his phone on the sink counter, knowing people embellished their texts. Kind loving person he wasn't so sure of. He held his head in his hands and stared at the white tiled floor. Was the virus starting here? He contemplated, while racking his memory about what went on last night between him and

Megan. He recalled them embracing and falling on to the bed, taking each other's clothes off as they rolled about and kissed. He couldn't recall what prompted the embrace, but it had led to pleasures for both of them and with no expectations, which further sensitized and enhanced their poetic actions.

He turned the shower on, able to reach it from his position. Once done on the throne, he hopped into it, washing off all the scented memories of earlier that morning. As he scrubbed he recalled grasping for her firm yet limber body. She was fit and strong and at times pulled him into positions of fulfillment for both of them. Smiling, he dried off, dressed quickly, and went to the hotel restaurant for breakfast. He now had Megan's phone number and texted her: I hope your mother is okay. Thanks for the text explaining your situation. Let me know if I can help in any way.

He still wanted to head north to the cabin, but also wanted to make sure Megan and her mother were okay as well. Maybe, I am a kind loving person, he thought laughing, trying not to invest too much stock in someone else's opinion of him, though he now reveled in it. His Denver omelet came, and the waitress made sure his glass was always full of Dr. Pepper, his morning caffeine. Virgil tipped the waitress then left and headed for the local hospital.

Saint Marks was also a division of the Grant Healthcare Group. Virgil knew Harmon and his father's vacation couple, Sylvia and Ernie, were connected to that group. Virgil wondered about that as he pulled into the parking lot a block from the glistening stainless steel, stone, and glass structure. As he walked Virgil realized he didn't know Megan's last name or her mother's first. He texted Megan requesting the information. He entered through the rotating door and the reply on his phone chimed with the response: We are the Petersons. Megan and Harriet.

Virgil informed the front desk who he was there to visit, and they gave him a mask and a pass with the room number, but only after he presented proof of vaccinations for anything in the air. He entered room 327 after a slight knuckle tap on the opened door. Harriet was in the bed with an oxygen mask on her face. Megan was not by her side as he had expected and hoped. The three stems and blooms he had cut off an untrimmed rose bush blocking the sidewalk he had navigated around to get here were now placed in a spare glass sitting on the tray bedside and over her mother's bed. The patient was sleeping after having consumed most of her breakfast. Only the dried wrinkly looking melon remained on the plate. Virgil grabbed the chair against the wall furthest from the bed, He waited, looking at his phone for any messages from anyone. He again texted Megan: Are you coming back to room 327 anytime soon?

The reply: It's room 326.

Virgil quickly stood up, took one of the roses out of the glass of water and walked across the hall then tapped his knuckles on the closed door. "Come in," he heard Megan's voice call out from the other side. He slowly opened it. He poked his head in first. "Everyone alright here?"

Megan stood quickly and grabbed Virgil's hand, trying to pull him out of the room. As he turned he saw a large gray-haired man he recognized as Doctor Harmon. The door closed behind him and his date from last night. He couldn't call out to the doctor so he confronted his companion. "Who the hell is that and what is going on in there?" he asked, pointing at the door.

"They called in a specialist," Megan answered then scolded. "You have to be quiet up here."

"How do you know Doctor Harmon?" Virgil asked in a softer tone.

"I told you he's a specialist," Megan confirmed then quietly asked, "How do you know him?"

"He treated me for a virus not too long ago," Virgil said. "I'm thinking we may be talking about the same one." He pulled Megan to the side of the doorway and towards him. He wanted to feel her touch no matter the situation.

"I'm not even sure of his name," Megan said, slowly pulling back from Virgil's embrace.

"I thought you saw him at the bar," Virgil asked.

"It's my mother," Megan replied with enough emphasis in her voice to convince Virgil he was overstepping his intentions. "I will go in and find out his name." She smiled at Virgil, stepped past him, turned and entered the room.

Virgil smiled, wanting to trust her, but the coincidence of all of this raised questions. He liked Megan. Maybe even loved her, but after all the crap he and his dad had been through in the past two months his defensive mode was queued. He leaned against the wall waiting for the door to open, looking at his phone for any work updates of which there were none.

"Virgil, what are you doing here?" a masked Doctor Harmon asked when he opened the door and turned to his right.

"I was just wondering the same thing about you," Virgil replied.

"This is a hospital, and I am a doctor," Harmon said through his mask. Virgil nodded back at the doctor, "I get that, but I thought you were only in Illinois."

"Let's take a walk, Virgil," Harmon suggested, grabbing Virgil by the arm and leading him in the direction of an empty lounge.

"What about Megan's mom?" Virgil asked, pulling away from the grasp and stopping in the middle of the hallway.

"She will be fine, I assure you," the doctor confidently stated, then asked, "How do you know them?"

"I met her at a local bar," Virgil answered, noticing a nurse passing by with a cart. He waited until she was beyond them and hopefully her hearing range. "Is the virus starting here? Is that what she has?"

Harmon continued towards the lounge, finally stopping when he reached the farthest spot from the hallway. He stood in front of the large window, his back to the view of office buildings which surrounded the biggest hospital in the city. He lowered his mask so he could whisper and still be heard. "First of all, from what I know the virus is about two months away from getting serious. Second, it is going to kick the hell out of the south before it gets up here." Harmon, softly stated, "And, Misses Peterson will be fine. She received the shot you did. It's the best option we have right now."

"What do you mean it's going to hit the south?" Virgil pulled his mask down and asked in a soft tone as well. "My dad, Ernie, and Sylvia are in Mississippi right now."

"I know, and it's their choice," the doctor matter of factly replied. "I warned against it, they stand a better chance because they had the shot too, but it will get bad down there,"

"My own dad told me to get down there within a couple months. This isn't adding up," Virgil said in a calm but concerned tone and wanting to remain on the same level playing field as the good doctor.

"This Chung virus will spread quicker in a warmer climate. Believe me you are much better off here than down there," Harmon said then reached in his coat pocket and took out his buzzing phone. He turned his back on Virgil and answered it.

Virgil walked to the other side of the lounge and phoned his father. Earl did not answer. Virgil didn't leave a voicemail. He wanted to hear his dad's version of these events in his voice. He texted: Dad, call me as soon as u get this. Virgil waited another five minutes, looking out the window near him and back at his phone. The doctor finally put his phone back in his pocket, turned and faced him. "I'm waiting for a call from my father. He would never lie to me about something like this," Virgil brought Harmon up to date on his stance as he slowly approached him.

"He must have his reasons then," Harmon said. "I have to get to another room."

"You never did tell me why you came up here," Virgil said, referencing his prior inquiry. "Why aren't you in the south?"

"I can save more lives in the south from right here," Harmon said, then walked past Virgil down the hall in the opposite direction from room 326.

Virgil walked back to the room and once again tapped his knuckles on the door then slowly opened it when he heard Megan say, "Come in." He entered and closed the door behind him. "You guys okay?"

"Doctor Harmon said she will be just fine," Megan quietly informed him as she nodded towards her sleeping mother.

"That's great," Virgil said. He suddenly remembered the rose he had handed Megan and wondered what happened to it. He looked about the room for the red bud then saw the bloom in a half-filled glass of water on the stone counter in front of the window.

Megan noticed Virgil surveying the room, "You didn't have to bring a flower you know," she said, looking in the direction of the rose in its handy vase. "She thought it was very nice of you, then fell asleep. I think it's sweet."

Virgil smiled at Megan, and she returned the expression. He looked at her mother who was much younger than Earl; it exemplified the age gap between him and Megan. He looked out the window, letting his mind bounce around in a blank space for a while. Why would his father lie to him was the first question Virgil received from that space. He contemplated it for a few minutes. The oxygen machine was the only sound in the room, he resolved nothing within that time, noise and vacated space.

"I said that was sweet of you to bring my mother a flower," Megan said, snapping Virgil out of his daze. "A fresh rose no less."

Again he looked at her mother then Megan. He was trying to make sense of all of what he had just learned but stayed calm. He did not panic. This would play out in whatever manner God saw fit, he thought, trying to seek counsel from he and Earl's deepest roots. "I'm sorry, what did you say?" Virgil asked.

"It was nice of you to bring my mother a flower," Megan said laughing at Virgil, "And very sweet of you."

Virgil took a minute to acknowledge her compliment, "Actually, I found it on the way, you know, a local vendor."

Megan now stood and moved about the room to interrupt the monotony of her confinement within it. "You want to get some lunch?" she asked, swinging her arms across her chest to loosen herself up. She looked at Virgil's blank stare and asked, "You alright, Virgil?"

"I'm good," he answered, then asked, "You hungry?"

Megan covered her face with her hands and shook her head back and forward, "You sure you're alright, Virgil?" she asked, laughing.

"Where would you like to go for lunch?" Virgil asked, laughing at himself. "Your mom will be okay then?"

"She will be fine."

The destination for the close enough to noon meal was only three blocks away. A place called Nina's Cafe. Megan was friends with the owner and knew they offered good sandwiches. The corner location and cheaper prices made it a popular hangout for those frequenting the downtown. Nina's boisterous personality and challenge to anyone who could write something on the large white wall worth repeating, was the hook she presented to her many customers. There were arguments over comments, poetry, declarations, confessions, but eventually decisions were made.

Some were painted over and some remained.

Virgil looked at his phone for a response from his father, or anybody he had attempted to contact. There was nothing. He started to worry as he moved towards the red maple counter Nina stood behind.

"Megan," Nina shouted. "What are you doing in the city on a Wednesday?"

"Got a date," she said, nodding towards Virgil while hugging her friend. "His name is Virgil."

"Hi Virgil," Nina shouted at him then gave him a hug as well.

"Hello, it's nice to meet you," Virgil said, returning the hug.

Nina seated them in a corner booth by the window. Virgil noticed a TV mounted on the wall opposite them. There was a national news program on and the headline over the shoulder of the anchorwoman read: Virus in the south? Virgil wished he could hear it, but the lunch crowd noise made that impossible. He stared at the screen anyway in hopes of finding out any info he could. The headline faded to a map of the South with a focus on Florida and Georgia. From the graphic shown he deduced cases had been found in these two states. He looked at his phone.

"You ordering anything?" Megan asked.

Virgil looked at the TV again and then at Megan. "Sorry, but that news story on the big screen caught my eye." He looked at the menu about the time their waitress, Bella, showed up. "Ladies first," Virgil said, nodding in Megan's direction.

"I'll have a turkey club with chips and coffee," Megan said.

"And I'll have the ham and Swiss club with chips, and water is fine for me. Thank you."

"Thank you," Bella said, taking their menus. "It will be about fifteen minutes.

Virgil looked at his phone. He texted Mark for any business updates. He replied about a job in Rockford, Illinois. There was a number included which Virgil knew was already in his contacts. They needed him on Thursday to look at an old lathe he had rebuilt for them two years ago. He made a call to confirm it and was given a synopsis of the problem. "I'm sorry, Megan," Virgil apologized. "I had to confirm my next call." Bella returned with their drinks.

"I understand," she said. "You have a business to run. As long as you don't cut me off in mid-sentence, it doesn't bother me."

"Thank you," Virgil said. "I have a question for you, and I don't want it to appear as lunch and interrogation."

Megan laughed at the reference to her comment from the previous night. "Is it about the virus?" She asked.

"Yes. I was wondering if you knew anything about a new strain?" Virgil asked then explained what happened to him after he had left Benny's that night she had helped him out.

"They actually shot you?" she asked. "And someone in your garage?"

"Yes, but we're not sure what happened to the guy in the garage."

"Holy shit, Virgil," Megan said excitedly but quietly, leaning across the table so he could hear her. "That's like Jason Bourne stuff."

"Too bad I'm not an ass kicker like that."

"Hey, you're sitting across the table from me," she said, inflating his ego with the compliment. "There's something to be said for that, plus you spent two nights in the woods in shit weather."

Virgil smiled at Bella when she delivered their sandwiches. "Could we get refills on our drinks, please?" Virgil asked.

"Coming right up," Bella replied.

"This looks good," Virgil said, looking at their plates. "Thank you."

"Wait til you taste it," Megan said. "They cook the meat right here, no processed bullshit."

"So have you heard anything about a virus?"

Megan laughed, "That's right, you did ask me that question." She took a small bite out of her sandwich first, "I've been here every time I come to the city and this food never gets old."

Bella returned with a pitcher each of water and coffee. She filled their glasses. "Is everything good with the food?"

Virgil was chewing a bite from his sandwich like he usually did when any waitress in any restaurant asked about the food. He nodded his approval and mumbled it as well. Megan smiled. "It's great as usual," she said. "Thank you."

"Doctor Harmon said this was a different strain from a previous virus, but the shot he gave my mom is supposed to take care of it and protect against anything else that might come."

"Did he say anything about what might be coming?"

"No, he just said she is protected."

"Did he offer you the same shot?" Virgil asked, taking a sip from his tumbler of water.

"Yes, but I told him I wanted to wait," Megan replied. "I want to see if my mom has any side effects from hers. I'm no good to her if I'm sick too."

"Beautiful and smart," Virgil said, doing some ego stroking of his own.

"Well, thank you," Megan said. "If nothing else I'm practical."

"Are you going to get the shot when you feel it would be okay?"

"Probably, but for now I'm going to get her out tomorrow and take her home and make sure she is alright."

"And I have to go to the place in West Allis for a follow up then on to Rockford. I won't be back until probably Monday."

"Why, do you have another job up here?" Megan asked.

"Not as of yet, but I was planning on coming back to see you and find out how your mother is doing."

Megan stared at Virgil, taking another bite out of her sandwich and slowly shaking her head back and forth.

"What?" Virgil asked, smiling then laughing as Megan continued to chew.

"Why would you do that?" she asked.

"I feel a connection to you," Virgil admitted. "I have had a few nights like last night, but none that have equaled it."

Megan wiped her lower lip with her napkin, "That was pretty damn sweet, I will admit," she said then leaned forward, reached across the table and grabbed Virgil's forearm. "We will definitely keep in touch, but you aren't obligated to come back just for that. We do have phones ya know."

Virgil laughed, "I was planning on going to my cabin up North with my buddy Mark if he is willing." He wiped his mouth with his napkin and dropped it on his lap. "Either way I want to see you."

"I see," Megan said, taking her last swig of coffee. "Return to the scene of the crime."

"Last night was not a crime unless you're under eighteen."

Megan laughed, "I'm thirty-one," she admitted. "Just so you know."

"And I'm forty-seven," Virgil said. "As long as we are being honest."

"I would have guessed younger by five years."

"Too big of an age gap," Virgil asked, not sure he wanted an answer.

"My dad was thirteen years older than my mom, enough said."

Virgil smiled, then for the first time he considered the crimes that must have been committed up until now. He had been bothered by a lot of what had gone on but never considered the legal aspect. He took a long drink of water, looked at the TV again which was now showing baseball playoff highlights. He peeked at his phone for any message from his dad of which there was none, then took the last bite of his ham and swiss. "Did you know the other older man that came to Benny's was Doctor Harmon?"

"Not until now," Megan said. "Guess I didn't put two and two together. Not as smart as you thought I was," she said, laughing at herself.

"But still beautiful," Virgil said.

The Following Tuesday

He had never been one for watching the news at six, nine, or ten. Earl had always taken on that task especially in retirement, but more out of habit from his younger days. Now Virgil had news radio on in the work van as soon as he started on the road. This was after watching the national morning news while he ate breakfast. He needed information, no matter how controlled, edited, or sensationalized these sources had become.

He had left Megan in West Allis with her mother, having stopped to see them at their home before he left for Rockford. Megan had provided directions though she insisted everything was good. Harriet was touched and proud of her daughter's choice of men when Virgil had shown up. Another fresh cut rose put the icing on the cake of acceptance, though Virgil's primary intent was seeing Megan again. Their well-being allowed him to leave there feeling they would be alright.

On his way to Rockford, over the side roads and sluggishly past the fall roadwork which required completion, he finally got a call from Earl. It came over his hands-free OnStar system, but he still pulled over at the next available opportunity he could find. At the back of a gas station named Bucky's, near the car wash was where he took the call. "Dad, are you alright?" was Virgil's first question.

"I'm fine, we saw Vicksburg," Earl nonchalantly said.

"What the hell, Dad?" Virgil yelled into the microphone, embedded in the ceiling on the driver's side. "Why didn't you answer my calls or the text?"

"Probably because I never saw them on my phone," Earl informed his son.

"Is your phone not working?"

"Working just fine."

"Then you should get my texts, Dad. We're on the same plan. We have the same phones."

"Well you know we're down here, and I'm not sure of the reception."

Virgil looked at two kids trying to climb up a dumpster that also rested behind the gas station. One black, one white, helping each other in an effort to achieve their mission of securing empty aluminum cans from the big steel bin. The taller and stronger black kid helped the spindly shorter white one up the side. The accomplishment of their mission would result in another trek to the nearest recycling place. Virgil smiled, knowing he and his dad always recycled aluminum and many other things to help defray costs but with the intent of helping the environment.

Virgil let his father's cavalier attitude roll past any of his concerns and into a space of irrelevance. "How are you feeling?" he finally asked his dad in an effort to simplify the situation.

"I'm fine. We're all fine. Having a blast."

"I ran into Doctor Harmon at Saint Marks," Virgil mentioned and waited for Earl's reaction. There was a pause and Virgil could hear his dad relaying the information to either Ernie or Sylvia, probably both. "Did you hear me, Dad? I saw Harmon at a hospital in Milwaukee."

"Are you alright? Did you get hurt?" Earl shot back.

"I was visiting a friend," Virgil explained. "Harmon told me the virus will begin in the south, not the north." Again Virgil waited for a response. There was more background talk. "Is that Ernie and Sylvia you keep talking to?"

"Yeah, they're right here."

"Why did you guys say the virus will begin up here?"

"We came down here to help out some friends before it does start," Earl admitted.

"Harmon said he warned you guys to stay up here."

"We'll get out if it gets too bad," Earl countered.

"Okay," Virgil said sarcastically. "Then why would I need to come down there in two months?"

He could hear the three of them conferring. He heard Sylvia specifically and she kept saying, "Just tell him the truth."

"What's going on, Dad?" He finally asked.

Virgil watched the top of the two boys' heads bobbing about in the dumpster, disappearing at times when they stooped to gather another can. They climbed out, throwing their bag over the side to the ground, while Virgil waited for whatever answer Earl and team were concocting. The boys had obtained a pretty good haul and were fist bumping each other once they were finally on the ground.

"We may need you to come and get us at some point," Earl confessed. "We have had the shot, but at our ages it might not matter."

"When...when did you find that out?" Virgil stammered, caught off guard by the revelation.

"When we were hiding at Sylvia's and Ernie's house."

Virgil was getting angry, having been kept out of the loop on this info. His ire began to rise as he thought about the trust factor that had been ignored by the elderly trio. He took a deep breath to relax, knowing he could never be too upset at any of them. Besides Earl, Sylvia and Ernie had helped him out many times at different stages of his life. Ernie knew Ben Helper, the founder and CEO of Helper Plastics. He had put in a good word for him when he applied for a job there. He got the job, which eventually led to what he was doing now. Ernie also knew other business owners that he recommended Virgil for machine repairs they required. Sylvia always thought of Virgil as the child she could never bear. She always sent him birthday cards, Christmas presents, and called or texted him occasionally. Though, until their emergency stay, they had rarely seen each other in the past ten years, Earl had always maintained contact with his old friend.

"Well then, I guess I will remain up here," Virgil said calmly. "But I want you guys to get back up here."

"As soon as we get the shots to some friends of ours," Earl said.

"All in Mississippi?" Virgil asked.

"We are headed to Alabama, then Florida and possibly Georgia."

"You guys know that it has already begun on the east coast down there?" Virgil asked, the concern inflected in the volume of his voice.

"We are aware of that, yes," Earl answered like it was no big deal.

"Dad, you realize we are talking life and death here," Virgil said, his voice now getting a little louder.

"We're trying to help some people down here, Virgil," Earl restated his case for the risk in an equal volume.

"I just don't want anything to happen to you, or Sylvia, or Ernie," Virgil said, calming down once again.

"I know. But we need to do this," Earl reiterated. "It's as simple as that."

"It may be simple, but I'm talking about the consequences," Virgil said.

"We know," Earl admitted. "God will take care of us no matter what those may be."

"I will pray for you guys, but I want you to check in with me and return my calls," Virgil said and demanded.

"We will," Earl assured his son.

"Love you, Dad."

"Love you, son."

Back Home Again

The lathe repair in Rockford went smoothly but took a little longer than Virgil expected. The most experienced machinist in the shop was able to make a part which fixed and actually improved the performance of the old, tired machine which had only been kept for nostalgic reasons. Virgil made it back home Friday mid-afternoon. Once again it seemed like he had been gone longer, but it had been less than a week. He looked in every room of the house, making sure everything was the same as he remembered. When he reached the front living room he opened the blinds and noticed a squad car in the Kalsows' driveway. It was the only thing Virgil found out of sorts. Nothing had been disturbed within the house. The rest of the area had seemed fine when he arrived. The Kalsows' driveway had been unoccupied at that time. He called Mark.

"Hey, big guy," Virgil said when Mark answered. "Can you head north this weekend?"

"You know it's Friday, right?"

"Well aware, just hoping you have some free time."

There was a pause on Mark's end of the line then finally, "Let me call you back in a few."

"Fine, I have to check something out anyway," Virgil said as he continued to watch the house across the street. He saw a tall officer looking into the bushes at the front of the house. He leaned over to look behind an evergreen bush hedge at the left corner of the house that stretched the length of the house on the driveway side. Because of his girth he strained to hold his balance, placing his right hand against the tan brick front. He pushed himself away from the sturdy structure and quickly reached for his radio attached to the top of his left shoulder. Ten minutes later more squad cars pulled up with lights on. An ambulance soon followed. Virgil thought back to that night he rescued his dad and the Kalsows and captured Gustav.

He watched the officers survey the area, moving in and out of the bushes with plastic bags in hand. He saw a handgun placed in one bag while Gene and Ellen stood on the top step with concerned looks on their faces. Is this tied to that night and how can I get involved without implicating myself in anything that happened, he wondered. He put on his gray Under Armor running jacket and left through the backdoor. Red and blue flashing lights bounced around and off the area homes. He entered the garage. It was empty. Earl had left his car at Ernie's place. Virgil turned on the light and walked throughout the one and a half car sized structure. The floor was clean. No bloodstain by the workbench where there should have been one. No shards of glass from the pane of the door he had entered. The only mark that remained were the ones made by the pitchfork Earl had slammed into the concrete that morning. He looked about and didn't see the pitchfork. He knew where it hung, and it wasn't there. Who was ultimately responsible for covering all of this up, Virgil thought. He mulled it over, standing in the middle of the garage. He then walked outside, down the driveway to the front of the only house Virgil ever cared to call home. He nodded at two officers now looking around on his side of the street. He leaned against the railing affixed to the steps which led to the front door. The same steps Ivan and Gustav had burned the check he had given back to them. Then basically ordered him to meet them in West Allis again.

He heard the officers tell the EMTs their services were no longer required, because the body they had found lying in the bushes against the foundation of the house was cold. The muscular male EMT defiantly confirmed the status of the body himself, then waved his female partner over to let her get some experience of her own. She too checked the lifeless body. The owners had not noticed anyone around their house recently but were concerned their son was overdue from a fishing trip he had taken down south a week or so ago the officers explained further.

The Coroner, Bill Staber, arrived in his black van with the signage boldly stating his title on both sides. He examined the body while a photographer snapped pictures of the scene, then motioned for the paramedics to assist with the bagging of the body. "Ol Stabber got another one for the cooler," one of the officers leaned over and said to the other.

"You know it's pronounced Stayber, right?" the shorter of the two policemen asked the other, then walked back across the street as the taller one followed.

Virgil watched as Gene Kalsow left his wife leaning against their front door and walked over to talk with Staber who had motioned him to his side. Staber asked Gene if he would mind taking a look at the body to identify him if possible as he pointed towards the black bag the paramedics were now placing it in. Kalsow nodded his approval for the morbid task. He followed the coroner to the driveway where the body lay on a gurney with the EMTs standing next to it. The first-year lady medical tech opened the bag, folding the edges back for a definitive view. Staber and Kalsow approached, and Gene fell to his knees instantly recognizing his son. He had no doubt it was Tom but was baffled by his deteriorating condition and the wound to his forehead only amplified his emotions. "My God," Gene yelled, then sat down on the asphalt as the coroner patted him on the shoulder and leaned down to verbally comfort him. Ellen ran to Gene's side, recognizing her only child lying in the black bag as she approached. She bumped Staber out of the way and consoled her husband, kneeling beside him, then hugging him and burying her head into his right shoulder. The paramedic zipped the bag shut and with her partner's help loaded the gurney and body into the coroner's van.

Virgil left the front step, knowing Tommy, as he had known him, was gone. He walked to, then up the driveway, knowing now his neighbor was somehow in their garage that morning Earl had happened upon him. And that was where he was shot. He turned and looked at the Kalsow home again, watching Ellen and Gene slowly making their way back to their front door then disappear inside. He went back inside the way he had come out.

The police remained for another hour and a half, going over the entire property and knocking on neighbor's doors. Officer Simmons knocked on Virgil's door about a half hour after he had returned inside. "Could I ask you a few questions sir?" the officer asked.

"Sure, officer, if I can help I will," Virgil offered.

"Did you know the Kalsows' son across the street?"

Virgil explained his history with Tommy and how they played baseball together growing up, scouting, swimming in their pool together and that they had gone fishing together a couple of times. He admitted they had lost contact over the years and wasn't exactly sure where Gene and Ellen's son was even living now. He informed Simmons that he and his dad were in and out a lot lately so they hadn't been in touch with the Kalsows. He didn't implicate Earl or himself in anything that had occurred recently and apparently Gene and Ellen had said nothing of the events Gustav had perpetrated only a few weeks ago. The officer thanked him for his time and left a card with a number which he could call if he thought of anything he may have forgotten.

Virgil closed the door, locked it, and walked into the kitchen. His phone rang as he took a beer from the refrigerator and opened it. He set it on the counter and answered on the fourth ring. "Hello."

"Virgil, this is Ellen Kalsow from across the street," Ellen said nervously. "We have a problem over here."

"I see that. There was an officer Simmons that just left from over here."

"Tommy's dead," Ellen said bluntly while sniffling.

"I'm sorry, Ellen," Virgil said. "What happened?"

"They found him in the evergreens out front. It looks like he shot himself."

"No way," Virgil said. "I mean, I can't believe he would do that."

"We're not sure, but it looks that way," Ellen said, sobbing and handing her phone to her husband.

"Virgil, do you think that Gustav guy could have done this?" Gene asked.

Virgil was silent, knowing the question was certainly warranted, but reluctant to put his own spin on the situation. Though from his and Earl's experiences he definitely had formed his own theories. "We will have to wait and see what the coroner finds out," Virgil suggested.

"That sonofabitch had a gun with him that night, Virgil. He meant business," Ellen yelled from the background.

Virgil looked out the front window again and saw the last squad car pull out of his neighbor's driveway and roll down the street. He kept silent for a moment, trying to formulate a better answer. "He was never going to harm any of you. It was me Gustav wanted, not Tommy," Virgil explained. "Or anyone else for that matter."

"Tommy couldn't have done this to himself," the grieving and pissed off father said.

"We will see what the coroner says."

"We know he couldn't do it," Ellen yelled louder.

Virgil thought for a minute and realized she was right. Tommy had always been afraid of guns and adamantly refused to go hunting with Virgil when he had invited him for a weekend. "You will never see me holding a gun," were Tom Kalsows exact words as Virgil recalled. "I agree, Gene. Tom hated guns."

"Exactly. So tell me how Gustav isn't involved with this then?"

"I can't, but I will look into what I can and we will wait on the coroner until then," was all Virgil could offer his neighbor for now. Gene reluctantly agreed and hung up. Virgil walked about the house then back to the living room and closed the blinds. He returned to the kitchen and called his father and let him know what was going on. Earl was shocked and also wondered if Gustav could be a suspect and assured him he and his traveling companions would look into it.

Virgil knew he wasn't going anywhere for a couple days unless work required it. He texted Mark and let him know he was staying in town. His buddy and accountant acknowledge with a text of his own sarcastically telling him to go fuck himself. He sent back a GFY of his own with a laughing face.

He still wanted to go north to his cabin. It hadn't been booked much this fall. The slow economic recovery prevented past clients from accumulating the funds required to book a week at his place. When the virus hits it might be sought after, he thought. He knew it was equipped to handle frigid temps, because he and Earl once tried to spend a Christmas there, a whim they had both agreed on, then almost regretted when they couldn't make it to the main road above them. With the help of neighbors who had the same idea, but owned a four-wheel Jeep, they made it to the road. The seven-hour ride home that followed convinced both they wouldn't do it again, at least, not without a Jeep of their own. He knew he wouldn't have to worry about snow just yet and they had a furnace and fireplace to provide heat if needed.

He went to his bedroom and finished his second beer as he searched his laptop and the Ditch Machine Repair website. There was work locally on Monday which he confirmed with an email. The job appeared to be a new machine setup which always happened in the fall for company tax advantages. It was two days for sure. For Thursday there was a request from Chase Products in West Allis, wanting another production line running and a machine repair to their specs. He confirmed immediately, knowing it would take him to Megan. West Allis, for him, was the destination he wanted and knew he needed.

After closing his website he accessed his business bank account and noticed an unusual influx of money with the same account info as the defense department. The same info had been provided when Ditch Repair received its initial compensation. Why more, why now, and what was expected of him? These questions floated in the mental space he now seemed to be hoovering in.

He thought of God. The Father, Son, and Holy Ghost he knew as a child. The Triune which had protected him back then and he realized till now. Or, had he just been lucky until this very moment. He knew he didn't need to go looking for these answers today. He had enough questions to deal with. He hadn't been in a church for some time now and felt he deserved little or no grace with any of his problems. Somehow though, he felt His strength that provided resilience against all that confronted him or stood in his way. It would work out. Virgil might not always show it but he had that kind of trust in God.

He returned to the kitchen to get one more beer then went to the living room to watch the news. He turned on CNN and waited for a report on the Chang Virus. It came about twenty minutes into the broadcast, informing him that the southeastern states were seeing an uptick in cases and deaths but nothing that was too concerning to the CDC at this time. The Center for Disease

Control and Prevention made the call on how bad things were.

Other countries, specifically Russia, were getting hit hard and the death toll was mounting. Travel to and from Russia and smaller countries affected had been banned by most countries. People in any of those countries trying to get back to their homelands were, at this time, out of luck. If the World Health Organization had learned anything from all the diseases it monitored, it was to isolate them whenever possible. The report did confirm the virus found abroad and the one in the U.S. were the same variant, but somehow more lethal there than here.

Virgil could hear his phone ringing in the kitchen where he had left it on the gray marble counter. He looked at the display. It was Earl. "Hello, Dad. What's going on?"

"We talked to Gustav," he said, then paused.

Virgil waited for him to continue and finally tried to cue him, "And what did he say?"

"Tommy was sick," he said, then asked. "Did you know that?"

"No, I didn't. What did he have?"

"Besides the virus he had bone cancer," Earl said. "He was a goner for sure."

"I'm questioning the bullet hole in his forehead and so are his parents," Virgil informed Earl.

"It was suicide is all they will be told," Earl stated.

"But did the guys you're getting your information from know Tom was deathly afraid of guns?"

"I told them that, but they said the virus could not under any circumstances be allowed to spread."

"We're talking about Gustav and Ivan, correct?"

There was silence. Virgil couldn't hear any background noise so he assumed Earl was by himself this time. "Dad, you're alone, right?"

"Yes, Virgil, I am."

"Then tell me how they plan to pass that one over on Ellen and Gene," Virgil asked, knowing they would never accept the coroner's findings if he maintained Tom had taken his own life.

"People can do desperate things when they face desperate times, is what they told us," Earl blandly said.

"C'mon, Dad. We're talking murder here," Virgil replied loudly.

"Virgil," Earl yelled back then paused for a moment. "I'm telling you this only once and this is the end of any more info you will get about it."

"Just say it, Dad," Virgil said.

"Shut the hell up and listen," Earl shot back.

Virgil hadn't heard those words in a long time. Whenever he wanted answers about things when growing up, Virgil would pester his father past his limits. Earl would then stop the inquisition by using those exact words.

"Sorry, Dad," was Virgil's reply then and now.

"Neither of us pulled the trigger. That was Tommy's decision. He acted alone and on his own," Earl calmly explained.

"I will accept that and tell Ellen and Gene that when the time comes," Virgil relented. "But he was the guy who was in our garage that morning."

"He wandered into our garage when he got back from his fishing trip," Earl now confessed.

"What?" Virgil asked.

"He was messed up when he was dropped off. He didn't go to his parents' house."

"Why not?"

"He was directed towards our garage by Gustav," Earl said. "It was all planned. Tommy had to be taken out for what he was carrying."

"I'm sorry, Dad, but this doesn't make sense to me."

"All you need to know, Virgil, is that he had maybe four months to live. And the ones calling the shots weren't taking any chances," Earl explained.

"Ironic," Virgil said. "I mean them calling the shots. I guess they did."

"He was going to die anyway, Virgil."

"I guess only someone with more power than them could truly answer that," Virgil said.

There was silence at the other end. They were then disconnected. Virgil didn't know if his father had hung up, thus putting an end to the inquisition, or if it was actually a dropped call. He thought about calling his father back then decided to let the authorities handle the explanation of Tom's death to Gene and Ellen. Besides, Earl had made it clear it had been the end of the discussion.

Virgil returned to the living room and turned on the TV once again.

The news was still on, but he quickly requested Haim on YouTube with his remote. A series of dots rotated in a circle as it loaded the third-party app while he sat and got comfortable on the couch. He wanted some of their great guitar work, style, and energy. He chose their cover of the Fleetwood Mac song "Oh Well." The three pretty sisters could rock the song and it being a live recording made the piece even better. He turned up the volume on the sound system of the TV. He stretched out on the couch and just enjoyed something for a change.

He thought of Megan, wondering how she and Harriet were doing. He wanted to call her but didn't want to appear pushy. He wasn't even sure what they had. Did she like him as much as he loved her? He listened to the end of the song playing air guitar lying on his back. He followed with "Hallelujah" also by Haim featuring beautiful lyrics and harmonies. He woke Saturday morning about six A.M. turned off the set, then rolled over and finally got off the couch about seven.

He was rested. He hadn't struggled through an all-nighter with the questions he had and what he needed to do. He called Mark three hours later.

"What do you want?" the accountant sarcastically answered.

Virgil explained everything that had happened last night and Tom's death. He laid out his schedule and wondered if Mark could still go north or even had the desire to.

"I would love to, but I would have to meet you there," Mark said then explained. "Gotta take care of the boys first."

"Understood."

"I will let you know exactly when I can make it there."

"You can bring Diane as well, you know."

"Oh, I thought it was a boys only weekend," Mark said.

"Let's change it up, besides I might have someone with me."

"Oh, you mean Megan the bartender?"

"How did you know that?" Virgil asked.

"She was really concerned about you that Wednesday night when she called my number," Mark explained.

"Really? I just asked her to call you and tell you to call me."

"When she called she said that this nice, good looking guy wanted me to call you and have you call him back."

"I call bullshit on that," Virgil said, laughing. "You're exaggerating."

"And, when I asked what you looked like, things got interesting."

"Now, I know you are exaggerating," Virgil replied semi-seriously.

"She said you were a ruggedly handsome guy with two annoying bearded men bothering you at the bar."

"C'mon," Virgil said, nervously laughing again. He rarely had that type of reaction from a woman. In fact, he could only remember three. The tone of his reply confirmed that.

"I'm serious Virgil," Mark reiterated. "Diane can confirm it. I had it on speaker because we were talking with Ryan at the time the call came. I decided to take it knowing you were up there."

"She said that?" Virgil asked for confirmation.

Mark had apparently called Diane in to do exactly that. "That is what she said. I could tell that she was concerned about you," she said, serving the oral affidavit.

"I'm not sure I believe either of you, but right now I'll take it," Virgil said. "So you guys will meet us there, then?"

"If everything works out on our end," Mark said, laughing.

"Me too," Diane joined in.

"Thanks, guys," Virgil said smiling.

Back To Work

It was the first time Virgil had been back in Helper Plastics in four years. The previous time had also been for an install, a Van Dorn injection molding machine as this one would be. He had been certified to install Van Dorn machines two years after he had started Ditch Machine Repair. It had been another way to expand the business. The job, normally a day and a half, took two long days. People he had worked with at the plant still worked for the company and wanted to catch up. Virgil obliged many but not to the length he had really wished. He finished on Tuesday at six-thirty at night. He had to be done. Tom Kalsow's funeral was the next day at ten in the morning.

Virgil had called Earl when he learned of the arrangements the Kalsows had made for Tom. His father informed him, though not going to Georgia, he wouldn't be making it home either. "I have to help the ones who need me most," he had said.

Virgil didn't question his father anymore when it came to the virus or anything related to it, like Tom's alleged suicide. His dad obviously had Ernie and Sylvia on his side, along with Harmon, and apparently Gustav Peprov feeding them information. He was still confused why they wanted to be in the south after what Harmon had told him, but he respected his father's wishes. The Chung Virus, as it was being reported, was prevalent in the deep south and now hitting Mexico and South America. The death toll was beginning to make authorities take notice and travel restrictions were recommended for those parts of the world along with the ones already enacted.

After his third attempt trying to tie his tie, Virgil stormed away from his mirror and out of the bedroom. He stopped in the front room, opened the blinds then looked across the street. Gene and Ellen were getting into a black Escalade parked in their driveway. Virgil understood the stoic, shocked, and beaten down look on their faces, but not the vehicle. He looked to see who was driving, but never, despite moving about the room, could he get the view needed. I guess they hired a driver for the day, Virgil concluded, then added this curiosity to his bag of questions. He tied his tie, walking about the room with no mirror. Finished, he walked back to his bedroom and checked his attempt. It looked like he remembered it should, having not worn a suit since a wedding he had attended five years ago. With his father's blessing, Virgil took his work van to Ernie and Sylvia's to retrieve his father's Impala. He went to St. Mary's Catholic Church. He was there early enough for the visitation prior to the funeral. It was well attended by people who knew the family at some point in their lives. Ellen and Gene were congenial and receptive of all condolences.

Virgil expected Ellen to be still reluctant to believe what the coroner had provided as the cause of death and tell her view on it to everyone. It wasn't the case.

"Gene, I'm sorry about this," Virgil told Tom's father as he hugged him. "I still can't believe this even happened."

Gene returned the hug with a pat on the back, "Thank you, Virgil."

"My dad sends his prayers for you during this time."

"Thank him for us, Virgil," Gene said, backing away from the embrace. "Is he sick?"

"No, he's down south, helping friends. He would be here if he could."

"I know that," Gene said enthusiastically while holding tight to Virgil's forearms.

Virgil smiled, "You know, Tom was a good guy. We had some good times together."

"He always liked you," Gene said, releasing his grip and giving Virgil some room.

"Virgil," Ellen said, stepping in front of her husband. She hugged Virgil, almost catching him off balance. "Thank you for coming."

"That's alright, Ellen. You knew I would be here. Tom was a good guy."

"He was always there for us. He was a good son," Ellen said, pushing away from Virgil and facing him. He faced her, both had tears in their eyes. Ellen kissed him on the forehead. "I know now why he did it. He was sick and I don't blame him."

"I'm sorry, Ellen," Virgil said, knowing he and his father were in a way responsible for much of what had happened. His tears flowed. Guilt is an emotion no one seeks, because of the reprimand it brings. Virgil felt the full brunt of its hurt. He softly lowered his head onto her shoulder. "I didn't know he was sick," Virgil lied only to help Tom's mother with closure.

"He had cancer, Virgil," Ellen explained. "He would have lived another few months and probably suffer while doing it. Tommy found a quicker route to the same end."

Virgil was amazed how Ellen and Gene had bought into this elaborate ruse. He also knew there was nothing he could do about it at this point. "I'm sorry it ended this way."

"We've decided it was the way he wanted it," Gene said, stepping in closer to his wife and next to Virgil.

"I will talk with you both after the funeral," Virgil mentioned, then hugged both at the same time, one arm for each. He heard their thank yous as he turned to look at the array of pictures Ellen's sister had arranged on tables set up in route to the closed casket. He recognized one from a fishing trip he and Tom had taken in northern Minnesota. They were holding a stringer of three-pound Walleyes including a six-pounder Tom had landed. Smiles beamed on their faces and now one came to Virgil as he remembered that four-day trip. It would be how he would always think of Tom and remember him.

It was a solemn day for sure and Virgil returned home with a feeling of remorse for how things were playing out. The circumstances of Tom's death left a hollow pit in his stomach that he knew would never be filled with a reasonable explanation. For now, he had to move on. He had to be at Chase Products in the morning. He would go get his work van and head to West Allis this afternoon.

He made a phone call to The Ambassador on his way to Ernie and Sylvia's to get the van. He secured a room for two nights. Once in his van and heading North, he called Megan. After asking about their well-being the rest of the message he left, informed her of his schedule and an invite for dinner tonight at a restaurant of her choice.

He called Mark again. "Would you quit bothering me," Mark answered.

Virgil laughed, "Have you noticed the influx of money in our business account?"

"Yes I have," Mark admitted. "Thought you were saving up for my Christmas bonus."

"Not sure why they keep sending it," Virgil said. "Thought we had received all we were getting."

"Well, it's obvious they know how good I am and want you to reward me."

Virgil laughed. "That will happen anyway," he assured him.

"I'm just messing with ya," Mark said. "I would suggest we put it into a separate account and not spend any of it. You know, in case they want it back."

"Earl and I invested some of the earlier money as you recall," Virgil said. "But I was thinking the same thing you just suggested with the rest of it. Makes me wonder why I really need the added expense of an accountant."

Mark laughed, "Now who's fucking with who?"

"I just don't get what they're up to with this?"

"Let's wait it out then," Mark suggested. "Just don't mention it to anyone."

"You would be the only one, Mark," Virgil said.

"How about Megan?" Mark asked, offering up an option.

"Let me worry about her, my friend," Virgil stated.

"Will do," Mark said. "We still on for the weekend?"

"For sure."

"Great, see ya then," Mark said and hung up.

Virgil arrived at the Ambassador around four that afternoon. The manager recognized him and made sure he had the best room he could allow him to have. Virgil was a little uncomfortable at what lengths the effeminate manager seemed to be going to make sure he was happy.

"Thank you, sir," Virgil quietly said.

"My pleasure," the manager responded with a smile, handing him a small envelope with the room key cards neatly tucked into it.

Virgil accepted the envelope then turned and pulled his luggage to the elevator. Once in his room he put away his clothes and set up his toiletries on the bathroom counter. His phone rang. It was his dad. "Hello, Dad, how's the south?"

"Getting a little hairy down here, but we're surviving," he answered. "How did it go at the funeral?"

"Not sure how it was presented to them, but Ellen and Gene are now convinced Tom did kill himself."

"As it should be," Earl stated.

"When are you guys coming home?" Virgil asked.

"By Thanksgiving for sure," Earl replied.

"Come on, Dad, it's not even Halloween yet," Virgil said, trying to make his dad realize the length of time that would be.

"I know son, but we're still needed here," Earl said, then added. "Hopefully it will be sooner."

"Okay," Virgil relented. "Tell me why I'm still getting money dumped in my business account by the Defense Department."

"I will check, but I think it's because you are helping Chase Products get the lines up for the PPE needed for the Chung Virus."

"Makes no sense, because they are already paying me. Confirm it if you can," Virgil said. "Take care of yourself and get home as soon as you can. Love you, Dad."

"We will. Love you, too."

Virgil walked across the room and opened the curtains. He stood, looking out the window. He thought about Megan, wondering why she hadn't called. Benny's was only three blocks away, hopefully she was working tonight. He grabbed his jacket and returned to the elevator. Once again, he walked there.

Jeff, the bouncer, greeted him at the door. There was no line tonight. "I don't think Megan is here tonight. At least I haven't seen her yet."

"Thanks Jeff," Virgil said. "Think I'll have a burger anyway."

"The bacon burger has been great lately," Jeff suggested.

"She has been here since last week though?"

"Yes, I believe so. I'm out here most of the night and our paths don't always cross."

They fist bumped and Virgil entered through the door next to Jeff. He scanned the bar for Megan and didn't see her. He found a table as close to the bar as he could. He looked about the room. The stage was still there from the show he saw when he and Megan had made their exit.

There were maybe a hundred people here tonight and obviously a show was not forthcoming. There was a lone microphone and stand in the middle of the stage along with a tall stool.

"What can I get you?" Lana, a tall slender jet-black haired waitress, asked.

"I would like the bacon burger and a Smithwicks please," Virgil answered.

Lana waitressed sans pad and pen and through the meal proved she didn't need them. She returned with his beer a few minutes later and set it on the table. "Your bacon burger will be out in about fifteen. What condiments would you like?"

"Mustard, ketchup and some relish if you have it."

"I will get that," Lana said and started to turn.

"One other thing, Lana," Virgil said, stopping her. "Is Megan here tonight?"

"You mean the blond bartender?"

"Yes, have you seen her?"

"Last I heard she was heading for Florida," she answered. She waited for Virgil to ask her something else, but he sat there looking stunned. Lana returned to the kitchen.

Virgil grabbed the Smithwick's and drank half of it. He set it back on the table and stared out across the stage. She would have at least texted me, he thought. He stood and approached the bar, leaning against it like he wanted a drink.

A large dark-haired man about twenty-five to thirty nodded in Virgil's direction. "Be with you in a minute, sir."

"That's fine," Virgil said, nodding back. When the bartender made it down to him he only confirmed what Lana had told him about Megan. Virgil couldn't believe either of them, not because he suspected a ruse, but the fact it didn't make sense. Why would Megan take her recently ill mother to a part of the country dealing with a health scare? He didn't want to appear pushy or overbearing with Megan, but he needed to know. He called her but had to leave another message. His burger came along with the condiments, and he ordered another beer. He ate quickly, feeling like he needed to get back to the hotel to figure out what his next move would be, then realized he knew where she lived in town and would go see her there.

He finished his meal, the beer, and tipped Lana who thanked him again as he left. He fist bumped Jeff again after he passed through the double doors. Once outside he trotted for the first block back towards The Ambassador. His meal weighed on him though and he slowed to a fast walk. His mind was always a step ahead of his pace until he made it to the sidewalk in front of the hotel. He breathed in one more lung full of fall air and walked into the empty lobby and to the elevator. He pushed the up arrow button and stepped back. The door opened immediately. His stare went from the floor to the elevator. Megan stood there smiling. Virgil didn't recognize her because she was the last person he expected to see at that moment. They looked at each other for a moment too long. The doors began to close.

"Hi," she said, putting her arm out to block the door.

"Hi," Virgil said, blocking the other one. The doors receded and he entered. They looked at each other again as the doors finally closed. He leaned towards and past Megan to push the number three on the keypad.

Megan put her arms around Virgil and lightly kissed him on the cheek. He returned the embrace and turned his head so he could kiss her lips. They squeezed each other and moved their hands to feel again what they remembered from before. Their lips and tongues did their own exploring. They eased their grasps when the ride ended and the doors began to open. They smiled at each other with their eyes and minds in sync.

"I missed you," Virgil said.

"I missed you too," Megan said. "I was hoping I timed this right."

"What do you mean?" Virgil asked, confused but still smiling. He led her towards his room with his arm around her shoulder.

"Jeff called me when you left Benny's," she said, looking up at him and laughing.

"You mean that bullshit about you going to Florida was a joke?"

"Obviously a good one. I mean you bought it."

"Yeah, a little bit, but it didn't make sense. I didn't bite too hard on the bait."

Megan and Virgil laughed as he opened the door to his room. He followed her in. He walked across the room and closed the curtain. Megan sat on the edge of the bed.

"I'm so glad you're here," Virgil said, standing by the window.

"I've been told by the owner of the bar not to see you," Megan replied.

"What? Why?"

"He said you are under surveillance by our government and he doesn't need that around Benny's," Megan explained.

Virgil laughed. Megan expanded on the story, telling him how she let the owner know he wasn't going to tell her who she could be or not be with. "This thing keeps getting weirder and weirder," Virgil admitted. "I wish it would end."

"I know you do, and I want to be there when it does."

Virgil was stunned again. He had never heard anything like what Megan had just confessed. He walked to the bed and sat beside her; she leaned her head against his shoulder. He could feel emotions welling up inside of him. It affected his heart and his stomach. He knew one was just butterflies and the other prompted a confession of his own. "I love you," he said somewhat clumsily. He quickly rebounded from that effort, "I love you and I want you to be there when it is all over."

Megan put her arm around Virgil again. "You can count on it," she reassured him then looked up at him. "I love you, too."

They kissed again and fell back on the king-sized bed. Megan rolled on top of Virgil. They made love. Like two people who had just acknowledged loving each other and spontaneously taking the opportunity to physically show it. Everything was on the table, and they feasted on each other. No move or position went untried. When they finished, they laid naked on the still made but ruffled bed side by side just looking at each other, exhausted but smiling.

"So how is your mom?" Virgil asked.

Megan started laughing uncontrollably, rolling away on her side and back again. Virgil started laughing just watching her. "What?" he kept asking her as she continued the rolling back and forth pattern. She finally stopped and looked into Virgil's eyes.

"We just made beautiful love together and you ask me about my mother," Megan said laughing while trying to gain control. Megan added, "And that is just one thing I love about you." She said hugging and patting Virgil's arm, "She is fine, thank you for asking."

Virgil laughed, "Guess I need to work on my timing." He then explained his plans to meet Mark and Diane up at his cabin the coming weekend and Megan agreed to come along.

Chase Products

Virgil awoke the next morning a changed man. His father loved him, as had Miss Laudy, but this was way different. He couldn't get Megan off his mind. Love will do that to you, and Virgil basked in that feeling lying alone in the bed, waiting for the alarm on his phone to go off. Finally, he grabbed it off the nightstand, turned it off then jumped out of bed.

Megan had gone home to Harriet last night, but Virgil could still smell her. He breathed it in as he slowly walked to the bathroom. He quickly showered and shaved and during that time tried to think about what he needed to accomplish this day. It was what he always did on the morning of a job. Yet today was different. He was pleasantly distracted this day. He knew why but tried to concentrate on the job he was going to do.

The request from John had been for a machine tune-up to feed a new line they were setting up. A side note asked him if he had considered their offer of employment. He and John had a good rapport and the company reminded him of Helper Plastics in many ways. Plus it was in West Allis. But he knew he would never not be his own boss. He loved the fact he could do things his way as long as it pleased his customers and it usually did.

He arrived at Chase Products by eight that morning and John led him to the machine that needed tuning. In route he probed for Virgil's decision on the company's offer of employment.

"Let's get this machine running then we can talk," Virgil replied, and John stepped back and let him go to work. With John's input Virgil was able to diagnose and suggest a valve replacement that would take care of the problem. He replaced the valve in question with one from the company's stock. As lunch approached the machine was running but soon after a hose burst and sprayed oil everywhere. They were able to shut it down immediately, but at two-thousand pounds of pressure the oil sprayed out enough to bring five maintenance men and two plant employees to assist in the cleanup.

Virgil started to assist in the cleanup, but John suggested now was the time they should talk. "The guys can take care of the mess. Let's go to my office."

Once there, Virgil ended any suspense. "I know this company wants me and the offer is a great one, but I can't accept it."

"I'm authorized to offer you more money if that's what it takes."

There was a knock on John's office door. Phillip Chase, the CEO of the company and son of founder, Paul Chase entered.

John stood as did Virgil. Phillip extended his right hand to Virgil who did likewise. They shook hands. "Nice to see you again, Virgil."

"Always good to see you, sir," Virgil replied.

"Please, call me Phil," Chase offered. "How did the repair go, are we up and running?"

John quickly intervened, "Virgil got the machine running like we want, but then a hose blew. The guys are cleaning it up now."

"How long will that take?" Phil asked, then motioned for everyone to sit down. He took a chair against the wall facing both John and Virgil.

"Hopefully only a couple hours," John informed him. "We'll make sure everything is up and running before we let Virgil go."

"That's why I'm here, Virgil," Phil said, turning in his direction. "I want you to come work for us."

"I understand and I am flattered at your offer," Virgil started, sliding forward in his chair, "But I enjoy being my own boss."

"We are never truly our own bosses," Phil stated. "We are always answering to someone and carrying the weight of our decisions day after day."

"That is true, and I know the weight you carry is much heavier than what I do," Virgil said. "But I feel mine is just as important."

John's phone rang and he answered it immediately. He hung up. "Would you two excuse me? I have to go look at something for a couple minutes."

"Take your time," Phil said, standing and closing the blinds on the office windows as John left.

Virgil was feeling a little uneasy as Phil paced across the room, finally sitting down on John's desktop. To Virgil the owner was a bit more intimidating at this angle. He also sensed this was a setup since John left so abruptly and with little resistance from the CEO.

"You have other problems from what I hear," Phil stated frankly.

Virgil was stunned, "Excuse me?"

"We know about your health problems and what you've been going through," Phil continued.

"You mean the hernia surgery a few months back?"

"If you want to still use that story it's fine with me," Phil said.

Virgil was boiling inside, but forced a smile while still staring at the CEO. "Tell me what you know. Cause I have nothing to hide."

Phil laughed, clapping his hands together. "We know about your government involvement. Your illness and recovery, your being followed. And we even know about the death in your garage."

Virgil sat back in his chair. "What do you want from me?"

"All of that information and blame will never see the light of day, if you come to work for us."

"Mr. Chase, I will be here to fix your machines whenever you call me, but I will not be blackmailed into working for you," Virgil responded, standing up to face his wanna-be boss. "I have nothing to hide and no blame to carry."

Chase also stood and the two stared at each other for a moment. "Life could be so easy if you let it," he said, putting his hand on Virgil's shoulder. "You have more to hide than you may realize."

"Like what?" Virgil asked.

"Murder or laundering money, take your pick," Chase confidently stated.

"You may know everything about me, but those are not true," Virgil replied. "From the very beginning I have wondered why people can't just leave me alone," Virgil said, turning away from Phil. "I only want to fix machines and live my simple life."

"You know about the virus and what we are doing here," Chase said. "This is not the time to be selfish, Virgil. I mean Doctor Harmon saved yours so you can now help us."

"Why doesn't this country quit lying to everyone and come out and tell its people the truth?"

"The panic would be devastating to this country," Phil said.

"That's because this country and its media make us panic about everything," Virgil said with conviction.

"I have no control over that part of the equation," Phil answered.

"And you have no control over me," Virgil said and started walking towards the door. He was about to grab the doorknob when Chase stopped him cold.

"What about Megan Peterson?"

Virgil let go of the handle, turned quickly and faced the CEO once again. "Leave her out of this. She is not to be touched."

"And she won't be bothered after you come work for us," Phil assured him.

Virgil wanted to hit Phillip Chase. They had gone too far this time. He looked down at the floor. "Okay," Virgil said, relenting. "But at some point I will require my freedom with no strings attached."

"Let's see how it goes first."

"One other thing, Phil, after I'm done here tomorrow I need to have the weekend away."

"As long as we have the line running, I have no problem with it," he said.

"It will be running," Virgil assured him, then turned and left the office, leaving his new boss standing there. He felt helpless and used in the way the job acceptance turned out.

Virgil stopped in the nearest bathroom, made sure it was empty, then punched the mirror. It cracked from the force. Instantly, he felt relief and little regret. How can they do this to me?, he wondered. How did they know all of this and how had they gathered their information? The questions made him fume, but he knew he had to hold it together. Somehow he knew he would come out above all of this and he had to handle the pressure. He returned to the machine they needed running. John was standing next to the control panel, looking at one of the pages on the screen.

"Hey boss, how's it going?" Virgil said in a tone meant to imply displeasure.

"Let's you and me make the best of this situation, Virgil," John replied.

"I will do everything required of me, but eventually I will go back to my business," Virgil said. "That will be the first point of my contract."

"Let's get this machine going then we can talk about the contract," John assured him.

"Fair enough."

John and Virgil always worked well together and today was no different. They stuck to the task at hand. John knew better than trying to be buddy buddy with Virgil, especially in his present state of mind. The machine was making parts for syringes an hour later. They watched for another half hour and returned to John's office. The Director of Personnel, Michelle Stans, a tall brunette with an all business look in both attire and demeanor, awaited them.

Michelle introduced herself and got down to business immediately. Virgil knew he had nothing to lose and gave her a list of what he wanted, beginning with what he had mentioned to John by the machine. John mentioned options that favored Virgil and Michelle left with a we'll see what we can do comment.

Virgil left for lunch. He wasn't an employee until he signed the contract. He called Mark to let him know what had transpired and the fact there wasn't much he could do.

"We can talk strategy this weekend if you like," Mark offered.

"I'm not an employee yet. If something comes up I'll take it," Virgil said. "Is the website still up?"

"I'll check then text you."

"Thanks."

He returned to Chase Products an hour later and directly to John's office. John waved him in and Virgil took the chair he previously used.

"Machine still running?" he asked his boss to be.

"Yes, it is," John acknowledged, walking from behind his desk towards Virgil. He stopped, holding his hand out, offering him his business card with the back facing upwards. There was a handwritten note printed on it. "That's my home address. My wife and I would welcome you for dinner if you would like," John said. "I know it's short notice, but there is something you need to know."

"Just tell me, John," Virgil pleaded.

"I want to but not here."

Virgil suggested he bring his wife to the Ambassador for a night out. Ditch Repair would pick up the tab and it was in a public place which would make him feel more at ease. John agreed and called his wife to confirm. He called Megan quickly to see if she would join them. She was supposed to work tonight but she would get out of it if she could.

"She'll be ready," John said, then set his cell on the desk.

"I'm waiting for confirmation, but I'll make reservations for four at six o'clock," Virgil suggested.

"Works for us." John agreed. "See ya tonight."

"The machine doing what we want?"

"It's humming along," John said. "We got it from here."

Virgil put John's card in his pocket then shook his hand and left. On the way to the Ambassador he called its number and secured a reservation. When he returned to his room he received a text from Mark informing him the site was still operating. There was a company needing his services in two weeks for a start up on a machine. Virgil thanked him, took off his jacket, threw it on the desk chair, and crashed on the bed. He awoke an hour later to his ringing phone. It was Megan letting him know she couldn't get anyone to cover for her. He immediately notified John he was showing up for dinner solo. John texted back that he was going to come alone as well, informing him his wife didn't want to be a third wheel.

Virgil turned on the news as he got ready for the evening. The south was inundated with cases at the hospitals in Florida and Georgia, but it seemed to have peaked. The death toll was not as bad as some far eastern countries, but it was significant. He texted his dad and asked him how soon they were coming home. The news also informed him of western states starting to see cases of the same variant. Texas, Louisiana, and Mississippi were the only states in the deep south with minimal cases. He turned the set off, threw the remote on the bed, and left to meet John.

He arranged with the maitre d to be seated at a table for two out of the way so he could hear what John had to say. Once seated and the first beers ordered John began his story. He had gone through what Virgil had gone through before the original pandemic six years ago. His tale was interrupted by the waitress taking their steak orders. Picking up the story he informed Virgil it was how he too had come to work for Chase Products.

"So they came after you?" Virgil asked.

"I stopped at a bar one night to meet some guys and I got approached by two guys."

"Ivan and Gustav," Virgil inquired.

"I think that was their names. They both had beards and dressed alike."

"That would be them," Virgil acknowledged.

John continued his narrative after the steaks and two more beers arrived. He said he was in a low paying job at a company not doing too well and he wanted out. The twins as he referred to the duo seemed to know this and a lot more about him. They were recruiting him for a maintenance manager position at a company making medical equipment that would help the country during any pandemics that might be coming or still forming. He had asked for info on the pandemics, but none was forthcoming from them. He ended up taking the job because of the money they offered, benefits, and the fact the following week he was informed the place he was presently working at was going under. He knew the company was in trouble, but not that kind of trouble. Despite all that happened he was glad he was at Chase because he felt they genuinely were helping humanity, at least in this country. "I was told they had someone in mind for a permanent position for the medical line, but I didn't realize at first they meant you."

"Why did you need me?" Virgil asked. "You have had good mechanics here for a while."

"Problem is a lot of them have gone looking for what they feel are better jobs. One guy switched professions," John explained. "The talent pool is shrinking in this field."

"I guess they need to pay guys better," Virgil suggested.

"We tried with some of the guys, but they felt life would be better somewhere else."

They finished their dinners and ordered pie and more beers. Virgil explained his story to John beginning with Benny's. John nodded throughout knowing he had experienced many of the same situations. His nodding stopped when Virgil told him about the events at the bar, the cabin, and the garage.

"They weren't recruiting you, Virgil," John said. "They were hunting you."

"That's the way I felt," Virgil explained.

"Those guys never seemed like they would do anything like that," John adamantly stated.

"That was six years ago for you, John. Times have certainly changed and the twins have honed their craft."

They ate their French silk pie and ordered one more round for the road. Virgil told the waitress to give him the bill then continued his story about Ernie, Sylvia, and Doctor Harmon taking care of him and his dad. John's parents were located in the Dallas area, and he sympathized with Virgil on the plight of his dad and his friends. Before the last beers were consumed John assured his new employee that he had a long leash if he was always available to Chase Products. "We want you in the area" was his only request. Virgil assured him it would be easier to do, now that he was looking for a place to permanently be. They left on good terms, and both felt they had gained a better knowledge of each other. John left feeling he knew a little too much.

At eight a.m. the next morning Virgil met John again at Chase Products. They checked on the machine that was now pumping out syringe parts at a rapid rate. Virgil asked if there was anything else the company needed that day. John wanted him to check on a machine from a past visit. John made minor adjustments to it but couldn't pick up the second on the cycle he was seeking. He talked with John about his role with the fifty-six-year-old company. John told him more work was coming in another week or so and a third line would be added to what they were already doing. He and John agreed they were doing their part to fight this latest virus no matter how limited, and John assured Virgil it was all legal. Virgil was not enamored with the way he had become part of it. He still wanted to know who killed Tom and why it was necessary. He knew that sometimes sacrifices for a cause were necessary. He could accept collateral damage no matter how cruel if it was for the right cause. Murder he would never accept.

He left Chase products later that afternoon. He had signed some paperwork making him an employee and would sign his contract the following Monday or Tuesday. He was ready for the weekend. Mark had texted him to let him know everything was a go on their end. He texted him back that this weekend would be somewhat of a planning session. He then ignored the question marks sent back by his best friend. Finally, Mark called, "What the hell is going on?"

"We may be shutting down Ditch Repair on our own this time," Virgil informed him. "That is what we have to discuss."

"Okay," Mark replied with a tone of apprehension.

"Relax," Virgil shot back. "I believe we will both benefit quite well."

"Good," Mark said. "We will be there by four or five."

"See you then," Virgil said.

He had checked out of the Ambassador that morning and went to Megan's house after leaving Chase Products. Virgil stopped by a local florist he passed in route to her house to buy some roses. Yellow for Harriet and red for Megan. Three for each. He arrived at the house Megan grew up in and the home she had lived in most of her life. She greeted him at the door before he could even knock. He held the roses behind his back then presented the fragrant red flowers to her as she opened the door. She took them, took a long whiff of the aroma, and kissed Virgil on the cheek.

"You didn't need to do this," she said, letting him into the house.

"I know. And you didn't have to be waiting at the door," Virgil replied, smiling. "Besides I wanted to, and these are for Harriet."

"You are a suck up," Megan said, giggling.

"Why break with tradition."

They continued into the kitchen where Harriet was eating a late lunch seated at the breakfast counter. "Virgil," she mumbled loudly, setting her BLT down on the plate while chewing on a bite.

"Nice to see you again, Harriet," Virgil greeted her. "And not in a hospital or recovering from it."

"I couldn't feel better," Harriet stated clearly.

"Virgil brought you something," Megan mentioned, smiling.

"Oh...," Harriet said, wiping her mouth as her eyes got bigger.

Virgil pulled out the yellow roses from behind his back. Megan took a vase from a lower cabinet, filled it with water and put the flowers in it and set it on the counter next to her mother. Virgil hugged Harriet.

"You know. Every time I see you I will expect a flower," Harriet said, laughing. "Thank you, you are a good boy."

"Thanks, you are a sweet lady," Virgil said, looking at Megan who rolled her eyes while mouthing the words "Suck Up."

"He brought me some too," Megan said, holding up her red roses to show her mom.

Harriet squeezed Virgil's hands, "Take good care of my Megan."

"I intend to," he assured her returning the squeeze.

The Cabin This October

Everything would be on the table this weekend, Virgil imagined as he tried to achieve the seventy miles per hour limit while the urban area grew distant in the rear view mirror. They would be planning their next steps. Their immediate futures, set within the chaos that had been created, were at stake. They would need to listen to each other's opinions and ideas and agree on a plan of action. These were the thoughts running through Virgil's mind as he sipped on his Yeti tumbler filled two-thirds of the way with Coca-Cola. Soda was the only caffeine he ever drank. He had tried coffee one time when nothing else was available but never acquired the taste for it. Route 41 was the longest stretch of their journey on this cool early Friday afternoon in October. He and Megan alternated choices of their music as they headed northward in Megan's Chevy Malibu. Virgil drove and answered any questions she had about Mark and Diane. She had only talked to them on the phone from Benny's but had yet to meet them. She was nervous but not overwhelmed by the upcoming introductions. Virgil assured her his friends would like her and if they didn't then that was their problem. They arrived at the cabin around three that afternoon with the sunlight starting to fade behind the hill above them. Mark and Diane made it there about an hour later.

They got situated in the cabin. Mark and Diane would use the bedroom downstairs to the rear of the cabin. It was the one with the floor hatch Virgil had made his escape from. Virgil and Megan would take the upstairs bedroom which overlooked the lake through the lingering fall foliage. Diane had done the shopping for the trip and put a couple of pizzas in the oven for their dinner. Megan helped Diane set up the dinner table and they got to know each other. Mark and Virgil were on a walk outside, beers in hand, just to look around and make sure things appeared in order. It was light enough, and they walked around the cabin and to the path that had led to Virgil's wooded hiding place. "We need to talk some things over while we're here," Virgil informed his best friend.

"First thing I want to know. How did someone like you end up with a woman like Megan?" Mark asked, lightly punching Virgil in the shoulder.

"I can't claim her as mine and maybe never will," Virgil replied. "She is an independent woman, and we haven't known each other all that long."

"You know what I mean."

"Hey I'm not that ugly. In fact, I'm ruggedly handsome," Virgil said, laughing. "Her words not mine."

"She's kind of young though, isn't she?" Mark said. "Not that there's anything wrong with it."

"I'm sixteen years older, and she has no problem with it."

"So what do we need to talk over?" Mark asked, changing the subject.

"I took that job with Chase Products this week."

Mark stopped by the fire pit and stared at Virgil, "Why?"

"Turns out that was one of the other things they were after me for," Virgil explained.

"Then why all the cloak and dagger shit?" Mark asked.

"That still confuses me," Virgil admitted. "But I do know it is very important for Chase to pump out the parts this country and others will require."

"It's gonna be that bad?"

"Look at the south and how they're getting hit down there."

Megan opened the door to the cabin fifteen minutes later. "Hey you guys the pizzas will be ready in a few minutes," she yelled out, looking around to see where they were. "Oh, there you are."

Mark and Virgil both waved. "We'll be right there," Virgil said, watching Megan walk back in the cabin.

"Let's eat," Mark said. "We can talk after."

"Before we go in I have to tell you Chase Products CEO knows all that has happened to me."

"Everything?" Mark asked, finishing his beer.

"Everything," Virgil said adamantly. "He even brought up Megan by name.

But this is between you and me, she doesn't need to know that."

"If you really like this woman, you better not keep secrets from her," Mark suggested.

"I know," Virgil slowly admitted, "I'll tell her tonight when we go up to bed."

"Good luck."

They finished the two pizzas while talking about Mark and Diane's two boys going to the same college in downstate Illinois. Mark asked Megan about her parents. Earl was mentioned by Diane and Virgil excused himself for a moment to call his father.

"How are you guys doing?" Virgil asked Earl when he answered.

"We are okay."

"When you coming home?"

"When are you coming home?" Earl shot back.

"Not sure, we're up at the cabin right now."

"Well, I'll be here when you do," Earl stated.

"So you're home in Illinois?"

"Yes. Got back late this afternoon," Earl explained.

"Are you feeling alright? I mean health wise?"

"Yes. We're all fine."

"Do me a favor Dad and stay there for a while," Virgil asked.

"I plan on it," Earl replied. "I'm going to bed in a bit, I'm tired from the road trip. Take care son."

"Love you, Dad."

"Yeah, yeah," Earl answered sarcastically.

Virgil was laughing when he came back into the living room. "Your dad alright?" Megan asked.

"He's home, so he is good, but tired from the trip," Virgil explained. "I told him I loved him, and he was like yeah, yeah." Virgil laughed again. "Good old Earl."

"Sounds like a sweet old man," Megan suggested.

"Oh he is," Diane quickly added.

"He's a funny guy too," Mark said.

"Guess I know now where his son gets it," Megan said, grabbing Virgil's hand when he was within reach.

"Yeah, yeah," Virgil said, emulating his father. He squeezed her hand in return.

Once the dishes were cleared they migrated to the living room where

Virgil had a nice fire going in the hearth of the fireplace. The wood crackled as they got comfortable on the two sofas. Mark had found a legal pad and a pen and agreed to play secretary for the idea session. Virgil began by explaining his intentions of working for Chase Products while still being able to freelance at other companies. He told them of the long leash he had been granted but wasn't sure how long it would be. He wanted to keep Ditch Repair in operation and Mark on the payroll as well.

"That would be great," Diane chimed in, looking at Mark who shot a quick glance at Virgil in a way which looked like an apology.

"It's all good, Mark," he reassured his friend. "I want everyone's opinions on this." He looked at Diane, then Megan. "I mean everyone."

"We would be alright if you didn't need me," Mark offered.

Virgil sat forward on the sofa, "I will always need my best friend. We can make this work."

"Just giving you options," Mark offered.

"I have to get back home at some time to check on my dad, but Monday I have to be in West Allis again," Virgil explained. "Can you guys stop and check on him after you get home?"

"No problem," Diane said as Mark wrote down notes. "I can go over there Tuesday after I get out of school."

"Thank you. I'm not sure when I'm going to make it there, plus I have to get a hotel."

"No, you don't," Megan said, tugging at Virgil's arm. "You can stay at my house."

Virgil looked at Megan, "You better check with your mom, don't you think?"

"I will, but I'm sure her answer will be yes," Megan said, smiling.

"Tell her there won't be roses every day," Virgil mentioned with a laugh.

"She won't mind," Megan said.

Mark and Diane looked at each other, smiling and rolling their eyes sarcastically. Mark acted like he was presenting his wife with a single flower. Diane feigned appreciation. Virgil noticed it. "I remember when you guys were dating," Virgil said then pretended he was on the phone. "No, you hang up, no, you hang up. Okay, on the count of three."

They all laughed. "We're still together," Diane rightfully boasted.

"You two were meant for each other," Virgil confessed then paused, looking at the fire for a moment. He was unsure how committed Megan was to him though he knew he wanted to be with her for as long as she would have him.

"So you will be in West Allis," Mark said, giving Virgil a moment to segue to his next point.

Megan grabbed Virgil's arm and pulled him closer to her. Virgil eased back into the sofa next to her, smiling at Mark and Diane. "He's with me, if he wants," Megan said, leaning forward and kissing his hand she held in hers.

"So, I'll be in West Allis," Virgil said smiling. "I will try to get to the other company for the start up. Then I will get home to see my dad on Thursday or Friday, I hope."

Their discussion and plans labored on and before they knew it midnight was approaching. They agreed it was time to end this session for tonight. Virgil took one more walk outside just to check things over. Megan accompanied him this time, wanting to see the night sky this far north. She was not disappointed. The moon, though not full, emitted enough light to illuminate much of the forest. The lack of full foliage at this time of year allowed them to see its reflection on a calm Booth Lake. They made it around to the backside of the cabin, or the uphill side as Earl always called it. Virgil looked around and up the hill towards Forest Road while Megan admired the sky. He thought he saw a light flash at the top of the hill. "Did you see that?" he asked Megan.

"Yeah, isn't the sky beautiful," she said, still looking skyward.

"No, I mean at the top of the hill by the road."

Megan turned and looked in the same direction as Virgil. They waited for a few moments without any indication that they were being watched, "Sorry Virgil, I don't see anything."

"Thought I saw a light at the top of the hill by our driveway."

"Anyone else in the neighborhood?"

"There are other cabins," Virgil said looking to his right where the next cabin was visible in the moonlight though over a hundred yards away.

There was a light on there, shining faintly at that distance.

"There," Megan pointed in the direction of the cabin Virgil was looking at. "I just saw a car go down the driveway of that cabin."

"Oh, yeah," Virgil said, noticing it. "Good eyes Peterson."

They continued around to the door on the lakeside of the house and stood for a while admiring the cool crisp night sky. Virgil watched Megan for a moment. She finally noticed it and turned in his direction, "What?" she asked.

Virgil said nothing. He pulled her close and kissed her until they needed to breathe. They slowly gasped for air then quickly kissed again. They entered the cabin and locked up for the night, stopping to tell Mark and Diane goodnight again then continued upstairs.

"Megan, can you sit on the bed next to me for a minute?" Virgil asked. "There is something I need to tell you."

She sat next to him taking off her flannel shirt and tossing it towards a chair in the corner. "What is it?"

"I took that job at Chase because their CEO brought your name up when we were meeting."

Megan thought for a moment, then with a confused look on her face asked, "Why would he do that?"

"They want me for this job and these people are willing to do whatever it takes to keep me," Virgil explained.

"But what does it matter if you know me?" Megan asked.

"They're using you as leverage," Virgil said. "I don't like it any more than you do."

"Fuck them, they can't control me, or you for that matter," Megan said, quickly standing and walking about the room. "I should have told Ivan and Gustav to go fuck themselves that night they came in after you."

Virgil stood as well, "Megan, it's okay. I just don't want anything to happen to you."

"They threw money at me like I was a cheap whore," Megan ranted. "Just stay out of the way, they said."

"It's alright," Virgil assured her. "I will play along with their scheme."

"For what?" Megan asked. "You're not a pussy. They can't run your life."

"Thanks for the vote of confidence," Virgil said, trying to grab Megan and stop her from pacing. "In reality, I'm the real whore here and I'm still being pimped out."

Megan smiled a little then sat back down on the bed. "I just feel so stupid. Like I've been used."

"I do too, but we will find a way out of it together if you want," Virgil said. "We could always tell them you moved to Florida with your mother."

"I'm not sure how we could pull that off," Megan said. "These assholes seem to know everything."

"Let's try to sleep on it tonight. We can talk more tomorrow."

"Yeah, get me all riled up right before we go to bed," Megan scolded. "I doubt I can fall asleep now."

Virgil walked to the nightstand and opened the drawer. "We can have a nightcap," he said, holding out a joint for her to take. "Then we can work off the rest of your rant in other ways."

"I'll do the spliff with you, but you're on your own for anything else," Megan informed him.

"That's alright, I'm getting tired anyway," Virgil replied, then lit up the joint, took a hit and handed it to Megan. He retrieved an ashtray from the bathroom and set it on the nightstand.

They laid back on the bed, propping up pillows against the oak headboard so they could lean against them. They smiled at each other, passing the aromatic, end of the day calming influence. Tomorrow would be another day in this venture they had both decided to take with each other. It was time now to relax, think, reflect, and refrain from sharing any of it. They both knew, at this moment, they were there for each other.

"You guys getting up?" Mark yelled up the stairs to Megan and Virgil. "It's like noon."

Virgil looked at his phone on the nightstand and saw it was a little before nine. He laughed to himself then rolled over and cuddled with Megan, kissing the back of her neck to wake her. She rolled over and smiled at Virgil, "Good morning beautiful," he greeted her.

"Yeah, I'm sure I'm looking my best right now," she said smiling.

"You look fine to me," Virgil said. "I'm getting up. Mark is getting restless down there. He must be hungry."

"They are really nice people," Megan said, rolling off the bed and standing there in only a tee shirt and her panties.

Virgil noticed, standing next to the bed on his side. "You are beautiful."

"Thanks," she said, smiling. "I'm going to jump in the shower quick, if that's alright."

"That's fine. I'll get Mark settled down."

Mark laughed at Virgil when he entered the kitchen in a tee shirt and running shorts. "You guys up there doing it all night?" Mark teased.

Diane laughed from the sink where she was washing off fruit, "That's none of your business, Mark."

"I'm just kidding," Mark replied.

"I know you are, Mark. We caught up on sleep after discussing some things."

"Megan coming down?" Diane asked.

"In a bit. She's in the shower."

"Happy birthday by the way," Diane said, setting a bowl each of assorted melons and strawberries on the table. She hugged her husband's best friend.

"Yeah, happy birthday buddy," Mark said, shaking Virgil's hand.

"Thank you. I didn't realize it was today," Virgil said, looking at his phone. "Damn, you're right." His phone started ringing. It was Earl. "Dad, how are you?"

"I was just calling to wish you a happy birthday."

"Thanks, Dad. Wish you were here too."

"Yeah, just what you need an old man tagging along," Earl admitted. "By the way I'm going to call or text you later today or tomorrow with some information about the virus."

"You can't tell me now?" Virgil asked.

"We're waiting for some results from Harmon."

"Are we good?"

"I'm sure you won't die, Virgil," Earl said. "Like I said, we're waiting on results."

"Well, thanks for the birthday present," Virgil said. Earl hung up. He tried to call him back, but Earl wasn't answering. A minute later he received his text: Said I will call or text you. Later.

"Damn him," Virgil said. He looked at Mark and Diane then explained what was going on.

Megan came into the kitchen, her hair pulled back and still wet. She was wearing jeans and a sweater but barefooted. "Who are you damning?" she asked. Virgil turned and quickly explained the conservation with his dad. "Don't worry about it then," Megan said. "Besides, it's your birthday, Virgil."

"How did you know that?" Virgil asked.

"My good friend, Diane, informed me last night," Megan said, looking towards her new friend across the table from her.

"Sorry guys, but all the shit I've, I mean we've been through lately puts me on edge. I'll just wait for the results of whatever they are looking at."

The remainder of the day consisted of a sun-filled walk down to the lake where they sat on the pier and hashed over some minor details from their morning meeting. A fire in the fire pit followed where they cooked their own hot dogs for a late lunch on sticks they had found on their way back from the lake. Beer and wine flowed. They kept the fire going and as the day waned the pipe came out and Mark and Virgil toasted the birthday boy. Megan and Diane refrained. Later after more hot dogs for dinner, everyone enjoyed Smores. Thankfully all the plans made were during the brunch Diane and Mark had planned and served with Megan's help. At ten that night the last ember doused. The hissing steam rose from the fire pit. They all agreed on their plans and to go inside as a light rain began to fall. It was one in the morning when they officially ended Virgil's birthday. He and Megan quickly undressed and jumped into bed, falling asleep almost immediately.

The next morning they had a hearty breakfast. Mark and Diane once again took the initiative to lay out. Surprisingly, they ate, cleaned up, locked up and left by noon. The misty rain lingered on as Virgil and Megan hugged and said their goodbyes with Mark and Diane, then led the way up the driveway to Forest Road. They traveled in tandem for a while, passing by one another flipping each other off and waving. They went their separate ways as Mark mooned them at the turn to the route Diane had chosen for their trip home.

"They are great people," Megan said, still laughing at Mark's antics.

"Yes, they are," Virgil agreed. "Some of the best I've ever known."

West Allis

Pamela Drive

Virgil found a white rose at a Jewel supermarket that he presented to Harriet when he and Megan walked through the backdoor of her home that had been built in the sixties. The one-story home contained three bedrooms, one and half baths, a two-car garage, with an equally sized front and back yard. "It's a peace offering for you allowing me to stay here," Virgil joked as he handed it to her.

"I see ya brought her back in one piece," Harriet quipped, looking at her daughter.

"Hi Mom," Megan responded as she wheeled her suitcase in and carried her tote bag over her shoulder. "It was a great weekend."

"Do I have a grandchild yet?"

"Mom," Megan said, turning to face her mother.

"Misses Peterson, just accept the rose for now," Virgil calmly added. Harriet paused then quietly uttered, "Amen."

"By the way, Mom, Virgil is moving in," Megan said, leaning over and kissing her on the cheek. "Love you."

Virgil's phone buzzed with a text from his father: You need to come home soon. I will have more info in the morning. Love You.

He went to the living room just off the kitchen where Harriet usually read the paper on her phone. But on Sundays it was delivered, and she preferred the light of the kitchen. She also liked that she could hold it in her hands and feel the paper that provided the news, cartoons, and fashion of the day. She had it spread out over the kitchen table poring over info many people never considered or sought out.

Virgil texted his dad back: I'm in West Allis. Are you okay?

Earl: I'm fine. You need to get home.

Virgil: I'm committed to a job here tomorrow and Tuesday.

Earl: Be here Wednesday or Thursday.

Virgil: Thursday it is.

Virgil wasn't satisfied with texting so he called his dad. "Dad, what is going on?" he asked when Earl answered.

"You better sit down," Earl said.

Virgil didn't like his dad's tone and quickly sat on the sofa. "Give it to me straight, Dad," Virgil requested.

"First of all, Ernie died this morning."

"Why didn't you tell me that earlier?" Virgil asked, feeling his stomach getting upset.

"It was after I talked to you that Sylvia called. She said it was a heart attack. She said he was sitting in his easy chair drinking coffee. She went to the kitchen for something and when she came back his cup was on the floor and he was slumped over to his right side."

"God I'm sorry, Dad. I know how close you two were. How's Sylvia?"

"She's doing alright. Seemed shocked but not all that upset," Earl explained.

"That seems odd," Virgil mentioned. "I always thought they were head over heels in love."

"When we were down South I saw a different version of their relationship, but I didn't give it much thought because we were doing so much running around and were tired much of the time."

"You think it was a heart attack?" Virgil asked.

"I have to believe her unless I get different information."

"Not to change the subject, but did you ever hear back from Harmon?"

"He says we are all good to go," Earl said, "Except for Ernie."

"You okay, Dad?"

"I'll be better Thursday when you're home," he admitted. "I think there's a six pack in the fridge with my name on it."

"Enjoy it and toast Ernie when you open each one," Virgil suggested. "I'll be home on Thursday at the latest, maybe Wednesday."

"Good, I miss you son," Earl said, beginning to choke up.

"I'll get home as quickly as possible," Virgil assured him.

Earl thanked his son then hung up. Virgil stood and walked to the far end of the living room. He turned around and standing next to the sofa was Megan.

"What's going on, Virgil?" she asked.

He explained the news to her, and she came to him and hugged him, putting her arms around his waist at first then raised them to his back while resting her head on his chest. "I'm sorry, Virgil."

"Thanks, Meg," he said, returning the caress by rubbing her back.

They stood there for a few minutes in silence just holding each other. "I will go to Chase Products tomorrow and see if I can go home on Tuesday," Virgil said, breaking the silence.

"No, you are wrong Virgil," Megan said, stepping back from him and looking him in the eyes, "You tell them you have to go on Tuesday because your father needs you."

"You're right," Virgil agreed, then pulled her close to him again. "I have to let Mark and Diane know."

Megan let go of Virgil and headed to the kitchen, "I'll let my mom know what's going on and that I might go with you."

Virgil called Mark and broke the news. "We can go over there now if you want," Mark offered.

"He actually needs to be alone tonight," Virgil informed him. "I plan on being there Tuesday."

"Sorry to hear all of this, buddy," Mark said. "By the way I went on the business account just to check some things and that account topped at a million dollars."

"I'll be damned," Virgil said, "I thought we were done getting anymore."

"Me too."

"We'll talk on Tuesday one way or another," Virgil said then hung up.

The night was a restless one for Virgil. A new house and different bed, plus the concern for his father and the day he faced at Chase the next day. All that weighed on his mind. He and Megan had decided on separate bedrooms so he tossed and turned without bothering her. Harriet and Megan were making breakfast when Virgil came into the kitchen after his shower. "I appreciate this, but it's not needed," Virgil said as he pulled up a chair to the kitchen table.

"Who said this is for you?" Harriet quipped.

Virgil laughed, "Good one."

Megan set a plate in front of him, and Harriet quickly filled it with scrambled eggs and bacon. "Sorry to hear about your dad's friend," Harriet said as she served him. She patted him on his shoulder.

"Thank you," Virgil said, patting her hand in return. "Ernie was a good man."

Megan dropped a piece of buttered toast on his plate as well then kissed Virgil on the side of his head. "You need to have a good start to your day," Megan said.

Anxious to get to work and have that situation settled, Virgil ate quickly. He made it to work in twenty minutes. John was waiting for him.

"Have a good birthday weekend?"

"How did you know it was my birthday?" Virgil asked.

"I was looking over the contract we want you to sign and it had a job application attached to it with your birthdate on it. We had that from the info you gave us when you first started doing business with us," John explained.

Virgil smiled, "It was a good weekend, thanks."

"I want you to check over the lines and those machines and see if there is any fine tuning we can do," John informed him, "Then we can look over the contract and see if you agree."

"Sounds good," Virgil said. "I also have a bit of a problem with my dad back home. I need to talk over with you."

"That's fine," John agreed.

Virgil teamed up with Bill from the automation group in the shop to bounce ideas off each other. They were able to speed the line up by a second and a half which doesn't sound like much but by the end of the week the output of the line would be significantly higher. Virgil returned to the shop and after lunch he went into John's office to hash over the contract. They were joined by Michelle once again. Virgil pored over the contract, reading the five pages and smiling internally the whole time. He would get the money he wanted and the freedom to maintain his business as long as he spent three full days a week at Chase Products and would be on call during the week as long as he was in West Allis. This he could live with. He explained his situation with his father and Ernie's death and asked permission to leave tomorrow to go home for the rest of the week.

"Chase Products believes in family first," Michelle explained. "If John okays it, then it is fine with us."

"Can you stay until three tomorrow?" John asked.

"That would be great," Virgil said. "I will call you and let you know what's going on."

"I'm good with that," John said, looking at Michelle.

"Then just sign the contract and we should be set," Michelle said, handing Virgil her pen. He did as told, and she rose and held her hand out. Virgil stood and shook her hand. "Welcome to Chase Products," she said, smiling.

"Thank you."

The rest of the day was uneventful, and Virgil drove to Megan's home. When he arrived nobody was home. He parked his van in the street and waited on the front porch, enjoying the sunshine and for this time of the year, the warmth it brought. Twenty minutes later he called Megan. "Where are you guys?" he asked her.

"I'm at work," Megan said as the music pounded in the background. "Remember I told you I had to work tonight."

"That's right, but I can't get in the house," Virgil said.

Megan explained where the spare key was hidden, and Virgil soon let himself in and locked the door behind him. "Where's your mom at?"

"She's probably at the store or one of the neighbors," she explained.

"I see. By the way, I'm going home tomorrow after work."

"I'll see what I can do to come with."

"I'm afraid it's not going to be a fun time, Megan," Virgil explained.

"I don't care, I still want to be there for you. I want to meet your dad too."

Virgil wasn't sure how to respond to her comment. He had never had a woman that committed to him before. He knew for sure she was special. "Thank you for that."

"We'll talk tonight, I'm on until nine," Megan said. "Love you."

"I love you, too."

Back Home

Megan accompanied Virgil to his boyhood home in South Elgin though she needed to return to West Allis by Saturday. She had arranged to work only part time at Benny's. It would be three days a week with one of those being on the weekend. It was a requirement. Virgil told her to just quit her job and he would support her. It was the main topic during the hour and a half trip to Illinois which Megan hadn't been to in six years. She loved the idea but felt she wasn't ready to take that step. Besides, she felt emboldened in the fact she had negotiated a deal where she worked the least amount of time and made the most for her efforts. She was a great bartender with a personality that befriended most of the patrons. By the time they arrived at 1248 Raymond Street there were only compliments and support from Virgil.

They entered the house through the back door and found Earl sitting at the kitchen table looking at a letter. "Dad, I have someone I would like you to meet," Virgil said as they entered the room. "This is Megan Peterson. Megan, this is my dad Earl."

Earl rose from his chair and hugged Megan when he reached her. Megan returned the affection, "So nice to meet you Mister Ditch."

"Please, call me Earl."

Megan smiled, "Earl it is."

Virgil stepped forward and hugged his father, "I'm sorry about Ernie, Dad.

Megan stepped to the side but patted Earl on his back which was now turned in her direction, "Me as well Earl."

"Thank you, guys," Earl said, squeezing his son. "You know, Ernie and I had our differences, but he was still my best friend," Earl said, now stepping back towards the table where he grabbed the letter he had been reading. "And now this," he said, handing it to Virgil, then walking to the fridge.

"I'll leave you two alone," Megan offered, then looked at Virgil. "Where is your bedroom? I'll put things away."

"Down the hall, last room on the right, Meg...and thanks," Virgil said while poring over the letter.

Virgil looked at the signature first. It was Ernie's full name with a notary seal below it. In the letter Ernie explained what Earl and Virgil would have never guessed possible. It would cancel any plans that had been made the past weekend. Astounded, Virgil had to read the letter twice.

"Dad, I can't believe this is real."

"Oh, I believe it is," Earl countered.

"Did you call Sylvia?"

"Only to console her. This came the day after her and I talked," Earl explained, opening the fridge and grabbing a beer. "You want one?" he asked, holding one in the air for Virgil to see.

"Didn't finish the six pack the other night, Dad?"

"Got that fucking letter, I went out and bought a case."

"Dad, I'm sorry," Virgil said, taking the Miller Lite. "How do you know it's real?"

"Because it mentions the affair Sylvia and Harmon were having, I heard them arguing about it when we were down south."

"I see that, but you said Ernie died of a heart attack, not from the vaccine or an illness."

"There is something in that vaccine that killed him and will kill me as well," Earl said, twisting the cap off his beer and taking a swig.

"They said it was a heart attack."

"Come on, Virgil. You believe that shit, and Tommy Kalsow killed himself. Come on." Earl leaned against the counter, tilted his head back and drank half of the fine pilsner.

Virgil took a healthy gulp of his and sat down at the table with the letter still in his hand. He set it on the table, slid his jacket off and draped it over the chair next to him, then grabbed Ernie's findings again. "But how did he know all of this?" Virgil asked.

"Ernie knew a lot of people, Virgil. He did favors for politicians, which were all legal, and they recommended him to others as well. Hell, he did some construction work for Governor Fat Ass."

"So he had inside information about all of this?"

"To a certain point."

"Did he tell you about this when we stayed out there?"

"Yes," Earl said, tilting his head back and finishing the beer. He opened the fridge and grabbed another bottle.

Megan reentered the kitchen. "I need some water, or something to drink," she mentioned.

Earl twisted the cap off his next brew and handed it to her. "Will this do?" he asked.

"Works for me," Megan said then asked, "Am I allowed out here or do you two need more time?"

"Virgil can answer that one," Earl said, grabbing a bottle for himself.

Virgil had stood, turned, and was now looking out the window at the backyard, mulling over the revelations in Ernie's letter. He didn't respond, he just stared. Those above fifty-five will probably die from either the virus or the vaccine. Ernie had overheard Harmon tell Sylvia that when they thought he was asleep. This meant Harriet Peterson was at risk, like Earl. "You need to read this, Meg." Virgil said, holding the letter out to her as he turned again to take his seat, "Hey Dad, who's playing god in all of this?"

"I suspect it starts with those two assholes you met at that bar up in Wisconsin," Earl said, taking a sip from his bottle.

"You think so?"

"Yeah, Sylvia was talking with Gustav many times and on occasion Ivan. And for sure Harmon. I heard that shit myself," Earl adamantly stated.

"Why is it that we all know some of the same people?" Megan asked as she pulled out a chair opposite Virgil and sat down. She slowly took the letter from him.

"Good point, Megan," Earl said, joining them at the table to her right. He set his beer on the table and leaned back into his chair, raising his arms above him in a stretching motion. He was glad Virgil was home. He was even happier that his son had found Megan, knowing he deserved a woman in his life for a change. Virgil had never known his mother and that fact always saddened Earl. In time he had sought other women after becoming a widower. But he had never found a match, and that was his personal sadness. "You know I don't trust our government at times, but I would die defending this country. Now this administration is doing this shit," Earl offered.

"To what purpose, though?" Virgil asked.

"Sometimes I think it's because they can," Earl said. "But then I pray and hope none of it is true."

Megan threw the letter down on the table towards Earl, "Reading that I would say it's population control."

Earl was shaking his head in agreement, "I thought that too."

"Those fuckers are killing who they want," Megan said, raising her voice.

"Easy now, guys," Virgil said. "Let's think about this."

"Virgil, they're killing our parents and whoever else they want. This world we are wrecking can only have so many people. I've always expected it, but they already know it," Megan stated.

"Amen, Megan," Earl said, raising his bottle in a salute. "I agree. We need to kill the assholes."

"I like how you think, Earl," Megan said, high fiving her confirmation by swigging her beer.

"We need to meet with Ivan and Gustav again," Virgil suggested. "You know eliminate that element."

"Can't think of a better place than Benny's on a Saturday night," Megan suggested. "This weekend there's a band playing and there will be a good crowd."

"Wait a minute," Virgil said, standing and pacing about the kitchen, "I'm not sure I can kill someone. I'm not sure it's necessary."

Megan and Earl looked at each other, then at Virgil, "I'll pull the trigger myself," Megan said.

"If you can't I will," Earl stated.

Virgil stopped in the middle of the kitchen. "What then Dad?" he asked, looking at Earl. "The government would be all over it." He then looked at Megan, "No matter who pulls the trigger."

"If my mom dies from this Virgil, somebody is going to pay," Megan said. "And according to the letter your father is at risk as well."

"Believe me I want revenge on these bastards too but I'm not sure this is the way," Virgil said, opening the fridge and grabbing three more beers. He set a bottle in front of Megan and his dad then sat down at the table again with his own.

They sat in silence, drinking their beer and thinking about what to do.

"What's for dinner, Dad?" Virgil asked in an effort to ease the situation.

"Let's order a pizza or we can call Portillo's and order something from them," Earl said, then rose and retrieved menus for both places and set them on the table.

Megan grabbed the Portillo's menu and scanned over it. "Their roast beef any good?" she asked, catching Virgil's cue.

"It's my favorite," Earl quickly chimed in. "I'll even make the order."

"Make it three beefs, but make sure you get the peppers," Virgil requested. He looked at Earl and Megan, then began to laugh. He kept looking at both of them and his laughter became heartier.

Earl looked at Megan, "Have you ever noticed he has a weird sense of humor?"

Megan laughed, "Yes, I have witnessed it." She said looking at Virgil, "What is so funny at a time like this?"

"Is this how you always act after three beers?" Earl asked, joining the jousting.

Virgil's hilarity eased, "Sorry, but one minute we're talking about killing two people and the next we're ordering from Portillo's."

"I'll still kill the fuckers, but I'll do it on a full stomach," Earl said with a stoic tone that matched his look.

Now Megan started laughing and Virgil joined her. They looked at each other and laughed harder.

"A man's gotta eat," Earl said, smiling, "Believe me though, I will pull the trigger."

Virgil knew his father wasn't bluffing and he slowly quit laughing while still looking at Megan. "You can do it for you and Harriet," Virgil said.

"Who's Harriet?" Earl asked.

"My mother," Megan said. "She had the same shot you did and she's sixty-one."

"Sorry to hear that," Earl replied. "At least she has a chance."

"But she is over fifty-five," Megan reminded them.

"It's not an exact science, Meg," Virgil offered. "Harriet could survive all of this."

"I'd still kill those guys for your dad's sake."

"And that's why I love you," Virgil said. "But we have to think about the consequences when we decide to do something."

Earl and Virgil attended Ernie's memorial on that Thursday. They consoled and talked with Sylvia after it and asked her to give them Gustav's cell number. She was reluctant at first, but Virgil said he was ready to have the blood work done to see if his RNA was a good basis for a vaccine. She couldn't tell them she already knew it was, so she relented and gave them the number. Virgil was never able to make contact with the men who had started all of this but left a message via text as to when they would be at Benny's. Megan remained at the house not wanting to attend a funeral for someone whom she didn't know. She spent much of her time talking with her mother. She couldn't bring herself to tell Harriet what they had found out in Ernie's manifest. Her mother was feeling great and there was no need to alarm her. Megan watched the news and took note that as it had gotten cooler in the south the Chung virus had waned, though fatalities were still prevalent. Mississippi was oddly enough seeing an uptick in cases. Megan researched it further and found out it was the leader in vaccinations in the south. She looked at the age breakdown of the cases reported, eighty-seven percent were over sixty-five and only ten percent were under sixty.

Benny's On a Saturday Night

Earl had insisted on coming to Wisconsin with his son and driving his car. Virgil agreed but only if he was the one who did the driving. Earl relented but only after referring to the wild ride they had taken when they had made their escape. "Noted," Virgil said and they left shortly after lunch. Megan had left with her car in the morning. During their drive up Virgil insisted that his father remain at Harriet's when he went to Benny's later that day. He somehow got his point across without telling his dad it was a young man's fight. Earl in agreement said, "If you get the upper hand on those bastards though, give them a shot for me, Ernie, and Megan's mom."

To this Virgil pledged his compliance as they arrived at Harriet's home. "You can't tell Harriet about any of this," Virgil said as they walked up the driveway to the door. He knocked on the inside wooden door then stepped in. "We're here Harriet," he called out, then looked back at Earl who was nodding his head in affirmation to his son's request.

"I'm in the living room," she called back.

Virgil introduced his father as they entered the room and Harriet rose from her favorite recliner to greet him. They shook hands when their steps ceased and they were face to face. They stared. It was as if they had met before, but both knew they hadn't. It was a connection neither had counted on, though both welcomed. "I'm going to leave you two here and head to Benny's," Virgil said, walking towards his bedroom.

"You go ahead, son," Earl said, then looked at Virgil and smiled. "We'll stay here and talk."

"Easy, Dad," Virgil said, stopping and watching the pair holding hands. "Remember what we talked about."

"Hey Virgil," Harriet said, looking past Earl's shoulder. "Where's my rose?"

"Sorry, Harriet, I'll have to bring two next time."

"I'll forgive you this time," Harriet said, looking at Earl then back at Virgil, smiling, "Sometimes we need more than flowers."

"Do I have to stay here with you two?" Virgil asked, smiling.

"Have a good time, Virgil," Earl said. "We'll behave ourselves."

"I'm counting on it," Virgil said, then continued to his bedroom and dropped what he didn't need. He came back into the living room to see Harriet and Earl patting each other on their backs, then separating, each taking a recliner. Virgil left through the kitchen, feeling maybe this night might turn out alright or crazier than what he had already experienced.

On route to Benny's, Virgil realized there was no plan he was counting on or could remember. He and Megan had met with Mark and Diane at their house west of town yesterday. Recently time seemed to fly by, and he just couldn't think of any concrete plans they had made. He also started feeling some of the symptoms he had felt shortly after his confrontation with the bearded boys at his cabin. He was tiring, and though able to drive, he felt maybe he really shouldn't be. Fortunately it was a short trip to the bar which was featuring a band calling themselves Deception.

When he arrived unscathed, he perked up, knowing he was getting to see Megan again. She would be working, like the night he first met her. A flash of memory sent an image of her swirling blondish hair flowing and that beautiful body dancing about the bar. Then another one from Mark and Diane's reminded him to be careful of what he would be drinking. He would stick with Smithwick's, he remembered telling everyone. He wasn't sure where these thoughts were coming from; he just wanted to see Megan again and feel better. He found a parking spot in the rear lot. Before exiting the car, he scanned the lot looking for a black Escalade, seeing none he took a deep breath, exhaled, and got out. He walked around the side of the building, looking in all directions and finally making it to the front. There was a black van at the curb but not the ride of choice for the twins. He entered the bar to the double doors where Jeff sat perched on his tall stool. The crowd hadn't arrived yet for the entertainment, but he appeared on high alert.

"She's not here," Jeff said. "And it's ten bucks at the door tonight."

"I know she had to work tonight," Virgil said, handing the thirty-year-old weightlifter and shotput record holder at a nearby high school a twenty. "Keep it."

Jeff grabbed the green Jackson and Virgil by the arm, pocketing the bill with his left hand and pulling him closer with the stronger other. "I've got something for you," Jeff whispered into Virgil's right ear, then transferred a tube from his left palm to Virgil's left. "Put this in your pocket, but don't bend it or it will break. Give it to your love," Jeff said, pulling Virgil past him and through the double doors to his right.

Virgil entered the bar area and saw Megan immediately and felt some relief from what had just happened but averted locking eyes with her. As he glanced at her he tried to remember what part of the plan made this a covert action. He walked away from the bar to the other side of the room near a pool table where a young man and his girl were attempting to play, through their laughter. He took a quick look at the present Jeff had given him. It was a vial with a clear liquid in it. He had no idea what it might be, or what it was for. He tried to think back to the meeting with Mark and Diane. He was drawing blanks. He put it in the inside pocket of his jacket next to a glove for protection.

"Hey, it's Virgil," a voice suddenly blurted out loudly in his direction. It was from the young man playing pool.

Virgil looked at them shocked at first, but then remembered the couple from another time he was here. It was someone he had a run in with. "I know you," Virgil shot back.

"Yeah, you're the guy who cut in front of us when we saw Virus here," the girl said, jumping in next to her man.

"You're Billy and Barb," Virgil said, remembering the incident. "I bought you guys some drinks that night, remember?"

"Yeah, then you left with the bartender," Billy said.

"Ever take that bartender out?" Barb asked almost accusingly.

"Yes, I did, and we're doing just fine."

"That's great," Billy said. "And so are we." He then turned back to the pool table that had seen better days and lined up his next shot.

"See ya around, Virgil," Barb said, blowing him a kiss then turned to join her boyfriend.

Virgil patted the vial through his jacket and headed towards the bar. He found the same stool he sat on the Wednesday he met Ivan and Gustav before their trip and confrontation up north. He spun to face the bar, hoping to see a sweet, blond-haired woman behind it. She wasn't there. Virgil panicked for just a second then remembered from his past visits that it wasn't uncommon for her to disappear from behind the bar through the course of an evening. She was probably telling another employee what was needed at the bar and they were to get it. That's how things ran smoothly at Benny's. Especially when Megan was in charge of the bar.

"What can I get you?" a tall, large black man asked him.

"A Smithwick's," Virgil said, staring at and in awe of his size.

"A what?" the question boomed back at him.

"Smithwick's is on the label, but it is pronounced Smiticks," Virgil explained, spelling out each pronunciation.

"I got it," the bartender said, now standing fully upright, impressing Virgil even more with his size. "I'll get it."

"And those two playing pool across the room, get them whatever they're drinking," Virgil said, pointing in the direction of the young couple.

"I will take care of them too," the bartender said before turning and walking away.

Virgil looked about the room. It was only five-thirty in the afternoon, and the dinner and a movie crowd was predominant. Younger blue-collar couples eating within their budgets and enjoying the best burger in the area. Many seemed to be celebrating a night out. There was a vibe. Virgil ordered a mushroom Swiss burger when the bartender returned with his beer. "Where did Megan go?" Virgil asked.

"She had to step out for a minute," he said. "She told me to take care of you." He held out his right hand. "By the way my name is Herron."

Virgil shook hands, watching his disappear into Herron's massive palm. "Thank you, Herron." Virgil said, feeling a little better about the night, knowing guys like Jeff and Herron were on their side emboldened him a bit. He could still handle himself pretty well at forty-eight, but it was nice to have some young blood on the team. Still, he was uneasy he hadn't seen Megan since he had conversed with Barb and Billy playing eight ball. He looked around the room again and thought he saw her towards the rear of the room but after a second glance, realized it wasn't her. He was getting worried about Megan's absence. He turned back to the bar, watching Herron filling the trays with drinks for the two waitresses. He felt someone bump into him from behind.

He turned, expecting to see a man with a beard. A younger woman wearing a long tan colored leather coat and large tinted glasses was tending to her wavy brown hair and facing him.

"I'm sorry, did I bother you?" the lady asked Virgil as if the bother was his fault.

"No, you're fine," Virgil responded with a smile.

"I heard you had something for me," she said with a smile, then seductively, "I know I have something for you."

Virgil leaned back, "Do I know you?"

"You better," she said leaning towards him. "Your dad is at my mom's house."

Virgil looked around the room again, reaching inside his jacket to retrieve the vial. He fumbled for a minute then folded his hand over, pulled it out and dropped it into her coat pocket. "I don't remember this part of the plan."

"Just be yourself and play along," Megan aka Sara whispered into Virgil's ear when he had leaned forward enough.

"How am I supposed to meet the twins?" Virgil asked her.

"They have agreed to meet with your team of people," Megan explained,

Virgil was coming up blank, trying to remember how Megan's disguise played into any plan they had agreed to with Mark and Diane and what team? In fact, the only part he could recollect was that they were going to meet Ivan and Gustav at some point this evening. Sylvia had made sure it would happen when Earl told her they were only able to leave messages on the number she had given them. She assured Earl the Peprovs would be there by eight. Virgil looked about the bar again, wondering if Sylvia might be coming as well. Ernie's letter convinced both he and Earl that she was not someone to be trusted and Ernie had actually apologized for the fact that he had been fooled by her charade. The burger was set on the bar and Virgil turned around on his stool, ignoring Sara as he did. He picked up the sandwich and took a healthy bite followed by a taste of his beer. He glanced to his right and Sara was gone. He ate the burger slowly, occasionally scanning the room for anyone else he might recognize. So far there were none. Just be yourself, Sara had said. He realized it was a plan he could follow. So far the symptoms he felt earlier had subsided and after the loaded burger he felt stronger. He washed it down with his red ale.

He went to the bathroom and when he returned his new bartender was Megan. "Bout time you showed up," Virgil said to her when she got within distance.

She glanced at him without a smile. "Sorry, I was busy," she said, setting another bottle of his favorite brew on the bar, then moved in close enough to quickly kiss his cheek. She turned away and continued doing her job.

Virgil smiled, grabbed his red and white labeled bottle of beer then turned his back to the bar. He was waiting for something to happen. The tuning of the guitars for the band on the dimly lit stage was a pleasant distraction, but not what he needed. As he waited he finished the fries that had accompanied the burger. Time was crawling. How would this plan he couldn't remember ever happen? He got up and walked about the bar, leaving his jacket on the stool in order to claim it when he returned. He headed to the back of the room when he heard the ringtone from his phone. It was John from Chase. "What's up, John?" Virgil asked with his left index finger pressed in his left ear.

"Machine 110 is slowing down by two seconds on the cycle," John explained. "I've looked at the obvious, oil temp, ejection time, injection time, and the barrel heats. I don't see anything that stands out."

"Let me think for a minute," Virgil said, moving to the corner of the bar where he had first met the bearded duo. "Are you by the machine?"

"I'll be there in five minutes."

"Can you do zoom on your phone?"

"I'll set it up when I get there," John said then hung up.

John made the necessary connections and Virgil was looking at machine 110's monitor ten minutes later. He had his back to the bar so he could concentrate on the task at hand. He instructed John to bring up various screen numbers to look at the performance of the pump and valves that ran the machine. He had John tweak some values on each page and soon the cycle was where they required it to be. "Has anyone been messing with those numbers?" he asked his boss, not sure where the machine was failing, or going to fail.

"Not that I know of," John replied.

"Just in case let's change the password so nobody can get to that level except you and me."

"I was going to suggest that," John said, navigating to the page where he could perform that task. "I'll change it and text it to you so you have it on your phone."

"Great idea, John," Virgil said. "So we're good?"

"Yes, enjoy the rest of your weekend."

It was around a half-hour later when he returned to his stool. He scanned the room again and noticed Mark and Diane sitting at a table in the middle of the room facing the stage. He was sure it was them for the familiar mannerisms he had witnessed many times. Mark's habit was looking at his glass of beer for any foreign objects. He was doing it now. Diane would smell everything before she bit into it. She did it now before taking a bite out of her club sandwich. Their shape and sizes were the same, but their look was askew. Diane had long blond hair and Virgil knew she was a brunette. Mark wore a cap you would only wear while driving a British sports car. Its color was a mix of earth tone with a tartan pattern. Mark was also wearing a matching full length topcoat. Virgil laughed, thinking God only knows what is under there. He laughed again, just be yourself he reminded himself. This must be the part of the plan you're not privileged to. They must be the team Megan aka Sara spoke of. But what was his role, Virgil wondered.

A Deception band member called Satch, but whose real name was Walter Gunn, entered through the flimsy grayish stage curtain. He carried a dining room chair in his left hand and his guitar in the other. He placed the tall back chair with a wider seat at the center of the stage. A roadie quickly came forward and positioned a microphone stand in front of the now seated Satch. The mic was live, and you could hear Satch strumming his six string as he thanked the roadie, Jake, for his assistance.

"I'm Satch," he said to scattered applause in the room, "I'm with Deception but wanted to come out and try out a new song. Hope you don't mind." The applause grew in strength as he took a deep breath and leaned into the back of his chair. "This one is called "Inherent" because we all have something essential in life, something we need to make our lives work for us." He started out slowly picking notes and strumming chords on the Doc Martin six string. Then he sang the words of the song he had recently written. His deeper voice boomed out the lyrics with feeling. It wasn't just made up, it was a personal experience.

Youth is inherent
Means the time
Has come to take
Your turn in life

Had my chance,
Missed many clues

Those with potential
Now inconsequential

But, I wouldn't
Trade away the
Life I've known
For just anybody

So, it was you
That cold night who
Brought warmth and
Smiles to my face

Eyes locked on
Each other at a
Friend's house
A future beginning

Perfect doesn't exist
But that night
Came so close
You even drove me home

What we've done
Where we've been
Brought us here
As always, together

Our age is inherent
Another phase of
This life remaining
Pleasant times we pray

An inherent life
Of the choices and
Savored results, shared
With those we love

The applause started slowly when Satch finished, but as he rose from the chair, it became louder with shouts and whistles of approval filling the venue. He bowed to the audience, then took the chair and vanished behind the curtain though cries of, "encore and more," could be heard in the rear of the room where the rest of the band stood and cheered. Virgil clapped his approval as well. He hadn't heard a song like that or performed like that in a long time. John Prine was better, but Satch would have been welcomed by Virgil's favorite artist.

He turned towards the bar and Herron was once again making the drinks and taking care of the patrons. Megan was gone. Virgil looked about the room for her or her alter ego, Sara. He turned back to face Herron standing in front of him. "What's going on, Herron?"

"I'm told they're here," he said with both hands resting on the bar and leaning his imposing stature towards Virgil so he could be heard with little volume to his baritone voice.

"Who's they?" Virgil asked, holding his spot on the stool.

"The one's you've been waiting for," Herron calmly replied. "I hear you guys call them the twins."

Virgil slowly turned on his stool and looked in the direction of the front door. People were pushing their way in to get the best possible seats for the show. He saw some bearded men entering, but it wasn't them. He focused on the entryway for ten minutes before he thought of scanning the room again. He looked at the perimeter, thinking they may have entered by another door. They weren't there either. He took a quick look at the table Mark and Diane were seated at, then looked away, then back again. He couldn't believe what he was seeing. He felt a tap on his shoulder. He turned and Herron was still there. "You, ready to go to work?" he asked.

"Doing what?"

"Being yourself and serving that table in the middle," Herron said,

"They ordered two vodkas, a beer, and two glasses of wine."

"What?" Virgil shouted.

"Your role is to be the waiter that serves that table," Herron said, leaning towards Virgil.

Virgil looked back at the table again. It was definitely Ivan and Gustav sitting with Mark, Diane, and Sara or Megan. He couldn't imagine what roles Mark and Diane were now playing in this. Was I asleep when we made these plans, Virgil thought then turned again towards Herron. "They will know my voice," Virgil said in a tone that suggested this plan would never work.

"Just go put this on and come back here and get the drinks," Herron said, handing him a Benny's shirt, apron, and name tag that read Kurt.

Virgil took the items and headed to the bathroom. He found a stall in the near empty room and changed into his disguise. In the apron were a pair of glasses and a fake mustache along with a picture of him with them on. He now realized he didn't know any of this plan. After adjusting his mustache in front of the mirror he made his way back to the bar. It was getting crowded. Maybe the shot he received up North did other damage, he considered on his way back. Just be your new self and keep your discipline, he convinced himself. His new boss was waiting with an anxious look on his face. "We need to get these drinks to table one," Herron yelled over the house music now blaring to pump up the crowd.

"How do I disguise my voice?" Virgil asked, looking at the tray.

"Take the drinks over there and serve them, don't say a word and just nod," Herron explained. "But do it now."

He took the tray and put it in the palm of his right hand with his left hovering about to prevent the chance of spilling its contents. He looked at his anxious boss. "I have my own pace," he yelled back at the man who had been on the Green Bay Packer's practice squad trying to make the team or catch a break. This job was a go-between which he actually liked, but knew it wasn't a career. The crowd had grown as Deception would soon start their show. Navigating through it was a challenge but Virgil made it to the table. Sara smiled at him as he approached their table.

"You finally got here," she scolded. "I thought you were stomping the grapes to make this wine." She laughed, sarcastically in her role, nodding at Mark and Diane as well as at the twins.

"Sorry, it has become busy," Virgil, aka Kurt said with a Germanic tone. He placed the white wine in front of Sara, wondering why he had opened his mouth, but thinking he had covered pretty well. He silently distributed the rest of the drinks, Diane being the next to get hers. He gave Mark his beer, then turned to Ivan and Gustav, placing their vodkas in front of them, avoiding their eyes the whole time. He turned to leave.

"Hey Kurt," Ivan called to his waiter.

"Yes?" Virgil stopped and turned back, then replied in character, "What do you require?"

"You are the first one in here that ever got our drinks right," Ivan said, holding up his glass of vodka and ice. Gustav raised his pure glass of vodka in salute as well.

Virgil felt his mustache slipping, nodded, and turned away, mumbling incoherently as he left. He returned to the bar and Herron was laughing as he approached. "What are you laughing at?" Virgil said in his newly discovered voice.

That made Herron laugh harder, slapping his hand on the bar top. "You were great," he said now just chuckling, "Relax, the show is about to begin." Herron nodded at the stage. "Just give me the apron , name tag, and glasses. The shirt you can keep." The house lights flickered on and off to advise people to find a seat or somewhere to stand. "Two minutes," a voice announced the ultimatum over the PA. Two minutes later the lights were off.

Virgil quickly removed his disguise and handed the items to his boss. His Kurt persona would no longer exist, name tag and all. He could still hear his large mentor laughing behind him. As the lights came back on he turned to face him. He was gone. What the hell, Virgil thought, he was just there. He finished straightening his shirt and was tucking it in when the emcee walked to the microphone.

He started to feel nauseous. He sat on his stool and leaned on the bar looking up the length of it for anyone he might recognize. He spotted Don. He was the one whom Virgil had thrown two twenty-dollar bills to when he tried to leave Benny's the night the Peprovs first made contact. He waved at Don but to no avail. He turned again to face the stage. "Ladies and gentleman, it's my honor to introduce Deception," the same woman who had handled these duties the last time Virgil had seen a show here, said.

This time though her hair was blue with pink streaks in it.

The group entered through the curtain as it was opening. The front men took their time moving forward to the microphones awaiting them. A drummer, violinist, and two back-up singers completed the ensemble behind them, moving into their positions. The group teased the crowd with individual tuning and familiar chords within songs. Virgil looked towards the table he had just served. The lighting was dim in that area, and he only saw silhouettes of people. As they seemed to move he tried to remember the position of any of them. The music began slowly:

Let's play a game
Called life, where
We all exist
Like minded

Destruction of
Each other's ideas
Doesn't exist
Or consumes us

We still complete
Our lives, but
We get to live
Them our way

Satch sang the opening song to many cheers and applause.

Virgil realized he better get to the bathroom and grabbed his jacket off the barstool and headed in that direction. He made it, but all the stalls were occupied so he took the swinging lid off the waste can, dropped it on the floor under the sink, walked to the back corner, and heaved into the receptacle two times. He leaned against the wall to rest, then looked about the room when he saw Mark enter. Virgil carried the can back to its original position, intentionally bumping into his accountant. "Excuse me," Virgil said, looking at Mark to make sure he noticed him, then picked up the lid and put it on top of the container.

"You got a problem," Mark asked.

"What?" Virgil asked as he put the waste can back into its original place.

"You want to take this outside," Mark asked a little louder.

"What?" Virgil asked again, knowing he just had to go along with whatever it was his buddy had planned.

"I didn't stutter, pal," he shot back, then leaned towards Virgil. "Play along," Mark whispered then pushed Virgil back with his shoulder. "You wanna go?"

"I apologized, alright," Virgil said, grabbing a paper towel and wiping his mouth.

"Yeah, but it was intentional, and I don't like that."

"Deal with it," Virgil said, throwing the towel into the can.

"Why don't you two pussies get a room?" a tall lanky guy wearing torn jeans, an ACDC tee shirt, and a blue ball cap on backwards bumped into and through both of them then stopped at the sink.

Virgil and Mark looked at each other, smiling and nodding already knowing what they would do. "He's just pissed off because he came here on the wrong night," Mark said, referring to the hard rock fan to Virgil with enough volume the man at the sink had to hear the comment.

"He'll get over it like you need to get over it," Virgil said, aiding the ruse.

"Ours is going outside pal," Mark upped his volume.

The lanky man grabbed a paper towel, wiped his hands then threw it in the direction of the waste can, knowing he would miss his target and not caring. "You two homos need to get a room," he said, pushing his arms out in front of him to make a path between the two acting combatants.

Mark and Virgil had performed this maneuver maybe three times prior to this night. They had never really hurt anyone, only the dignity of their foe and that was repairable. Mark's left fist found the man's stomach with an upward thrust while Virgil gave a right clenched backhand to the genitals of the smartass. His blue hat popped off his head and landed in the sink as he crumpled to the floor. He would be alright, Mark and Virgil knew it. They bumped shoulders as they left the bathroom of Benny's, took a left, and exited the way Virgil had intended the first time he met the Peprovs.

Mark led the way. They navigated past some women waiting in line for their bathroom, then out the side exit. The green steel door was closer to the back parking lot where Earl's Impala was parked.

"What the hell is going on?" Virgil asked his leader and best friend.

Mark looked around, tugging at his sporty hat. The lot was full of cars but nobody had missed the opening number of Deception so no one was walking around. "You don't remember the plan?" he asked, now tapping the top of his hat.

"I really don't," Virgil admitted. "I'm just being myself."

"That was the plan," Mark said, looking at Virgil while still tapping his hat.

Virgil wasn't quite sure what was happening or how he might survive it all. Hell, he didn't even know the plan. He recalled being able to continue his business while agreeing to work with another company. That was a fact, then why couldn't he remember this plan they had somehow agreed to just yesterday, he wondered. At times he wasn't even sure what the truth was about any of this. At this moment he was even questioning the use of disguises. He leaned against the wall of Benny's, trying to sort this all out. He wondered if the media was embellishing facts that weren't confirmed, like during Covid. It was a common theme these days. Throw out an idea.

Get enough to say it's true, then guess what, it's true even if it wasn't. Maybe that's the way our government wanted it, he thought, suddenly feeling faint. He looked at his disguised friend waving his hat now above his head, "What the hell are you doing?"

Mark stopped waving his cap, "Right now?" he asked, staring at Virgil.

"Yes, right now," Virgil said, staring back and for some reason feeling his strength dissipating.

"I'm probably saving your life," Mark replied.

The Cabin

A Day Later

Virgil awoke, wondering where he was at. He looked at the ceiling constructed of pine logs and thought it looked familiar but wasn't sure. He felt weak as he tried to sit up and look about the room. He settled for leaning on his right elbow to survey his confines. There was a large, curtained window at the other end, and he knew he had to open it. He pulled his legs over the side of the bed and pushed off the mattress to bring the other half of him to an upright sitting position. The blankets from the bed had followed his motions and he pushed them aside and slowly rose to his feet. He remembered the last time he felt like this was when Earl had found him in the woods and got him back to their cabin. He felt just as drained but without the wounds. He shuffled his feet forward, testing his balance and strength. The rest of the way he took short steps to reach and brush back the curtains covering the window.

He looked through the glass at bare trees adorned with one or two rogue leaves hanging on. Beyond the sloping land he saw a sunlit body of water with a lone fisherman aboard a Jon boat trying his luck one more time before the actual cold weather set in. This place was somewhere he knew he had been to recently but not sure why.

"You alright?" a woman's voice asked from behind him.

He didn't turn around. He wanted to place the voice while staring at the boat bobbing on the rolling white capped waves.

"Are you alright?" the woman asked again, raising her stronger matter of fact tone.

Virgil knew that voice. It comforted him now, and in many ways had guided him. He watched the fisherman who decided he had had enough and reached for the rope to start his seven and a half horsepower motor. Virgil turned and faced her, knowing the boater would be okay. Megan stood there in black jeans and a maroon sweater. He felt he knew her by sight, but in his state of mind inquired anyway. "Megan?" he asked, then lowered his head into his hands and hid his shame. "What the hell happened to me?"

Megan walked to Virgil, suddenly wiping away tears of her own, "It's me, Virgil." The man she loved had survived this and was hopefully free from all of it. She grabbed his shoulders, shaking them at first in a playful effort to get him out of his funk. Then relented and pulled him towards her. They stood in the middle of the room. Virgil gently wrapped his arms around her at first, then firmly hugged her, making sure she was real.

"Where are we and how did we get here?" Virgil asked, holding the embrace while awaiting an answer. He was in no hurry for a reply but felt Megan squirm in his arms as she pushed against his chest to make some space between them.

She knew she owed Virgil an explanation. Once she was back a few steps she wiped her cheeks with the heel of her hands. "This is your cabin, Virgil. We're in northern Wisconsin. We got here yesterday. Today is Sunday," she explained, then asked, "Do you understand me?"

Virgil nodded. "Yes, I do. I now know where we are but not sure what is going on, or what happened." As he looked about the room again. He turned and glanced out the window again. The fisherman was moving around a bend to calmer waters. "Are we the only one's here?" he asked, turning to face her again.

"Mark and Diane are downstairs with my mom and your father," Megan informed him.

Virgil knew those mentioned. "What happened to me? I think I was at Benny's and got sick. I remember going to the parking lot with Mark and him for some reason he was waving his hat over his head. After that I woke up here. Did I sleep that entire time?" Virgil stated and inquired.

"You actually got up and went to the bathroom a few times and that was it," she explained. "Mark was signaling the vehicle to pick us up. Diane and I followed you guys out the side exit and you passed out while Mark was waving his hat."

"Okay, but what made me sick?" Virgil asked. He remembered having the burger, steak fries, and a couple Smithwicks at the bar, but that was it.

"Virgil, sit down," Megan said. "There are some things you need to know before we go downstairs."

Virgil slowly walked to the bed and sat on the edge of it. "What things?"

"Do you remember the bartender Herron from that night?" Megan asked.

He thought for a moment. The huge black guy?"

"That's him," Megan confirmed. "Well, he is with the FBI as is the front door man Jeff. The older bartender, Don, used to work on the West Allis police force and knew what was going on with the FBI and was included."

"What was the FBI doing there?"

"They have been watching Gustav and Ivan along with Doctor Harmon, Sylvia, Ernie, then you and Earl and your neighbors across the street."

"For what?" Virgil asked, suddenly standing up and slowly pacing to the window and back.

"You are all connected, but it was the Peprovs we wanted above anything," Megan explained. "Their only interest in you was if you would survive the vaccine."

Virgil stopped pacing. He was looking out the window again. He could see the spot where Earl had found him that day in the wind and rain. He hadn't remembered those two days that week either, he now recalled.

"Have I?" Virgil asked.

"From what I have been told you should be fine," Megan said.

"Okay, so why did they want the twins?"

"For one thing they killed your neighbor Tommy after loading him up with enough of their vaccine that would kill him anyway," Megan explained. "He was full of cancer as well."

Virgil started pacing about the room again, this time at a slightly quicker pace. He stopped by the dresser and stared at his reflection in the mirror mounted on the wall. He had installed it for Megan when she had come here as well as one in the guest bedroom. He didn't remember doing it. Right now he looked at an old man in a black Benny's tee shirt. His hair had a tint of gray and his face was drawn and showing its age. The only thing he recognized was the scar on his cheek. "Are our parents okay?"

"They insisted on helping and coming up here," Megan said. "They are fine."

"How did they help?"

"They drove the getaway car and Mark and Diane followed."

Virgil turned from the mirror and looked at Megan. She was smiling. He chuckled. They knew they were both imagining their only remaining parents as Bonnie and Clyde. "Are they feeling alright? Our parents I mean," he asked.

"Yes, they are," Megan said. "I'm sorry Virgil."

"Sorry for what?" Virgil asked, looking at her and wondering why she might feel that way.

"I wish I could have told you earlier, but that wasn't my part in all of this," she said, stepping back.

"What are you talking about?'

"I was told to keep an eye on you and keep you coming back to Benny's. That was all I had to do," Megan explained as tears followed her confession.

Virgil was stunned. His memories of them together were always good ones as he recalled. The only exception, their last night at Benny's and that had been just odd. He turned and walked to the window again. He could see clouds, dark and ominous, moving across the lake towards them. It would storm soon, he knew. He watched the sudden fall thunderstorm rumbling closer, then spoke louder, "So, you were in on this from the start. I mean, you were working for the FBI?"

"Yes," Megan said, moving closer so Virgil would hear her. She stood in the middle of the room. "They knew Gustav and Ivan were recruiting you and they needed someone close to you."

Rain began to beat against the window, blurring the view of the lake like Virgil's thoughts. He wanted to slam his head through the pane of glass to punish himself for being stupid enough to not catch on to what had transpired between Megan and him. Thinking back, he realized she had connected with him way too easily. He leaned his head against the pane, feeling the beat of the rain. "So, I guess I should actually thank you for staying close to me."

"There's no need for that, Virgil."

The way she said it Virgil felt the distance between them growing larger, "How much did they pay you to be my friend?" Virgil asked, accusingly.

"There's no need for that either," Megan shouted at him in her defense.

Virgil turned and faced her. He smiled and shrugged his shoulders, feeling like he was the butt of a bad joke. He felt humiliated. Not knowing what to say he asked for more facts, "What happens to those involved?'

"You know, Virgil, it wasn't an easy choice for me either," she explained.

"What happens to the others?" Virgil quickly asked again.

Megan hadn't seen this side of Virgil. She doubted he was capable of spite in the little time she had known him. Her tears flowed harder from the sting of his assumptions. "They are probably going to prison. The twins, Harmon, and Sylvia," she informed him through an occasional sob. "Herron and Jeff took the twins away that night at Benny's. The Peprovs were sedated."

"And why the money in my business account?"

"Pure compensation for any losses you may have incurred."

Virgil laughed out loud, "Ha! Guess I know now what my life is worth."

"They were never going to kill you, Virgil," she explained, starting to get perturbed herself. "We were never going to let that happen."

"They sure as hell tried though, didn't they? Almost got my dad right along with me," Virgil offered. "What about Tommy and Ernie?"

"Sylvia injected Ernie with a syringe of air. Ivan shot Tommy to shut him up. He was about to tell your dad about the bad vaccines," Megan informed Virgil, loudly.

"How long have you worked with the FBI?" Virgil snapped back.

"Just over nine years," Megan confirmed, then confessed, "I didn't want to hurt you, Virgil. You have to believe that." She turned away and raised her voice. "I was doing my job," she said. "Until I couldn't anymore."

Virgil felt it, but ignored the last of what she had said. "So what do I do with the money in my account?"

"Anything you want. It's yours to do as you see fit," Megan said, now trying to face him.

Virgil stood in silence for a moment, trying to make sense of all Megan was telling him. "Are our parents going to survive the shot they were given?"

"That is one thing we are not sure of and is the one regret," Megan said, avoiding making eye contact by looking at the floor. "They are not the only ones. Don't forget Ernie's letter."

Virgil walked to the bed and sat down again as a loud clap of thunder exploded in the sky outside. He looked at the window, seeing a flash of lightning, he waited for the next boom. Megan moved closer but remained standing. Virgil sat in silence staring at the floor, listening. The next boom resounded across the lake, echoing through the bare trees. Megan shook at the surprise.

"It's five miles away yet," Virgil said.

"What is?" Megan asked, looking at Virgil.

"The storm is five miles away," Virgil explained. "Count from the time of the lightning to the thunder and that is the distance it is away from you."

"I'll take your word on that," Megan said. "Well, I should probably get out of here and head home," she said. She turned, starting to walk away.

Virgil quickly stood and took her hand. Another flash in the window was immediately followed by the loudest clap of thunder yet. The lights flickered then went out. The noise and darkness startled both of them, and they once again found themselves in an embrace. Virgil held her tight. "You better stay for a while," he suggested.

"For what?" Megan asked, trying to pull away from Virgil.

"Earlier you mentioned you couldn't do your job anymore."

"And you ignored it," Megan reprimanded, standing her ground.

"What did you mean?" Virgil asked.

"I fell in love with you," Megan said, turning her head away.

Virgil now slumped in regret. He hugged her tighter as one more boom of thunder put an exclamation point on her confession and gave him no reason to doubt her. He kissed the top of her head then rested his cheek on it. "When you told me you worked for the FBI, I figured everything was part of the job," Virgil said as the remaining sounds and flashes of the storm grew distant.

"I love you, Virgil Ditch," Megan said, turning back and raising her head so she could be heard and able to look Virgil in the eyes.

The lights came back on and they looked at each other for the first time since the storm began. They were both smiling now.

The End